PRAISE FOR
RUTH RENDELL
AND HER
INSPECTOR WEXFORD MYSTERIES

"Chief Inspector Wexford is an erudite, thorough investigator....He is a compassionate man, who can put the screws on if need be."

—*Los Angeles Times Book Review*

"The page-by-page storytelling—wry, superbly paced, full of arresting character—details—is still unsurpassed in the mystery field."

—*Kirkus Reviews*

"Ruth Rendell is the finest living practitioner of the mystery genre."

—*New York Daily News*

"There aren't many writers like Ruth Rendell who are highly prolific and yet maintain a consistently high standard.... Miss Rendell is a plot prestidigitator who has mastered all the tricks of her trade... including writing."

—*The New York Times Book Review*

SPEAKER OF MANDARIN

A New Inspector Wexford Mystery

Ruth Rendell

BALLANTINE BOOKS • NEW YORK

Originally published in Great Britain by Hutchinson & Co., Ltd.

Copyright © 1983 by Kingsmarkham Enterprises Ltd.

The poem quoted on p. 59 'To Wang Lun' by Li Po, the poem quoted on pp. 99 and 109, 'Drinking Song,' by Shen Hsun, and the two lines on p. 177 from 'Song of a Chaste Wife' by Chang Chi are all from the *Penguin Book of Chinese Verse*. Translated by Robert Kotewall and Norman L. Smith, translation © Norman L. Smith and Robert Kotewall, 1962, and are reprinted here by permission of Penguin Books Ltd.

Library of Congress Catalog Card Number: 83-47745

ISBN 0-345-30274-5

This edition published by arrangement with Pantheon Books

Manufactured in the United States of America

First Ballantine Books Edition: September 1984

21 20 19 18 17 16 15 14 13 12

For Don

Author's Note

For the transcribing of Chinese words and Chinese proper names into English I have used both the Wade-Giles and the Pinyin systems. While Pinyin is the officially endorsed system in the People's Republic, Wade-Giles, which was evolved in the nineteenth century, remains more familiar to Western readers. So I have used each where I felt it to be more appropriate and acceptable, e.g., the modern Pinyin for Lu Xing She, the Chinese International Travel Service, but Ching rather than Xing for the name of the last imperial dynasty, and I have used Mao Tse Tung in preference to the Pinyin Mao Zedong.

PART ONE

Part One

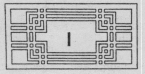

THE PERFECTLY PRESERVED BODY OF THE WOMAN THEY CALL the Marquise of Tai lay, sheathed in glass, some feet below them on the lower level. Two thousand odd years ago when she died she had been about fifty. A white shift covered her thin seventy-five-pound body from neck to thighs. Her legs were a fish-like pinkish-white much marked with striations; her right arm, on account of a mended fracture, was rather shorter than her left. Her face was white, puffy, the bridge of the nose encaved, the mouth open and the tongue protruding, the whole face bearing an expression of extreme agony as if she had died from strangulation.

This, however, was not the case. According to the museum's brochure and Mr Sung, the Marquise had suffered from tuberculosis and a diseased gall bladder. Just before she died of some kind of heart attack she had consumed a hundred and twenty watermelon seeds.

'She have myocardial infarction, you know,' said Mr Sung, quoting from memory out of the brochure, a habit of his. 'Very sick, you know, bad heart, bad insides. Let's go.'

They moved along to look down through a second aperture at the Marquise's internal organs and *dura mater* preserved in bottles of formaldehyde. Mr Sung looked inquiringly into the face of his companion, hoping perhaps to see there signs of nausea or dismay. But the other man's expression was as inscrutable as his own. Mr Sung gave a little sigh.

'Let's go.'

'I wish you wouldn't keep saying that,' said Wexford irritably. 'If I may suggest it, you should say, "Shall we go?" or "Are you ready?" '

Mr Sung said earnestly, 'You may suggest. Thank you. I am anxious to speak good. Shall we go? Are you leady?'

'Oh, yes, certainly.'

'Don't reply, please. I practise. Shall we go? Are you leady? Good, I have got it. Come, let's go. Are you leady to go to the site? Reply now, please.'

They got back into the taxi. Between the air-conditioned building and the air-conditioned car the temperature seemed that of a moderate oven, set for the slow cooking of a casserole. The driver took them across the city to the excavation where archaeologists had found the bodies of the Marquise, her husband and her son, clay figures of servants, provisions, artefacts to accompany them on their journey beyond the grave. The other bodies had been skeletons, their clothing fallen to dust. Only the Marquise, hideous, grotesque, staring from sightless empty eyes, had retained the waxen lineaments of life, wrapped in her painted gown, her twenty layers of silk robes.

Wexford and Mr Sung looked through the wooden grille at the great deep rectangular burial shaft and Mr Sung quoted almost verbatim a considerable chunk from *Fodor's Guide to the People's Republic of China*. He had a retentive memory and seemed to believe that Wexford, because he couldn't decipher ideographs, was unable to read his own language. It was even Wexford's *Fodor's* he was quoting from, artlessly borrowed the night before. Wexford didn't listen. He would have given a good deal to have been rid of baby-faced pink-cheeked slant-eyed Mr Sung. In any other country on earth a bribe equivalent to a month's wages—and here that would easily have been within Wexford's means—would have freed him for good of his guide-interpreter. Not in China, where even tipping was banned. Mr Sung was incorruptible. In spite of his youth, he was already a party member. A fanatical light came into his eyes and his flabby muscles tautened when he spoke of the great statesmen, Mao Tse Tung included, his own native place of Hunan Province had produced. Wexford sometimes wondered if the day would come, twenty years hence perhaps, when if he still lived he would open his *Times* and read that the new Chairman of the Chinese Communist Party was one Sung Lao Zhong, aged forty-seven, from Chang-sha. It was more than possible. Mr Sung came to the end of his memorized paragraph, sighed at the call of duty but refused to shirk it.

'Light,' he said. 'Shall we go? We visit now porcelain factory and before evening meal teacher training college.'

'No, we don't,' said Wexford. A mosquito bit him just above the ankle bone. The heat was enormous. Like the imagined casserole, he was slowly cooking, a gravy-like viscous sweat trickling stickily all over his body. It was the humidity as much as the ninety-eight degree temperature that did it. 'No, we don't. We go to the hotel and have a shower and a siesta.'

'There will be no other time for porcelain factory.'

'I can't help that.'

'It is most necessary to see college attended by Chairman Mao.'

'Not today,' said Wexford. The ice-cold atmosphere in the car stimulated a gush rather than a trickle of sweat. He mopped his face.

'Velly well. I hope you not leglet,' said Mr Sung, indignation, as any emotion did, causing acute confusion in the pronunciation of liquids. 'I aflaid you be solly.' His voice was vaguely threatening. Much more rebellion on the part of this obstinate visitor, Wexford thought, and Mr Sung might even insist that no such omissions were open to him. If Lu Xing She, the Chinese Tourist Board, whose vicar on earth, so to speak, Mr Sung was, required Wexford to see factories, kindergartens, colleges and oil refineries, these institutions he would see and no doubt about it.

Mr Sung turned away and looked out of the window. His face seldom expressed anything but a ruthless affability. The top of his head came approximately to Wexford's shoulder, though for a Southern Chinese he wasn't particularly short. He wore a cotton shirt, white as driven snow, a pair of olive green baggy cotton trousers and sandals of chestnut brown moulded plastic. His father, he had told Wexford, was a party cadre, his mother a doctor, his sister and own wife doctors. They all lived together in a two-roomed apartment in one of the city's grey barrack-like blocks with Mr Sung's baby son, Tsu Ken.

Hooting at pedestrians, at cyclists who carried on their bikes anything from a couple of live fat piglets and a chicken to a suite of furniture, the car made its way through drab streets to the Xiangjiang Hotel. There were very few buildings in Chang-sha that pre-dated the Revolution of 1949, only the Kuomintang general's house with green curly roofs just by the hotel and a ruined European church of grey stucco whose provenance no one seemed to know anything of. Mr Sung got out of the car and came into the lobby with him. There he shook hands. Any more casual mode of behaviour wouldn't have satisfied his sense of duty. It was all Wexford could do to prevent his accompanying him to the eighth floor in the lift. He would be ready, please, by seven, said Mr Sung, for an open-air showing of a film about the history of the Revolution.

'Oh, no, thank you,' said Wexford. 'Too many mosquitos.'

'You take anti-malaria pill evly Fliday, I hope?'

'I still don't like being bitten.' Wexford's ankle bone felt twice its normal size. 'Mysteriously enough—' he caught sight in a rare mirror of his sweat-washed, sunburnt, never even adequately handsome face, ''—I am particularly attractive to *anopheles* but the passion isn't mutual.' Mr Sung looked at him with uncomprehending relentless amiability. 'And I won't sit in the open inviting them to vampirize me.'

'I see. Light. You come to cinema in hotel and see *Shanghai Girl* and Charlie Chaplin in *Great Dictator*. *Shanghai Girl* very good Chinese film about construction workers. I sit next so you don't miss storly.'

'Wouldn't you rather be at home with your wife and your baby?'

Mr Sung gave an enigmatic smile. He shook Wexford's hand once more. 'I do my job, light?'

Wexford lay on his iron-hard bed on a thin quilt. The undersheet, for some quaint reason, was a blue and white checked tablecloth. Cold air blew unevenly over him from the Japanese air conditioner, while outside the window the general's house and the brown pantiled roofs of Chang-sha lay baking in moist sizzling heat. He had made himself, with water from the thermos flask that was one of the amenities of his room, half a pint of green tea in a cherry-blossom-painted cup with a lid. They made you eat dinner here at six (breakfast at seven; lunch, appallingly, at eleven-thirty) but there was still an hour and a half to go. He couldn't stomach the lemonade and strawberry pop and Cassia fizz you were expected to pour hourly into yourself to combat dehydration. He drank green tea all the time, making it himself and making it strong, or else he bought it from the street stalls for a single *fen*, something like a third of a penny, a glass.

Presently, after a second cup of tea, he dozed, but then it was time to shower and put on a fresh shirt for dinner. He would write to his wife later, there wasn't time now. Hong Kong, where she was staying, waiting for him, seemed infinitely far away. He went down to the dining room where he would eat at a table by himself with his own private fan, discreetly half-concealed from the only other foreign contingent, Italians sitting at the next broad round table by a bamboo screen. He sat down and asked the girl for a bottle of beer.

The Italians came in and said hallo to him. The girl

turned their fan on, tucked their screen round them and began bringing Wexford's platters. Chicken and bamboo shoots in ginger sauce tonight, peanuts fried in oil, bright green nearly raw spinach, fried pumpkin and fried fish. Setting off with his nephew Howard and those other police officers who all ranked so much higher than he, he had brought a spoon and fork in his suitcase because he was afraid the Peking Hotel might not have Western cutlery. How green he had been, as green as the tea! The Peking Hotel was like an austere Ritz with arctic air-conditioning and a huge shopping arcade and curtains that drew and undrew electrically. But somehow none of them had ever bothered with the silver that was offered them but had eaten from the first as the Chinese eat, and now he was as proficient with chopsticks as might have been any dignitary in the Forbidden City. He could even, he now discovered, pick up a slippery oil-coated peanut with chopsticks, so skilful had he become. The girl brought him a bowl of rice and the big green bottle of Tsing-tao beer.

A feeling of tremendous well-being invaded him as he began to eat. He could still hardly believe after two weeks in China that he, Reg Wexford, a country police-man, was here in Tartary, in Cathay, had walked on the Great Wall, set foot on the Stone Boat in the Summer Palace, touched the scarlet columns in the Temple of Heaven, and was now touring southwards, seeing as many marvels and experiencing as many delights as Lu Xing She would permit.

When Chief Superintendent Howard Fortune of Scot-land Yard, who was Wexford's dead sister's son, had first told a family gathering he was going to China in the summer of 1980, his uncle had felt something he wasn't usually a prey to—envy. Howard would spend a good deal of time, of course, over the conference table. The particular branch of the Chinese Government who were his hosts wanted advice on crime prevention and crime detection and they would no doubt want to indulge in that favourite communist pastime of showing off national institutions—in this case, probably, police stations, courts, prisons. But Howard and his team would still have leisure to see the Imperial Palaces, Coal Hill and the Marco Polo Bridge. All his life Wexford had wanted to see the Forbidden City and been pretty sure he never would. But he had said nothing of this and had jollied Howard along and told him, as everyone else did, to be sure to buy jade and silk and to bring back a fragment of the Great Wall as a souvenir.

A week after that Howard had rung up to say he had to go to Brighton and would call in on his uncle in Kingsmarkham on the way back. He walked in at about six on a Saturday night, a cadaverous giant of a man who, though perfectly healthy, had always contrived to look twenty years older than he actually was. His parents-in-law lived in Hong Kong. After the China trip he would be joining his wife in Hong Kong. What would his aunt Dora think of joining Denise out there for two or three weeks?

'Reg too?' Dora had said quickly. She was used to being left for long hours, days, by him. But she would never go off and leave *him* of her own accord.

'Can't be done,' Howard said, shaking his head. 'He'll be occupied elsewhere.'

Wexford thought he meant Kingsmarkham. He cocked an eyebrow at his nephew, though, at this curious choice of words.

'I shall need him in Peking,' said Howard.

There was a silence. Wexford said, 'You have to be serious, don't you, Howard?'

'Of course I'm serious. I've got *carte blanche* to pick my own team and I'm picking you as about the best detection expert I know, bar none. And I'm giving you plenty of notice so that you can get your own visa. These group visas are such a bore if you want to go wandering off on your own round China, which I'm sure you will.'

And that was what he was doing now while Howard,

the amateur antiquarian, prowled about the yellow-roofed pavilions of Peking at his ecstatic leisure, and the other team members, nursing incipient coronaries, hastened back over the skies of Asia to British worries and British crime. It was two weeks of his own annual holiday Wexford was taking now. He had flown down from Peking three days before and been met at Chang-sha airport by Mr Sung. He would never forget that flight, the stewardess bringing a strange meal of hard-boiled eggs and sponge cake and dried plums wrapped up like toffees, and the passengers—he had been the only Caucasian—the boys and girls in blue cotton, the high-ranking Korean army officers, military and correct in khaki-green uniforms, yet fanning themselves with fans of black silk trimmed with gold.

Wexford was disturbed in his reverie by a discreet cough. Mr Sung was standing over him, waiting no doubt to take him to the cinema. Wexford asked him to sit down and have a beer but Mr Sung wouldn't do that, he was a teetotaller. He did, however, sit down and began lecturing Wexford on higher education in China with particular reference to the Peking Institute of Foreign Languages which he referred to as his alma mater. Had Wexford visited the university while there? No? That was strange, he would certainly regret it, he would be sorry. Wexford drank two cups of green tea, ate four lichees and a piece of watermelon.

'Mind you not swallow seeds like two-thousand-year-old lady,' said Mr Sung, who had a sense of humour of a kind.

The Great Dictator was dubbed in Chinese. Wexford stuck it for ten minutes. It seemed to him that all the children in Chang-sha must be in the cinema, all laughing so much that they nearly fell off their mothers' laps. He excused himself to Mr Sung, saying with perfect if strange truth that he was cold. The air conditioning was blasting away over his left shoulder and down his neck. He strolled out into the street where the air had a warm furry dusty feel to it like the inside of a muff. Opposite was a shop where they sold tea. Wexford thought he would buy more tea there in the morning, he had almost exhausted the packet the hotel supplied.

He walked. He had a good sense of direction which was as well since the ideographs in which the street signs were written rendered him illiterate. The city was dimly lit, a warren, exotic and fantastic without the least pretension to beauty. In a broad intersecting highway people were playing cards on the pavement by the light of street lamps. Remembering what the hotel's name meant, he headed back for the river. Crowds thronged the streets, friendly people too polite to stare, though their children looked and pointed and giggled at this blue-eyed giant. Ten o'clock is the middle of the night when you have to be up again at six. Wexford made himself a cup of tea, went to bed and to sleep and plunged soon after into the kind of dream he never had, or hadn't had for years.

A nightmare. He was in China but it was the China of his own youth, before the Communists came to power, long before the Cultural Revolution destroyed the temples of Taoists and Buddha and Confucius, when the cities were still walled-in clusters of pagodas. And he was a young man, Chinese perhaps. At any rate he knew he was on the run—from the Nationalist soldiers, it could have been, or the Communists or the Japanese. He was walking barefoot and with a pack on his back along a path to the north of the city, outside the city walls.

The stone door in the hillside stood a little open. He went inside as into a place to shelter for the night, finding himself in a cavernous passage that seemed to lead into the heart of the hill. It was cold in the passage and close with a dank, ancient kind of smell, the smell of the Han Dynasty perhaps. On and on he walked, not exactly afraid, no more than apprehensive. The passage was dark, yet he had no difficulty in finding his way into the big rectangular chamber, its walls shored up with

11

wood, its dimness relieved by the light from a single small oil lamp of green bronze.

The lamp burned by the side of a wooden table or bench that looked to him like a bed provided for his own night's rest. He went over to it, lifted off the painted silk cloth which covered it and looked down upon the Marquise of Tai. It was a sarcophagus that he had uncovered, set in a burial chamber. The dead woman's face was convulsed in a grimace of agony, the cheeks puffed, the eyes black and protruding, the lips curled back from shrunken gums and sparse yellowed teeth and swollen tongue. He recoiled and started back, for there came from the misty, gloomy depths of the coffin a sweetish smell of putrefaction. But as he took hold of the silk to cover once more that hideous dead thing, a shudder seemed to pass along the striated limbs and the Marquise rose up and laid her icy arms about his neck.

Wexford fought his way out of the dream and awoke with a cry. He sat up and put the light on and came round to the roar of the air conditioner and the beating of his own heart. What a fool! Was it going to the cinema or eating fried fish spiced with ginger or the heat that had brought him a dream straight out of *Curse of the Mummy's Tomb*? It certainly wasn't as if he had never seen a woman's corpse before, and most of those he had seen had been a good deal less well-preserved than that of the Marquise. He drank some water and put out the light.

It was on the following day that he first saw the woman with the bound feet.

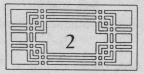

2

SHE WASN'T THE FIRST WOMAN OF HER KIND HE HAD SEEN SINCE coming to China. The first had been in Peking on one of the marble bridges that cross the moat towards the Gate of Heavenly Peace. She was a tiny little old woman, very shrunken as the Chinese become with age, dressed in a black jacket and trousers, clasping a stick in one hand and with the other holding the arm of her daughter or daughter-in-law, for she could do no more than hobble. Her feet were like nothing so much as hooves, dainty hooves perhaps when she was young, shuffling club feet now in pinkish stockings and black slippers the size for a five-year-old.

Wexford had felt fascination, then a rush of revulsion. Foot-binding had come in about AD 500, hadn't it, and gone out with the Kuomintang? At first only aristocrats had practised it but the fashion had caught on even among peasants, so that you could scarcely have found a girl in China with normal unrestricted feet. He wondered how old the woman was who crossed the marble bridge on her daughter's arm. Perhaps no more than sixty. They used to begin the tight bandaging of feet, turning the toes under and up into the sole, when a girl was little more than a baby and the bones were pliable. Such was the power of fashion that no man would have wanted a wife with normal feet, a wife who could walk with ease. In the nineteen thirties the custom had been banned by law and feet that were not beyond remedy

13

unbound. Fascination conquered revulsion, pity and distaste, and Wexford stared. After all, everyone stared at *him*.

How would that woman feel now? What would she feel? Self-pity, resentment, envy of her freer descendants and, worse, her liberated near-coevals? Wexford didn't think so. Human nature wasn't like that. For all the pain she had suffered, the curtailment of movement, the daily agony of dressing and cleansing and rebandaging, no doubt she looked with scorn on those girls who ran across the bridge on large whole healthy feet, and with a sniff of snobbish contempt shuffled the more proudly on her own tiny pointed deformities.

She was the first of several such women he had seen, maybe ten in all. They had caused him to look with curiosity at the shapely flexed feet of the Marquise of Tai, even though he knew she had been born centuries before the custom came into vogue. His dream seemed to him ridiculous when he reviewed it in the morning. He didn't have nightmares, never had, and had no intention of starting on them now. It must have been the food.

Breakfast was by far the last palatable meal he got and he viewed the spread before him with resignation. Fried bread rolls, sliced soda bread, rancid butter, plum jam, chocolate cream cake and coconut biscuits. Tea was brought in an aluminium kettle and he drank two cups of it. Mr Sung was hovering before he had finished.

He had a fresh pink shirt on—he was one of the cleanest-looking people Wexford had ever seen—and his black hair was still damp from its morning wash. How could you achieve that sort of thing when you shared a bathroom not only with four or five members of your family but with the other tenants on the same floor besides? It was wholly admirable. Wexford now recalled uneasily how it was said that Westerners smelt bad to the Chinese, owing to their consumption of dairy products. If this was true his own smell must lately be much improved, he thought, pushing away the nearly liquid greenish butter.

'You will not mind come on bus with party?'

'Not at all. Why should I?'

As if Wexford had protested rather than concurred, Mr Sung said in a repressive scolding way, 'It is not economic drive bus fifty kilometre for one man. This is very wasteful. Much better you come with party, very nice Europe and American people. Light?'

The very nice European and American people were trooping off to the bus as he came out of the hotel. They looked weary and somewhat dishevelled and as if the last thing they wanted was to be driven out into the scorching Chinese countryside to the scenes of Mao Tse Tung's birth and infancy. However, they had little choice about that. Their guide, with whom his own was chatting in rapid Mandarin over a post-breakfast menthol cigarette, looked as relentless, determined, cheerful and clean as Mr Sung. He was a little taller, a little thinner, his English a little worse, and was introduced to Wexford as Mr Yu. They shook hands. It turned out he was a fellow alumnus of Mr Sung's from the alma mater of foreign languages.

Of all green growing things the greenest is rice. Wexford looked out of the window at rice seedlings, rice half-grown, rice near to harvest. This was the very quintessence of greenness, perhaps Aristotle's perfect green which all other greens must emulate and strive for. Men and women in the age-old Chinese blue cotton and conical straw hats worked in the fields with lumbering grey water buffalos. To distract Mr Sung and Mr Yu from their enthusiastic disquisitions on Mao's political career, Wexford asked what the crops were and was told peanuts, aubergines, castor oil plants, cassava, taro and soya beans. Sheets of water—ponds, lakes, canals—studded the neat landscape like jewels on patterned silk.

After a while Mr Yu got up and went to the front of the bus and began translating items from a newspaper into bad English for the benefit of the tourists. Wexford was trying to decide what was meant by a pirates' strike in Hungary and measles in Afghanistan when one of the men from the party came and sat in the seat next to him. He was a small man with a lined red face and a shock of sandy hair.

'Mind if I join you?'

What could he say but that he didn't mind?

'My name's Lewis Fanning. It was either coming to sit with you or jumping screaming off the bloody bus. You can't be worse than that lot and there's a chance you're better.'

'Thanks very much.' Wexford introduced himself and asked for an explanation of Mr Yu's news disclosures.

'He means pilots and missiles. If I'd known he was coming on this jaunt I wouldn't have myself. I'd have stayed in my room and got pissed. As it is I don't reckon I'll make it sane to Canton.'

Wexford asked him why he had come if he hated it so much.

'Dear God in heaven, I'm not on my hols. I'm *working*. I'm the tour leader. I brought this lot here by train. D'you wonder I'm going bananas?'

'On the train from where?'

'Calais,' said Fanning. He seemed cheered by Wexford's incredulity. 'Thirty-six days I've been in trains, the Trans-Siberian Railway among others. Ten lunatics to shepherd across Asia. I nearly lost one of them at the Berlin Wall. They uncoupled the carriage and she got left in the other bit. She jumped out yelling and came running up along the track; it's a miracle she's still here. There's another one an alcoholic and one who can't leave the men alone. To my certain knowledge she's had four in various wagons-lits en route.'

Wexford couldn't help laughing. 'Where's your destination?'

'Hong Kong. We leave tomorrow night on the train via Kweilin. I'm sharing sleeping quarters with two guys who haven't been on speaking terms since Irkutsk.'

Wexford too would be on that train, sharing his four-berth compartment, as far as he knew, only with Mr Sung. But he hesitated over inviting Lewis Fanning to

16

join them and in the end he didn't. Instead he listened to a long account of the alcoholic tourist's propensities, how she had drunk a bottle of whisky a day and had had to be carried by four men back on to the train at Ulan Bator. This lasted until they reached Shao-shan and were drinking tea before climbing the hill to the Mao farmstead. The countryside here had that fresh sparkling look you occasionally see in England on a rare fine day after a long spell of rain. In front of the house the lotus reared its round sunshade leaves and pink lily flowers out of a shallow pond. The rice was the soft tender green of imperial jade. But for all that the heat was intense. Thirty-nine degrees, said Mr Yu, which Wexford, multiplying by nine, dividing by five and adding thirty-two, made out to be a formidable hundred and two Fahrenheit. In the shade it became suddenly and shockingly cool, but they weren't in the shade much and when they walked back down the hill, their heads stuffed with Maoism, they still had the museum of Maoiana to inspect, before lunch in the hotel.

Wexford was one of those Englishmen who aver they find a hot drink more cooling and refreshing than a cold one. Once they were in the dining room of the hotel he drank about a pint of hot strong tea. Mr Sung sat with Mr Yu at a table with two local guides. The train party, for some inscrutable, Chinese, culinary reason, were placed behind a screen and once more Wexford found himself alone.

He was rather annoyed at being so affected by the heat. He misquoted to himself, 'My mother bore me in a northern clime'. Was that the reason for his feeling felled and bludgeoned in this temperature? Behind him a fan moved the warm heavy air about. Two girls brought a banquet in to him, no less than seven platters. Hard-boiled eggs, battered and fried, lotus buds, pork and pineapple, duck with beansprouts, mushrooms and bamboo shoots, prawns with peas and raw sliced tomatoes. He asked for more tea. From the moment he picked up the carved wooden chopsticks and began to eat the

17

sweat rolled off him, wetting the back of his chair through his shirt.

Across the room the guides were eating fried bread rolls and hundred-year-old eggs and what Wexford thought might be snake.

'As long as it moves they'll eat it,' Lewis Fanning had muttered to him on entering the room. 'They'll eat mice if they can catch them.'

A murmur of soft giggling voices came from the girls. It was like the twittering of birds at sundown. The men's voices rose and fell in the strange purity of ancient Mandarin. Wexford wondered how it had come about that Europeans called the Chinese yellow. The skins of those four were a clear translucent ivory, a red flush on their cheeks, their hands thin and brown. He turned away, compelling himself not to stare, and looking instead into the shadowy part of the room from which the waitresses emerged where he saw an old woman standing by the doorway.

She was looking at him intently. Her face was pale and pouchy, her eyes black as raisins. Chinese hair scarcely ever turns white, remains black indeed long into middle age, and hers, though her age seemed great, was only just touched with grey. She wore a grey jacket over black trousers and her bound feet were tiny and wedge-shaped in their grey stockings and black child's slippers. She stood erect enough but nevertheless supported herself on a cane.

The mother of the proprietor or the cook, Wexford supposed. Her stare was almost disconcerting. It was as if she wanted to speak to him, was girding herself up to find the courage to speak to him. But that was absurd. The overwhelming probability was that she spoke nothing but Chinese. Their eyes met once more. Wexford put down his chopsticks, wiped his mouth and got up. He would go to Mr Sung and ask him to interpret for them, so evident was it that she wished to communicate something.

But before he reached Mr Sung's table the woman was gone. He looked back to where she had stood and there was no longer anyone there. No doubt he had imagined her need. He wasn't in Kingsmarkham now, he reminded himself, where he was so often consulted, grumbled at, even pleaded with.

Lunch over, they went once again into the relentless sunshine to visit the school Mao had attended and the pond where he had swum. On the way back to the bus Wexford looked again for the old woman. He peered into the dim lobby of the hotel on the chance she might be there, but there was no sign of her. Very likely she had gazed so intently at him only from the same motive as the children's—because his height and size, his clothes, ruddy skin and scanty fair hair were as remarkable here as a unicorn galloping down the street.

'Now,' said Mr Sung, 'we go to Number One Normal School, Chairman Mao's house, Clear Water Pond.' He jumped on to the bus with buoyant step.

Wexford's last day in Chang-sha was spent at Orange Island and in the museum where artefacts from the tombs at Mawangdui were on show. There, reproduced in wax this time, lay the Marquise of Tai, still protected by glass but available for a closer scrutiny. Wexford drank a pint of green tea in the museum shop, bought some jade for Dora, a fan for his younger daughter made of buffalo bone that looked like ivory—Sheila the conservationist wouldn't have approved of ivory—and a painting of bamboo stems and grasshoppers with the painter's seal in red and his signature in black calligraphy.

There was an English air about the old houses on the island with their walled gardens, their flowers and vegetables, the river flowing by. Their walls were of wattle and daub like cottages in Sewingbury. But the air was scented with ginger and the canna lilies burned brick red in the hazy heat. Off the point where Mao had once swum, boys and girls were bathing in the river. Mr Sung took the opportunity to give Wexford a lecture on Chinese political structure to which he didn't listen. In

19

order to get his visa he had had to put down on the application form his religion and politics. He had selected, not without humour, the most stolid options: Conservative, Church of England. Sometimes he wondered if these reactionary entries had been made known by a form of red grapevine to his guide. He sat down in the shade and gazed appreciatively at the arch with its green pointed roof, delicate and jewel-like against a silvery blue sky.

Through the arch, supported this time on a walking stick with a carved buffalo-bone handle, came the old woman with bound feet he had seen at the hotel in Shao-shan. Wexford gave an exclamation. Mr Sung stopped talking and said sharply, 'Something is wrong?'

'No. It just seems extraordinary. That woman over there, I saw her in Shao-shan yesterday. Small world.'

'Small?' said Mr Sung. 'China is a very big country. Why lady from Shao-shan not come Chang-sha? She come, go, just as she like, all Chinese people liberated, all Chinese people flee. Light? I see no lady. Where she go?'

The sun was in Wexford's eyes, making him blink. 'Over by the gate. A little woman in black with bound feet.'

Mr Sung shook his head vehemently. 'Very bad feudal custom, very few now have, all dead.' He added, with a ruthless disregard for truth, 'Cannot walk, all stay home.'

The woman had gone. Back through the arch? Down one of the paved walks between the canna lily beds? Wexford decided to take the initiative.

'If you're ready, shall we go?'

Astonishment spread over Mr Sung's bland face. Wexford surmised that no other tourist had ever dared anything but submit meekly to him.

'OK, light. Now we go to Yunlu Palace.'

Leaving the island, they met the train party under the leadership of Mr Yu. Lewis Fanning was nowhere to be seen, and walking alongside Mr Yu, in earnest conversation with him, was the younger and better-looking of the two men who had quarrelled on the Trans-Siberian

Railway. His enemy, a tall man with a Humpty-Dumpty-ish shape, brought up the rear of the party and gazed about him with a nervous unhappy air. The women's clothes had suffered irremediably from those thirty-six days in a train. They were either bleached and worn from too frequent washing or dirty and creased from not having been washed at all.

Already, and without difficulty, Wexford had decided which was the nymphomaniac and which the alcoholic: a highly coloured woman and a drab one respectively. Apart from these four apparently single people, the party consisted of another lone, and much older, woman, and two elderly married couples, one set of whom were accompanied by their middle-aged daughter. On the whole, Wexford reflected, it would seem that the young and the beautiful couldn't afford five-week-long tours across Asia.

That evening the screens were drawn closely around their table and he had no further sight of the party until he and they were boarding the bus for Zhuzhou where they would pick up the Shanghai to Kweilin train.

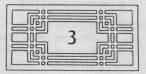

3

It would have been easier and quicker to fly. Fanning's party, of course, had to make every leg of their journey by train but Wexford would happily have gone on by air. It wasn't a matter of his will, though, but the will of Lu Xing She and Mr Sung.

He had a double seat to himself on the bus. Silently he observed his fellow passengers. A couple of days in the hotel at Chang-sha had gone a long way towards reviving them and they looked less as if they had been pulled through a hedge backwards.

Each of the enemies had also secured a double seat, one of them behind the driver, the other on the opposite side of the aisle to Wexford. Out of the corner of his eye Wexford read the label tied to the older man's handcase. A. H. Purbank, and an address somewhere in Essex. Purbank was perhaps forty-five, unhealthy-looking, thin, dressed in baggy jeans and an open-necked pale green shirt. His sprucer, dark-haired adversary was also in jeans, but a snugly fitting pair of denims which looked smart and suitable with a 'friendship' tee shirt. He had swivelled round in his seat and was talking to the woman in the seat behind him. This was the daughter of one of the elderly couples and after a little while Wexford saw her get up and sit in the empty place beside him. Wexford, with another glance at Purbank, thought how uncomfortable it must have been travelling all those miles from Irkutsk away up there on Lake Baikal with a man with

22

whom you weren't on speaking terms. What quarrel had sprung up between these inoffensive-seeming travellers? Both were English, both middle-class, prosperous presumably, adventurously inclined surely, having a fair bit in common, yet they had fallen out so bitterly as purposely not to have exchanged a word across all those vast stretches of eastern Asia. At table in the hotels they must have sat, if not together, near enough to each other, perhaps have been allotted adjoining rooms. Now they were to share a sleeping space some eight feet by five and lie breathing the same warm air in the rattling darkness for eight or nine hours. It was grotesque.

Was one of them or perhaps each of them among the four men with whom Fanning alleged that pretty, painted, ageing creature in the spotted blouse and white pants had engaged in sexual relations during the trip? Fanning, of course, exaggerated wildly. Certainly he couldn't have been indicating as among her partners the fair woman's father, asleep now with his white cotton hat drooped over his eyes, or the austere silver-haired man with the ugly wife. Of course, Wexford reflected, he hadn't exactly specified members of the party and presumably there had been plenty of other men in the Trans-Siberian train.

The bright sky had clouded over and a little warm rain had begun to fall. It was still raining lightly when they came on to the station platform. By each door of the train stood a girl attendant in grey uniform and with the red star of the People's Republic on her cap. Wexford was shown to the carriage that was to be his for the night. Though clean and with comfortable-looking berths, it was insufferably hot, the thermometer on the wall telling him the temperature was two degrees short of a hundred. Once the train started, he opened the window and switched on the fan. A very slightly cooler air blew in through the fly screen.

As soon as they were off Mr Sung came in. Wexford, who had discovered a thermos flask and was busy with the Silver Leaf he had bought in Chang-sha, offered him a cup of tea but Mr Sung refused. Here, as elsewhere, he contrived to give the impression of always being busy and involved. The restaurant car would open at eight, he said, and drinks would be available: beer, red and white wine, Maotai, maybe Japanese whisky.

Wexford drank tea and read his *Fodor's*. It was dusk now, growing dark, and was no longer unpleasantly hot, though smuts came in through the fine mesh of the screen. Hunan Province, blanketed in darkness, fled past as the train reached a steady speed. After a while he went out into the corridor to establish the where-abouts of lavatory and bathroom.

Next to the bathroom, in the first compartment of the carriage, four Hong-Kong Chinese in Palm Beach shirts and white trousers sat playing cards. The door of the next one was opened as Wexford passed it and a voice said, 'Oh, excuse me. I wonder if we could possibly trouble you a moment?'

Wexford went in, not entirely reluctantly. He had been curious enough about these two women to want to make a closer personal estimate. The one he had privately styled the alcoholic was lying in one of the lower berths, her shoes tumbled on the floor and her swollen feet raised up on two pillows. She gave him a wan smile.

'It's so awful constantly trying to make oneself under-stood to these Chinese,' said the other, 'and that beastly Yu has disappeared again. He always disappears when you want him. I suppose he thinks playing hard to get makes him more desirable, do you think? Oh, by the way, I'm Lois Knox and this is Hilda Avory—I already know your name, I *spied* on your luggage—and now, please, please, do you think you could be awfully sweet and make our fan work?'

The attendant who had shown Wexford to his carriage had worked his fan for him, so he had no difficulty in finding the switch which was rather cunningly hidden under the back of the table.

Lois Knox clasped her hands together girlishly.

'And since you're so clever, could you be even more

24

of an angel and find out how to suppress that bloody radio?'

The martial music which had greeted him on entering the compartment—interrupted now for what was presumably a political harangue—Wexford had supposed to be on at the desire of the occupants.

'Oh, no, we hate it, don't we, Hilda? There should be a knob under there but it's broken and it won't move. How shall we ever get a wink of sleep?' Her eyes were a brilliant sea-blue, large beautiful eyes which she fixed intensely on his face. The muscles of her face sagged rather and her jawline was no longer firm but she had something of a youthful look as the gyrating fan fluttered her black hair about. It was dyed hair, greyish-brown at the roots after five weeks away from a hairdresser.

'You're all by yourself, aren't you?' She didn't wait for confirmation. 'We're on that beastly train tour but never again, so help us God. How we should love an aircraft or even a humble bus for a change, shouldn't we, Hilda?'

Hilda Avory made no reply. She put out a hand for her teacup and drank from it with a shudder. She had a damp look, skin glistening, tendrils of hair clinging to her forehead, portions of her dress adhering to thin flesh, as if she had been out in the rain or had sweated profusely.

Wexford set about hunting for the controls of the radio. 'I could fix it for you if I had a pair of pliers.'

'Imagine trying to explain pliers to that inscrutable little Yu! Do have a cup of tea, won't you? Or some *laoshan*?'

'That's Chinese for mineral water,' said Hilda Avory, speaking for the first time. She had a gravelly voice, unexpectedly deep.

'I'm terribly afraid we haven't anything stronger but the fact is Hilda is drying out, aren't you, darling? And she doesn't feel it's very wise to have spirits about, such an awful temptation, you know.'

There seemed no answer to make to this. He accepted

25

a cup of tea. The music burst forth once more in a kind of Chinese version of 'Washington Post.'

'What shall we do?' cried Lois Knox. She brought her hands together appealingly. The red nails were as long as a Manchu's. 'We shall be found stark raving mad in the morning.'

'How about cutting the wires?' said Wexford.

The deep voice from the other berth said, 'Not a good idea. I heard of someone who did that in China and they had to pay to have the whole train rewired. It cost them thousands of *yuan*.'

'I'll see what I can do,' said Wexford. He drank up his tea and went off down the corridor to find an attendant.

The only one he came upon, a very young boy, had nodded off to sleep, his head against the hard wall, in a little cubby-hole next to the bathroom. Wexford went on over the intersection into the next carriage, the sweat gathering on his body now and breaking out on his forehead and upper lip. Away from the fans the heat was as great as ever. There was nothing but dense blackness to be seen outside now and, dimly through the upper part of the windows, a few faint stars. In a compartment with Mr Yu and another young Chinese sat Mr Sung, the three of them poring over a map of the Li River spread out on the table.

'Restaurant will open eight o'clock,' said Mr Sung as soon as he saw him. All the guides seemed to think that visitors from the west needed to eat and drink all day long in order to maintain equilibrium, and that any requests they received from tourists must necessarily be for food or tea or beer. 'I come fetch you when restaurant open.'

'I want a pair of pliers,' said Wexford.

Mr Sung, Mr Yu and the other man looked at him in blank inquiry. Wexford recalled how, in Peking, he had asked an interpreter where he could buy a packet of aspirin and had been directed to an ice-cream shop.

'Players,' said Mr Sung at last.

'You want cigarettes?' said Mr Yu. 'You get plenty cigarettes when restaurant open.'

'I don't want cigarettes, I want pliers.' Wexford made pinching movements with his fingers, he mimed pulling a nail out of the wall. Mr Sung stared amiably at him. Mr Yu stared and then laughed. The other man handed him a large shabby book which turned out to be an English-Chinese dictionary. Wexford indicated 'pliers' and its ideograph with his fingertip. Everyone smiled and nodded, Mr Sung went off down the corridor and came back with a girl train attendant who handed Wexford a pair of eyebrow tweezers.

Wexford gave up. It was a quarter to eight and he began to look forward to a beer. In the intersection he met the little elderly woman who was travelling in what he had mentally dubbed—though it certainly was not—a *ménage à trois*. She was carrying a packet of teabags.

'Oh, good evening,' she said. 'This is quite an adventure, isn't it?' Wexford wasn't sure if she spoke with seriousness or irony, still less so when she went on to say, her head a little on one side, 'We English must stick together, is what I always say.'

He knew at once then, he intuited, he hardly knew how, that she was getting at him. It was neither witty nor particularly clever, though she intended it to be both, and she was referring to his brief association with Lois Knox which she had perhaps observed from the corridor. Her expression was dry, her mouth quirked a little. She was as small and thin as a Chinese and the dark blue trouser suit she wore unsexed her. What was she to the man Fanning had told him was a retired barrister? Sister? Sister-in-law? Wife's confidante or best friend's widow? As she went on her way into the next compartment he observed that her left hand was ringless.

In the cubby-hole next to the bathroom the boy was still asleep with his head against the wall. Wexford saw what he hadn't noticed before, a cloth toolbag lying beside the boy's legs on the floor. He went in, opened the toolbag and helped himself to a pair of pliers.

Outside the windows a few feeble clusters of light showed. They were passing a village or small town. For a moment the outline of a mountain could be seen and then the darkness closed in once more as the train gathered speed. Wexford stood in the doorway of Lois Knox's compartment. The radio was still on, playing a selection from *Swan Lake*. Hilda Avory still lay in the lower berth and on the end of it, beside her feet, sat Purbank. He seemed to be addressing them on the very subject which had been the reason for Wexford's visit to China in the first place, crime prevention. Lois's face wore the expression of a woman who has been taught from childhood that men must at all costs be flattered. Hilda's eyes were closed and slightly screwed up.

'These Communists make a lot of high-flown claims about how they've got rid of crime. Now that's all very well but we know in practice it just isn't true. I mean, where did I have my watch pinched and my Diners Club card and all that currency? Not in Europe, oh, no. In the Union of Soviet Socialist Republics. And that, mark you, was in a train. Now why should it be any different here? Same lack of material possessions—worse, if anything—so you can bet your life they can't wait to get their hot little hands on rich capitalists' property—and that means yours. So don't leave it in the compartment, carry it with you, and when you . . .'

Wexford coughed. Lois saw him and jumped up, clasping her hands. In his absence she had put on more lipstick and eyeshadow and had changed into a low-necked dress of thin yellow material with a black pattern on it.

'Oh, what a fright you gave me! Tony has been scaring us out of our wits with tales of robbery and murder.'

Purbank gave a very *macho*, reassuring-the-little-woman haw-haw of a laugh. 'When did I mention murder now? I never said a word about murder. I merely counselled the inadvisability of leaving valuables around.'

'Quite right too,' said Wexford.

He groped under the table, got a grip on the broken

knob with the pliers and wrenched it anticlockwise. The music stopped.

'Oh, you wonderful, wonderful man!' cried Lois. 'Listen to the blessed silence. Peace at last! Don't you adore the masterful way he *strode* into the compartment? You couldn't do that, Tony. All you could do was say we'd have to put up with it all night and get robbed as well.'

'Give the man a cup of tea,' muttered Hilda into her pillow.

'I'll give him anything he wants!' She extended the teacup to Wexford, holding it in both hands and bowing over it in what she perhaps thought was the manner of an emperor's concubine. 'Oh, if only you hadn't drunk up all the Scotch, Hilda!'

But at that moment Mr Yu appeared in the doorway, announced that the restaurant was open and please to follow him. Mindful perhaps of Purbank's warning, Lois gathered up purse, handbag, hand case and what looked like a jewel box. Wexford gulped down the by now lukewarm tea, realizing he was about to be trapped into a foursome with the two women and Purbank. This being China, though, the restaurant would hardly be open for long. Everywhere he had been so far what night life there was came to a halt at about ten. But was there much chance of sleep in this stuffy train? He felt himself being overtaken by those sensations which result from an insufficiency of sleep, not so much tiredness as a lightness in the head and a feeling of unreality.

They walked down the corridor, Wexford at the rear with Lois immediately in front of him. The boy was still asleep, his head having slid down the wall and come to rest on the table. Wexford slipped in to replace the pliers in the toolbag. Lois hadn't noticed his absence and had gone on in the wake of the others. Wexford stood a moment by the window, trying to make out some indication of the terrain in the darkness that rushed past. He heard a footstep not far from him, the way they had come, turned round and saw approaching him, though still some yards away, the old woman with the bound feet.

This time she was without her stick. Had she followed him on to the train? He closed his eyes, opened them again and she was gone. Had she turned aside into one of the compartments? A hand, red-taloned, was laid on his arm; he smelt Lois Knox's perfume.

'Reg? Do come along, darling, we thought we'd lost you.'

He followed her down the corridor to the restaurant car.

Blue velvet curtains, lace curtains, and on the seats those dun-coloured cotton covers with pleated valances that cover the chairs all over China in waiting rooms and trains and airports and even aircraft. Lois patted the chair next to hers and he had no choice but to sit there. On the table were a plate of wrapped sweets, a plate of wedges of sponge cake, a wine bottle which contained, according to Purbank, spirit and a spirit bottle containing wine. Both liquids were the colour of a Riesling. Wexford asked the waiter for a bottle of beer. Purbank, lighting a cigar, began to talk about the frequent incidence of burglaries in metropolitan Essex.

The restaurant car was full. Chinese passengers sat eating noodles and vegetables out of earthenware bowls. The guides were drinking tea, whispering softly together in Pu Tong Hua. Behind Wexford the two married couples shared a table and the older of the men, in the high-pitched, jovially insensitive voice common to many surgeons, was instructing his companions in the ancient art of foot-binding. A gasp of revulsion came from the barrister's wife as he described toes atrophying.

The beer arrived. It was warm and sweetish. Wexford made a face and signalled to the waiter who was walking round with a tea kettle. Under the tablecloth Lois's knee touched his. 'Excuse me,' Wexford said and he got up and walked over to Mr Sung's table. 'Let me know when you're ready for bed. I don't want to keep you up.'

One of those complex misunderstandings now arose. Why did Wexford want him, Mr Sung, to go to bed? He was not ill. It was (in Mr Sung's words) only twenty-one hundred hours. The dictionary was again produced. Mr Yu smiled benignly, smoking a cigarette. At length it transpired that Mr Sung was not sharing Wexford's compartment for the night, had never intended to share his compartment, would instead be sharing with Mr Yu and the other man whom he introduced as Mr Wong. Because the train wasn't crowded Wexford had his accommodation to himself. He went over to Lewis Fanning and offered him one of the spare berths in his compartment.

But Fanning rejoined in a fashion very interesting to those who are students of character.

'Good God in heaven, I couldn't leave those two alone together! They'd be at each other's throats in two shakes of a turkey's tail. They'd tear each other to pieces. No, I'm frightfully grateful and all that but it'd be more than my life's worth.'

From which Wexford gathered that Fanning was by no means dreading the night ahead and looked forward to extracting from it the maximum of dramatic value for the delectation of those willing to listen to him. Mr Sung, Mr Yu and Mr Wong had begun to play cards. The surgeon was drawing diagrams of the metatarsals, before and after binding, on a table napkin. Wexford sat down again. His teacup had been refilled. Having apparently postponed her drying out, Hilda Avory was drinking steadily from a tumbler filled out of the wine bottle Purbank said held the Chinese spirit Maotai, while Purbank himself told anecdotes of thefts and break-ins he had known. Lois Knox's knee came back against Wexford's and he felt her bare toes nudge his ankle, her sandal having been kicked off under the table. The train ran on through impenetrable darkness, through a dark that showed no demarcation between land and sky and which was punctured by not a single light.

The little woman in the blue trouser suit came into the restaurant car and hesitated for a moment before making for the table where the two married couples sat. The barrister jumped up and pulled out a chair for her. And then Wexford understood it was she he had seen. It was she who had been coming down the corridor when he turned away from the window, she who, while his eyes were closed, had vanished into her own compartment. She too was a small slight creature, she too was dressed in a dark-coloured pair of trousers and a jacket, and though her feet had certainly never been subjected to binding, they were not much bigger than a child's and they too were encased in the black Chinese slippers on sale everywhere. He laughed inwardly at himself. He must be very weary and light-headed if he really believed that the Chinese woman he had seen in Shao-shan and then on Orange Island was following him by train to Kweilin. He drank his tea, accepted a glass of Maotai. Who knew? It might help him to sleep.

Hilda Avory got unsteadily to her feet. She said in a shaky tone, 'I think I could get a little sleep if I try now. Please don't be long, Lois. You'll wake me up if you come bursting in at midnight.'

'Darling, I never burst,' said Lois. She edged a little closer to Wexford. 'Be an angel and give her a hand, Tony, this awful awful train does jerk so.'

Purbank hesitated, torn between being a gentleman and ordering another bottle of laurel flower wine before the bar closed. Fanning, alerted, had half-risen from his seat. 'Allow me,' said Wexford, seizing his opportunity. Lois made a petulant little sound. He smiled at her, rather as one might at a difficult child who, after all, is not one's own and whom one may never meet again, and taking Hilda's arm, shepherded her away between the tables and out into the corridor.

She was sweating profusely, deodorized, French-perfumed sweat, that trickled down her arm and soaked through his own shirt sleeve. Outside the window a box of a building, studded all over with points of light, flashed out of the darkness and receded as the train passed. Wexford slid open the door of the compartment next to his own and helped her in. It was silent in there now. The fan had been switched off so that the air was heavy and thick and densely hot with a faint smell of soot. The thermometer read ninety-five degrees or thirty-five Celsius. He switched the fan on again. Hilda fell on to the left-hand berth and lay face-downwards. Wexford stood there for a few moments, looking at her, wondering if there was anything more he could do and deciding there wasn't, moistening his lips, passing his tongue over the dry roof of his mouth. The Maotai had set up a fresh thirst. He closed the door on Hilda and went into his own compartment.

The fan was off there too. Wexford switched it on and turned back the sheet on the lower left-hand berth. His thermos had been refilled and there were two teabags on the table. He had never cared for teabags. He put a big helping of Silver Leaf into the cup and poured on the near-boiling water. A pungent aromatic perfume came off the liquid, as unlike supermarket packet tea at home as could be. For a moment or two, drinking his tea, he peered into the shining, starless darkness that streamed past the window and then he pulled down the blind.

Lois Knox and Purbank were coming along the corridor together now. He could hear their voices but not what they said. Then Purbank spoke more loudly, 'Good night to you, ladies.' His footsteps pattered away.

Wexford waited for the corridor to empty. He made his way to the bathroom. The lavatory was vacant, the bathroom engaged, the barrister having stolen a march on him and got there first. In the lavatory it was hot and there was a nauseous smell of ammonia. The train rattled and sang. Wexford waited in the corridor, looking out of the window at nothing, saying goodnight to the doctor and his wife who passed him, waiting for the barrister to come out of the bathroom and leave it free. Purbank's enemy and the doctor's daughter, he reflected, hadn't been with the rest in the restaurant car. A holiday romance? The bathroom door opened, the barrister came out, said rather curtly, 'Good night to you,' and walked off, carrying his dark brown towel and tartan sponge bag.

Wexford washed his hands and face and cleaned his teeth, trying not to swallow any of the water. Of course he should have brought some of the water from the thermos flask with him.

All the compartment doors were shut. The light that burned in the corridor wasn't very powerful. Wexford wondered, not for the first time, if there were such a thing as a hundred-watt bulb in the whole of China. He slid open the door to his compartment.

In the right-hand berth, on her back, her striated pinkish-white legs splaying from under the white shift, her face white and puffy, the bridge of the nose encaved, the mouth open and the tongue protruding, lay the Marquise of Tai.

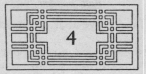

4

HE DIDN'T CRY OUT OR EVEN GASP. HE CLOSED HIS EYES AND held his fists tightly clenched. Without looking again at the dead thing, the mummified, two-thousand-year-old thing, he turned swiftly and went out into the corridor. He didn't know whether he shut the door behind him or not.

He walked down the corridor. The bathroom window was open and he went in, inhaling the cooler air. He put his head out of the window into the rushing darkness. None knew better than he that this was an unwise thing to do. Years ago, when he was young, he had been to an inquest on a man who put his head out of a train window and was decapitated as the train entered a tunnel. He breathed deeply, closed his eyes again. Any attempts at thinking were impossible. He would have to go back there and *do something*.

The bathroom door opened and someone said, 'Oh, sorry.' It was the old doctor.

'I'm just going,' said Wexford.

He wondered if his face was as white as it felt. The doctor didn't seem to notice anything. Humming to himself, he began to wash his hands. Wexford walked swiftly back down the corridor the way he had come, blindly as well as fast, for he almost collided with Lois Knox who was sliding open the door to her own compartment. She wore a short, white, crumpled negligee of broderie anglaise and her face had the stripped look women's faces have that are usually coated with make-up.

He apologized. She said nothing but drew the door across with a slam. Drawing breath, tensing himself, he opened his own door and looked at the berth. It was empty.

Wexford sat down. He closed his eyes and opened them and looked at the berth and saw it was still empty. He would dearly have liked a stiff whisky or even a glass of Maotai, but he was pretty sure he wouldn't get either at this hour—it was after eleven—even if he knew how to summon an attendant, which he didn't. He scattered Silver Leaf into a clean cup and poured hot, no longer boiling, water on to it.

There was no doubt of what he had seen. The corpse had been lying there. And what he had seen had been precisely what he had seen when he had looked down through the cavity in the museum floor at the glass sarcophagus below. It had been the same even to the shortened right arm, the flexed feet, the yawning tongue-filled mouth. *He knew he had seen it.* And now, gingerly, then more firmly, touching the opposite berth, he saw that something had indeed lain there. There was a distinct indentation in the pillow and a creasing of the upper sheet. Something had lain there, been put there, and in his absence had been removed.

He found there was no way of locking his door, but it was possible, by stuffing the side into which the door slid with the Peking *Blue News*, to prevent anyone's opening it from the outside. He drank his tea. The fan had gone off for the night and, in spite of the open window, a close heavy warmth filled the compartment. A nasty thought came to Wexford as he undressed. By means of the metal step which let down out of the wall, he climbed up and checked there was nothing in either of the upper berths. He had just recalled a particularly unpleasant story by F. Marion Crawford in which a traveller at sea finds a drowned corpse, or the ghost of a drowned corpse, in the upper berth of his cabin.

When he had had a second cup of tea he put out the light. After several hours of tossing and turning he got about an hour's sleep but no more. It was still only three when he awoke and he knew he wouldn't get any more sleep that night.

He sat up, switched the light on and asked himself a question. Was it possible that what he had seen lying in that berth was Lois Knox?

Wexford was a modest man with a humble idea of his own attractions insofar as he ever thought about them. To his own wife he seemed to be unfailingly attractive after thirty years of marriage, but this was something to be thankful for and dismissed rather than speculated about. His life hadn't been devoid of feminine admiration; he had taken none of it very seriously. He hadn't taken Lois Knox seriously at all, yet now he came to think of it . . . if what Fanning said was true, or even partly true, this holiday was for her a kind of sex tour. Wexford knew very well that a woman of this sort need not even find her selected partner attractive; it would be enough that he were a man and accessible, someone to boost her drooping ego, for an evening or an hour, someone to quell her panic, push old age and death an inch or two further away.

Foolishly, he had smiled at her on leaving the restaurant car. Had she taken this smile for an invitation? She had been in the corridor when he came back from the bathroom. She had been wearing a short white shift or at any rate a short white dressing gown, and she had seemed offended with him, in high dudgeon. Had it been she, then, lying in that berth, waiting for him? What must she have felt when he recoiled, closed his eyes in horror and stumbled out without a word?

Wexford was aware that a good many people would have found this funny. After all, the woman, no longer young, no longer attractive, but as forward and brazen as any young beauty, had only got what she deserved. At least, thank God, she didn't know he had mistaken

her for a two-thousand-year-old, diseased, disembow-
elled corpse. But had he? Again, closing his eyes in the
dim warm jogging compartment, he saw what he had
seen. The Marquise of Tai. The face wasn't Lois's face—
God preserve him! And that shortened right arm? Those
thighs, scored with deep striations?

Perhaps he needed glasses for daily wear, not just for
reading. Perhaps he was going mad. Presumably if you
developed schizophrenia—which was quite possible, there
was such a thing as spontaneous schizophrenia coming
on in middle age—presumably then you had hallucinations and didn't know they were hallucinations and
behaved, in short, just as he had. Don't be a fool, he
told himself. Get some sleep. No wonder you see visions
when you never get any sleep. Towards morning he
dozed, until the sunrise came in and the fan came on
again.

Things always seem different in the morning. We reiter-
ate this truism always with wonder perhaps because it
is such a remarkable truth. It is invariably so. The fearful,
the anxious, the monstrous, the macabre, all are washed
away in the cool practical morning light. The light which
filled Wexford's compartment wasn't particularly cool
but it performed the same cleansing function. He wasn't
mad, he could see perfectly, and no doubt he shouldn't
have drunk that big glass of Maotai on the previous
evening.

Events quickly confirmed that it had been Lois Knox
in the lower berth. In the restaurant car she and Hilda
Avory were sharing their table with the barrister, his
wife and the wife's friend, and all but Lois looked up to
say good morning to him. Lois, who had been reading
aloud from her guide to Kweilin, paused, stared out of
the window, and once he had passed on, continued in a
gushing voice.

Wexford took a seat opposite Fanning.

'How was your night? I see they haven't killed each
other.'

'Mr Purbank and I slept soundly, thank you. Mr Vinald didn't honour us with his presence, thank God. As far as I can gather, and I can't say the subject fascinates me, he had the vacant berth in Dr Baumann's compartment.'

'Unconventional,' said Wexford.

'There's nothing like a few days on the Trans-Siberian Railway to make you forget all the dearest tenets of your upbringing. Not that there'd be anything like that with the Baumanns and Mr Vinald. Daddy and Gordon up top, Mummy and Margery down below.'

Wexford glanced at the plump fair-haired woman who now sat next to her father and opposite Gordon Vinald, eating the Chinese version of a Spanish omelette which always appeared under the sweeping generic title of 'eggs' and which was served up without fail each break-fast time wherever he had been. She was pleasant-looking with a serene face and she hadn't made the mistake which Lois had of cramming an hour-glass shape into trousers and tee shirt. His glance now fell upon Lois herself. Her hair was carefully dressed, her face painted to a passable imitation of youth. She bore not the least resemblance to the Marquise of Tai and it would have been a cruel libel to suggest it. Her eyes met his and she looked away in calculated disdain.

'Mrs Knox given you the old heave-ho yet?' asked Fanning innocently.

'Good God, no,' said Wexford.

'I only wondered.'

Mr Sung, Mr Yu and Mr Wong were eating with chopsticks from bowls of noodles with rice and vegetables. Purbank came in and Wong immediately got up to speak to him. Whatever it was he said, it brought an expression of edginess to Purbank's face; for a moment he looked almost panicky. He walked away from the Chinese and sat at a table by himself.

Wexford felt relieved. He was noticing people's behaviour again, he was himself again, he had cleansed his thoughts of what hadn't, after all, been a corpse in the berth. He held out his cup as the waiter came by with the tea kettle.

Another grey barrack of a hotel, its design so uninspired that Wexford felt sure no true architect had had a hand in its building. But when he crossed his room and looked out of the window the view was enough to dispel any speculations about man-made things. The mountains that formed the skyline, and in front of the skyline a long ridge, were so fantastic in shape as to resemble almost anything but the karst formations the guidebook said they were. These mountains were shaped like cones, like cypress trees, like toadstools. They rose, tree-studded, vertically out of the plain, their sides straight and their peaks rounded curves. They were the mountains of Chinese paintings that Wexford had until now believed to be artists' stylizations. While you gazed at them you could forget the grey blocks, very like this hotel, that had sprung up too frequently all over the town, and see only those curvy cone mountains and the little red-brown roofs and the water everywhere in ponds and lakes and the Li River twining silver amongst it all.

It was unusual in China for one's guide to accompany one on a train journey. Generally, Mr Sung would have parted from him at Chang-sha station and he would have been met by a fresh guide at Kweilin. It appeared, though, that Mr Sung was a native of Kweilin and hadn't been above fiddling this trip for reasons of his own. Mr Yu, in company with Mr Wong, had disappeared at Kweilin station and Fanning's party were now in the charge of a cadaverous man, exceptionally tall for a Chinese, called T'chung. This new guide had relentlessly organized his tourists into an excursion to caves.

They had only two days here. No doubt they had to make the most of it. Wexford eluded Mr Sung and took himself for a quiet walk about the town, under the cassia trees. You could get knocked down by the bicycles which thronged the streets here just as you could in Peking. Men with bowed shoulders and straining muscles pulled carts laden with concrete blocks while women, wearing the yoke pole with a loaded basket at each end of it, jogged by with their curious coolie trot. Among the cassia leaves flew green and black butterflies. Wexford paid a few *fen* to look at an exhibition of paintings and brush calligraphy and to walk in a bonsai garden. He went into one of the dark spice-scented grocery stores, stacked with sweet jars, and bought more green tea. In there he lingered, examining the wares, dried seaweed in bundles and barrels of rice, pickled fish, root ginger, casks of soya sauce, *tofu* in tanks of water. When he turned round to look at the cakes and pastries displayed under glass, he saw across the shop, leaning on her stick, peering as he had just been doing into a drum of rice, the old woman with the bound feet.

It was no more than a split second before he realized that this wasn't the same woman. She straightened and turned her head and he saw a face like a brown nut, scored with a hundred wrinkles, spectacles on her tiny snub nose. Her eyes passed indifferently over him, or at least there was no more in them than a spark of natural curiosity, and then she began speaking in a rapid singsong to the assistant she had called over to her. The shops here were like they had been in England forty years ago, Wexford thought. This was the way they had been in his early youth. Assistants were polite to you, served you patiently, took trouble, made you into the customer who was always right. How times had changed! The old woman bought her rice, her two pastries, her bag of roasted soya beans, and set off at the clumping pony trot which is how you have to walk if you have no toes and your instep is bowed like a U.

At dinner he was glad they continued the discreet custom of giving him a fan and a carefully screened table to himself. On the other side of the screen he could hear Purbank and Lois Knox grumbling about the miles they had been expected to walk in those caves, and on top of that train journey too. The waitresses brought him fried carp, pork and aubergines in ginger sauce, glass noodles with mushrooms, slices of duck, boiled eggs dipped in batter and fried. They made the tea very strong here and aromatic. When he had finished he went up on to the roof to the new bar the hotel seemed so proud of.

It was evident that its creators had never seen any sort of bar in the west. Perhaps they had read of bars or seen old films. The effect was of a mixture of a bun fight in an English village hall and a one-horse town saloon in a western movie of the thirties. On the concrete of the roof with its concrete parapet, large bare trestle tables had been set out and folding wooden chairs. Light came from bare bulbs and the moon. At the counter you could buy fireworks and on a distant unlit part of the roof a group of Chinese were setting off firecrackers.

Whatever amenities the rooftop bar lacked was made up for by the view. The sky glowed with moonlight and above the river's thread the mountains floated like black storm-clouds. As Wexford, a glass of cassia wine beside him on the parapet, leaned over to gaze at the town and the mountains, music burst forth from a record player set up on a card table. It was an LP of Christmas music they were playing. The syrupy voices of an angel choir began with 'Silent Night', went on to 'Santa Claus Is Coming' and then Bing Crosby started his soft crooning of 'White Christmas'. It was hotter here than in Changsha, stickily humid, the treetops rich with foliage, a bright June moon illuminating it all. As the record went relentlessly on, the Americans at the next table to Wexford's began laughing. The neat smiling Chinese boy who supervised the player and had put the record on beamed at them with gratification. He had made the foreign tourists happy, he would make them even happier by starting it all over again.

As 'Silent Night', with all its evocations of bitter cold, of church bells, of the star of Bethlehem, crept for the second time over the still, hot air, Lois Knox came up the stairs from the floor below. She came from under the concrete canopy which sheltered the bar out on to the roof and she was accompanied by a large paunchy Australian with whom Wexford had gone down to dinner in the lift. Lois's make-up was fresh, she had at some time contrived to visit the hotel hairdresser, and she was wearing a newly pressed blue linen dress and high-heeled blue shoes. She was looking better than he had ever seen her and the Australian seemed smitten already. Wexford understood that he was forgiven, she could afford to forgive him now. She waved, calling out, 'We won't intrude on your reverie!' The Australian took her arm and led her away to a part of the roof where neither the moon nor the lights penetrated.

He sat down at a table alone. After last night it might be wise not to drink too much. Besides, the cassia wine was sweet to the point of cloyingness. Presently Gordon Vinald and Margery Baumann came up on to the roof together. He talked to them for a while and then he went off to green tea and bed.

Going out of the hotel in the morning was a little like walking into a cloud of steam. Already, at a quarter to eight, the temperature was soaring into the eighties. To Wexford it seemed absurd to board a bus for a three- or four-hundred-yard journey to the landing stage. He walked, attempting to shake off the light-headed unreal feeling that was still with him. The roar of his air conditioner had awakened him at two, and when he turned it off the oven temperature returned, closing in like a thick soft blanket. Moreover, the bed was the hardest he had ever attempted to sleep on, a wooden cot with a thin layer of cotton wadding over it. He had lain there, reading, shifting his aching limbs about. Having already got through most of what he had brought with him, *Vanity Fair* (a third reading), the poetry of Lu Yu (because he was coming to China) and last year's Booker winner, he had started on a weighty anthology called *Masterpieces of the Supernatural*. The first story in the collection was 'The Upper Berth' and he was glad he hadn't tried to read it in the train.

Gradually coming round, shaking off the miseries of

43

the night, he walked along the avenue of cassia trees. The boat was in and the American party and the Australian businessmen were already going on board. As Wexford started to follow them the minibus drew up and Mr Sung came bounding out, cross and pompous.

'This is very bad. Must not go alone. Why not wait bus like I say? Cannot board ship without tickets.'

He thrust a piece of coloured cardboard at Wexford. Mr T'chung gathered up the train party by waving his arms like one making semaphore signals. Wexford took the ticket stub that was handed back to him. It had a map of the Li River on it and their route down to Yang-shuo marked, a number of ideographs in pink ink and the somewhat pretentious words printed: Ship's papers. But the boat itself was nice enough, a typical river boat, with a saloon and a big upper deck with deck chairs.

'Good scenery begin ten-thirty,' said Mr Sung.

'Isn't this good scenery?' Wexford asked as the gangway went up and they cast off. The Li River, broad and bronze-coloured, wound out of the town between green cone mountains.

'Ten-thirty,' said Mr Sung. 'Then you take photographs.'

Wexford was tired of explaining to him that he didn't have a camera. Impossible to make Mr Sung understand that to be without a camera was to be free. Gordon Vinald, the barrister's wife and her friend were already up on deck, grumbling, changing films, struggling with telescopic lenses. Wexford sat at a table in the saloon with Margery Baumann, drinking tea that was just being served. Sometimes it is possible for a middle-aged woman to look as fresh as a girl and that was how Margery Baumann, in blue and white checked cotton and with her fair hair newly washed, looked at eight-thirty in the morning on the Li River.

'I'm looking forward to this trip,' she said. 'It's going to be wonderful. And after that—well, we can't get home soon enough for me.'

'I don't imagine you're doing the homeward trip by train as well?'

'Oh, no, thank goodness.' She had a nice light laugh and laughed a good deal but not, Wexford thought, from any sort of nervousness. 'Train to Canton, train out of China to Hong Kong, then the flight home with dear old comfy Swissair.'

'You haven't enjoyed your holiday?'

'In some ways tremendously.' For a moment her eyes had a dreamy look as of delightful, perhaps romantic, things remembered. She became practical. 'But I've had enough, six weeks is too much really. And then I'm needed at home. I'm beginning to feel guilty.'

'What job do you have, Miss Baumann?'

'I'm a GP.' He didn't know why he was so surprised. The children of doctors are often doctors themselves. But she looked so much more the sort of woman who had devoted a gentle life to her old parents. 'I hadn't taken a holiday, not more than a long weekend, in three years. So I got a locum and took the lot owing to me in one—well, not fell, but super swoop!' She laughed.

'The practice is in London?' He really mustn't ask so many questions. It was the habit of an investigating officer. She didn't seem to mind.

'No, Guildford.'

'Really? I'm not far away in Kingsmarkham.'

'Then the Knightons are even nearer to you. They come from a place called Sewingbury.'

'The Knightons?'

'Those people,' she said, as the barrister and his wife walked past the windows. Lois Knox came into the saloon with her Australian. She introduced him as Bruce. Wexford, keeping a straight face, shook hands. Bruce began to talk loudly and vituperatively about Chinese double-think, the way everything was the people's—the people's money, the people's hotel, the people's school—while the people themselves had nothing. He button-holed Mr T'chung who was peaceably drinking tea with Mr Sung.

'You say it was slave labour built the Ming Tombs, right? It's wrong to force men to build a grandiose tomb for some lousy emperor?'

'Of course,' said Mr T'chung.

'But it's OK to make men build a damn great tomb for Mao Tse Tung in Tien An Men Square, is it? What's the difference?'

Mr T'chung looked at him calmly. 'That is a question,' he said in his little clipped voice, 'no one can answer.'

Bruce threw up his hands and gave a bark of laughter.

'Don't let's talk dreary dreary politics,' said Lois.

Wexford went up on deck. The Knightons' friend and Hilda Avory were sitting in deck chairs, drinking tea and Maotai respectively. Hilda said in her gravelly voice with its dying fall, 'Some people who did the trip yesterday told me the boat broke down in midstream and they were three hours repairing it.'

'Then the odds are against it breaking down today.'

'It's not a matter of odds, it's a question of efficiency. My only comfort is this place isn't quite so bad as Russia.'

There were boys swimming in the river on one side and water buffalo on the other. High up on the cliffside, against the limestone, wheeled a pair of birds that might have been eagles. Wexford sat in silence, watching the life of the river go by, a village in which was a little curved bridge over an inlet, a temple with a blue roof that the Cultural Revolution had managed to miss, men fishing with cormorants . . .

He stayed up there in the sun for as long as he could stand the heat. Mrs Knighton came up on deck and indefatigably took pictures of everything she saw, water buffalo, cormorants, peasant farmers in the fields, boats with square orange sails, even a utilitarian building Wexford suspected might be a sewage works. By the time it was ten-thirty he had gone below, scorched off the deck. But it was true what Mr Sung had predicted. The scenery suddenly became spectacular, the mountains looping like fantastic clouds, the water clear as glass but with a fierce current running.

Lunch was served at the favourite Chinese time of eleven-thirty and it was the worst meal Wexford had so far eaten, the main course being mainly those organs and entrails which in the west are not eaten by human beings. It amused him to consider how Chinese food, which is usually thought of in Rupert Street or at Poon's as crisp and delicate, may have its slime and lights side too.

It was during lunch that, looking round, Wexford saw the man who had been introduced to him in the train as Mr Wong. He was very surprised. But perhaps it wasn't Mr Wong, perhaps he was confusing him with someone else. But he didn't think so. To say that all Chinese look alike to Europeans was as great a fallacy as that all Chinese had yellow skins. Ah, well, there must be some reason for his being there, not mysterious at all probably to Lu Xing She.

There was just room to wedge a chair into one of the shady companionways. He sat there sleepily while the boat chugged along from Kao Ping to Hua Shan through the deep water, past the drifting boats on which whole families lived, past the cormorant fishermen, between the domed mountains on which trees grew like moss on boulders. When he didn't want to sleep he couldn't keep awake . . .

A commotion awoke him to an immediate awareness that the boat was no longer moving. Normally, his was a quick rousing from sleep, but after so many white nights and in the slumbrous steamy heat he came to gradually and slowly. His first thought was that Hilda Avory had been right and the boat had broken down. But the engine room was just behind where he was sitting and, turning round, he saw it was deserted.

Then he saw the heads bobbing on the water. He got up and tried to go forward but after a few yards his passage was blocked by the press of people. The saloon was empty, twenty or thirty people were in the bows.

Wexford turned back and made his way up on to the upper deck. Here too was a similar craning crowd but the river could be seen. He could see Mr Sung swimming, fully clothed, and what seemed like the entire crew of the boat in the water. And not only the crew—Margery Baumann, Gordon Vinald, Tony Purbank, all swimming or treading water, searching for something, someone . . .

Mrs Knighton, holding her camera in thick red hands, said to him, 'A man went overboard. He couldn't swim, they can't find him.'

'Who is it?'

She began to take pictures, and said with indifference, 'Not one of us. A Chinese.'

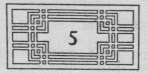

5

It was an hour before they gave up trying. Before that they had put one of the crew ashore and he had set off to walk, a distance of four or five miles, to the nearest place where there would be a telephone. Wexford watched the little figure in the blue shirt walking along between the river bank and the ricefields until it was swallowed up by the richer blue and the green.

Margery Baumann was the first of the would-be rescuers to reboard the boat. She was in a one-piece black swimsuit. Wexford thought she was exactly the sort of woman who would never take this sort of trip without wearing a bathing costume under her clothes. She said nothing, went down to the bathroom to get dried and dressed. Purbank came next, shivering in spite of the heat. The crew member who had stayed on board—young, though older than the others, who all looked to Wexford about eighteen—seemed to be the captain. He helped haul Purbank aboard, tried to say something to him in very halting English, failed, and shrugged, holding up his hands.

Gordon Vinald was still swimming among the reefs which reached in places almost to the surface of the water. But as, one by one, the Chinese gave up the search, he too swam reluctantly towards the boat in a slow crawl and allowed himself to be hauled in. Now the search had been abandoned, almost everyone had either gone up on deck or retreated into the saloon. The river was empty, a shining sheet of turquoise under a pale blue sky, the mountains behind making a horizon of misted blue loops. Such a beautiful, gently smiling river! A river artists had been painting for two thousand years and would paint, no doubt, for a thousand more. Under its silken rippling surface, trapped in the teeth of one of those reefs, hung a drowned corpse, small, thin, white as a root.

'What happened?' Wexford said to Purbank. 'I was asleep.'

Purbank, in blue underpants, the sun drying him, pushed his fingers through his wet hair. 'Nobody knows really. It's always like that, isn't it, when someone goes overboard? This chap was up here in the bows where we are now. He must have been alone and he was sitting on his haunches, I reckon, the way they all do, and somehow or other he toppled in. Couldn't swim, of course. Captain Ma got everyone who could swim to go in after him but he'd gone before I was even in the water.'

'Who was it?'

'Who was what?'

'The man who was drowned. Who was he?'

'God knows. To tell the truth I never asked. I mean, we wouldn't know anyway, would we? He was Chinese.'

'Not one of the crew?'

'I wouldn't know. Anyone would think you were a policeman, the questions you ask. I daresay we shall get enough of that from the Chinese cops when we get to what's it called, Yang Shuo.'

But Captain Ma, apparently, had no intention of continuing the journey to Yang Shuo. They were within a bend of the river of a village with a landing stage and it was to there, Mr Sung told Wexford, that they were now heading. The engines started up and the boat began to move. A bus would come and pick them up. It was best, there was nothing to worry about, the incident was unfortunate, that was all.

'Who was the drowned man?' Wexford asked. 'One of the crew?'

Mr Sung hesitated. He seemed to be considering and he looked far from happy. Wexford, from long practice in studying the reactions of men, thought that what he saw in Mr Sung's face was not so much sorrow at the death of a fellow human being as fear for his own skin. Eventually he said with reluctance, 'His name Wong T'ien Shui.'

'Mr Wong?'

Mr Sung nodded. He stood looking over the side at the reefs, one of which the boat's bottom had slightly scraped. 'Impossible navigate here at all January, February,' he said brightly.

Wexford shrugged. He went into the saloon and helped himself to one, then a second, cup of green tea. The pungent tea revived him with almost the stimulus of alcohol. The passengers were gathering up their belongings—bags, carriers, raincoats, umbrellas, maps—preparatory to landing.

'What the hell was that Wong doing on this trip anyway?' grumbled Fanning to Wexford. 'I thought he was supposed to be a student? I thought he was supposed to be at university in Chang-sha? Chinese can't just run about the country like that, going where they please. They're not *free*. I bet you fifty *yuan* there's going to be hell to pay. Heads will roll over this. Thank God I'm whizzing my little lot off to Canton tomorrow.'

They went ashore. On a little beach sat an old man with a sparse beard and two strands of moustache. Three small children played about him in the sand. The beach was also populated by a hundred or so chickens and ducks and two white goats. The old man looked at the people from the West with a kind of impassive polite curiosity. He put a few words to Captain Ma and nodded his head.

The village lay above them, at the top of a sloping lane. It was the hottest part of the day. Wexford had never before experienced the sun as an enemy, something to retreat from, to fear. The party wound its way up the street where mirages danced ahead of them in the light. The ground was thick with reddish-brown dust which rose in spirals at their tread. Dust coated everything, the hovels that lined the lane, the walls, the grass, even the legs and arms and faces of the children who came out of their houses, chewing on handfuls of glutinous rice, to stare at the visitors.

At the top of the hill half a dozen men and a girl were building an apartment block. The smell of the river and the dust gave place to a pleasanter one of sandalwood. There was a shop next door into which the entire party, with the exception of Wexford and Fanning, immediately disappeared, and at the end of the village a big house with a walled-in court which had perhaps once been the home of the local warlord. Fanning squatted, oriental fashion, on the broad veranda of the shop and lit a cigarette.

'I make call Yang Shuo,' said Mr Sung. 'Bus come very soon.'

'*I* make call,' Mr T'chung corrected him in a very admonitory voice. He began lecturing the other guide in a hectoring sing-song, wagging his finger. Wexford began to think that if it were to be a question of finding a new Chairman from this part of the world, T'chung Bei Ling might stand a better chance than Sung Lao Zhong.

It was too hot to explore the village, though Wexford walked down one or two narrow lanes. Children followed him in a giggling huddle. As he returned once more to the square or marketplace where the shop was he saw an old woman standing in the deep shadow of an overhanging roof. He stood still and looked at her, from her black hair laced with grey, her white puffy face—the Marquise of Tai's face—down to her tiny wedge-shaped feet in child's slippers. He approached till he was no more than a yard from her.

'You want to speak to me?' he said, enunciating clearly.

She made no answer. He repeated what he had said. She seemed to shrink, from shyness or fear. From the other side of the square Mr T'chung began calling, 'Bus has come. Please come quick down hill to bus. Come along, bus has come.'

When Wexford turned from the voice and looked where the old woman had been she was gone. Into the house? It was impossible she should keep vanishing into the abodes of strangers. He went up to the dark doorway and looked inside. It was a dirty hovel in which a child sat eating rice on the floor and a small pig rooted in the far corner. No old woman and no other exit for her to have departed through. If for one moment he were prepared to entertain the idea of the supernatural . . .

Talking excitedly about their purchases, the drowned Wong for the time being forgotten, the train party and the Australians made their way down the hill to where the bus waited. It was parked by the beach and beside it was what was very evidently a police car. Police were on the boat, talking to Captain Ma. An officer came up to Mr T'chung and fired a string of questions at him.

'People's police will come to hotel this evening,' said Mr T'chung.

All this would normally have interested Wexford very much. The reason it didn't was that he had been aware, all the way down the hill, of the old woman with the bound feet following him at a distance. He turned round once or twice, like Shelley's traveller, he told himself, and saw not exactly a frightful fiend but this old creature, hobbling on her stick, who was becoming fiendish enough to him. Now about to enter the bus, the heat thick and gleaming, radiated off the still blue water in a dazzling glare, he made himself turn round and face behind him boldly. She was gone. There was nowhere for her to disappear to but she was gone.

For the rest of the passengers the bus ride back was as rewarding as the boat trip had been on account of the scenery through which the route passed. They drove along lush valleys, green with young rice. Wexford thought about the old woman whom he had now seen three, or possibly four, times. Was she real? Was she a real woman

53

who, incredible as it might be, was for some reason following him across China? Or was she a hallucination such as he supposed schizophrenics might have?

He was sitting next to Tony Purbank, who was as silent as he. Purbank was also a fair-skinned person who reacted badly to the sun and his face hadn't been protected as Wexford's had. Moreover, he had a big bald patch on top of his head. His forehead and his bald pate began to glow a fiery red as soon as he was in the air-conditioned shelter of the bus. He spoke not a word, he looked as if he were suffering from a mild degree of heatstroke. Mr Sung too made the return journey in total silence. From the back seats, where Lois Knox sat with Bruce and the Knightons, Wexford could hear a continuous hum of speculation as to how Mr Wong had come to fall overboard.

Wexford expected to see the old woman get off the bus after him but she didn't. It was an absurd relief. He went straight off upstairs and made himself a cup of Silver Leaf. He lay on the bed, thinking about schizophrenia, wondering what he was going to do if she moved in with him, if she came into his room in the night and lay down in the other bed. Presumably, the truth was that she had never existed at all. He thought back. At Chang-sha he had heard the tap of her stick, her voice as she spoke to her companion. Besides, if his mind was going to produce figments to haunt him, why produce *her*? Out of what recesses of experience, unconscious processes, even trauma, was his mind conjuring an old Chinese woman?

The tea, as always, made him feel better. Could he convince himself it was a mirage he had seen in that river village, a trick of the heat and light?

'People's police say no need talk with you,' said Mr Sung, coming up to his table as dinner was being served. 'No need ask questions any tourists, ship's crew only.' He paused, said, carefully choosing his words, 'They have find dead body Wong T'ien Shui.'

'Poor chap,' said Wexford. 'He can't have been more than twenty or so.'

'Age I don't know,' said Mr Sung. 'Very young, yes. Body cut and—what you say?—brushed very bad by rocks.'

'Bruised?'

'Bruised, yes. Thank you. Many bad rocks there under river so body all cut and bad bruise.'

There was as usual a screen between Wexford and the table at which the train party sat. From beyond it he could only hear a general buzz of conversation. The girl came round with the tea kettle and he had two cups, strangely disturbed now by the death of Wong T'ien Shui. It was still only seven and the sun was just setting. He walked out of the hotel, crossed the road and took the little causeway to the island in the middle of the lake. Somehow—sentimentally, no doubt—he couldn't help imagining Wong as he must have been when a little boy, not so long ago, attending the kindergarten, being met by his mother with her hair in two braids, having a doughnut bought for him in a dark, scented grocer's shop, flying a kite shaped like a butterfly or a dragon, going home to loving grandparents. It was a very young life to have been cut short like that.

It should have been pleasant out on the island but because of the weighty thickening humidity, it wasn't. The undulations of mountains looked blue now, veiled in mist, and the air hung full of sluggishly moving mosquitos. After being bitten for the second time, he went back to the hotel. Malaria and dengue fever might now be avoidable, but you could still have a leg or an arm swell up like a balloon.

Up on the roof it was too high for the mosquitos. He knew he shouldn't drink, because of his blood pressure and an ever threatening weight problem, but he had to get some sleep somehow. He bought a smallish bottle of cassia wine. The Baumanns, the Knightons and Gordon Vinald called him over to the table they were sharing, only a second before he was similarly summoned to the other—necessarily a few yards away because of the Purbank-Vinald feud—shared by Lois Knox, Hilda Avory and Purbank. There was no sign of the Australians, Fanning or Mrs Knighton's friend. Lois looked sour and Hilda ill, and it was a relief to Wexford to follow the rule of first come, first served.

The people at the table he joined were indulging in the favourite tourist pastime of showing off to each other the souvenirs they had bought that day. As Gordon Vinald began talking, Mrs Baumann whispered to Wexford that he was an antique dealer.

'Jade is always cold to the touch,' he was saying. 'That's one of the best ways for the amateur to tell if it's jade or not. If it stays cold in a hot room or against the skin the chances are it's jade.'

He told them of various jade frauds. How the unscrupulous dealers of Hong Kong would arrange a display with five items of plastic to one of jade, five items of plastic to one of ivory. China was safe, though. The Chinese were either too high-principled to deceive or too innocent to understand the mechanics of deception. But if, of course, the jade they were selling had been imported into China they might themselves have been deceived . . . Wexford thought of the little pieces he had bought for Dora. Were they cold to the touch? He couldn't remember. He put a tentative question about it to Vinald.

'You're in the room next to mine, aren't you?' Vinald replied. 'No doubt we'll be keeping our usual nursery hours, so why don't you bring them in at the witching hour of nine-thirty and show me?'

Margery Baumann laughed. She took a tissue-wrapped parcel out of her handbag and out of it tumbled half a dozen little cups, medallions, a ring and a pendant in the shape of a turtle. She put the ring on to her finger. Vinald examined all the pieces and pronounced them to be jade, one indeed very close in colour to the imperial jade beloved by the emperors. Then suddenly, as if no one else was there, he lifted her hand in his and brought it up against his cheek. Ostensibly, he was testing the temperature of her ring on his own skin, yet the gesture had a very lover-like air to it. Wexford saw Mrs Baumann smile with pleasure and Margery blush.

Vinald released her hand. 'That's your true nephrite. You've done well, Margery. If you hadn't a worthier profession already I'd say you've a flair for my business.'

She said nothing, only laughed again. And yet the remark, delivered in such a tone and after such a gesture, could almost have been leading up to a proposal of marriage. Wexford thought he wouldn't be surprised if an announcement were made to the party on the following day.

He offered his wine round the table. The beer drinkers refused but Mrs Baumann and Mrs Knighton each took a glass. His bottle wasn't going to last long at that rate. He went off to the bar to get another as 'Silent Night' came crooning out of the record player.

Standing at the bar, in the company of an older woman, was the best-looking girl he had seen since he came to China.

The best-looking Caucasian, that is. Of Chinese beauties there had been plenty but it had seemed to him that women with the looks of his daughter Sheila or his niece Denise weren't interested in visiting the People's Republic.

This girl, though, would have compelled glances in the most sophisticated milieu. She and the older woman were standing by the counter, talking to the three Australian businessmen about the topic which commanded the attention of the whole hotel, and probably the whole city of Kweilin, the drowning of Wong T'ien Shui. Wexford heard her say, 'There's always something with that boat. If I believed in things like that I'd say that boat had bad joss. Maybe the place they built it was on a dragon's eye or something.'

She laughed. The Australians laughed uproariously. Her accent, he thought, was that of New Zealand. The older woman—her mother?—spoke to her.

'Are you having that red wine again, Pandora, or the Japanese whisky stuff?'

Pandora pondered. She was tall and extravagantly slender, somewhere in her early twenties. Her hair was as black as Lois Knox's raven dye, but Pandora's was natural and it fell as straight to her shoulders as if it were wet. There was no make-up on the dazzling white skin but for a stroke of emerald green on her eyelids. Her eyes were hazel green and the lashes as thick and sooty as a black kitten's. She had on a bright green dress with a pink and black cummerbund and pink sandals. Deciding on the whisky, she turned away and walked out on to the roof. Bruce took a tray and piled bottles and glasses on to it.

Wexford bought his wine and went back. For a moment he thought he saw the old woman with the bound feet standing up against the parapet, but when he looked again he saw only a Chinese boy with a firecracker in his hand. Back at the table they were once more on the topic of Wong's death. Dr Baumann couldn't understand how anyone could have drowned where there were so many reefs to provide footholds. Margery wondered if he had struck his head on one of those reefs as he fell. Mrs Knighton, with an unpleasant little laugh, said be that as it might it had ruined what had promised to be an interesting day out. And then Wexford's attention was caught by the action of Lois Knox who, seeing her Australian come out on to the roof with a woman and two other men, seeing him home in on the table where Pandora had sat down, got up, muttered 'excuse me' to her companions and walked swiftly away towards the stairs. Purbank said something inaudible but Hilda Avory's reply carried on the night air.

'Of course it makes her unhappy. What does she expect if she goes on like that at her age?'

Knighton was staring ahead of him. He had contributed little to the conversation but now he had extracted himself from it entirely. Gazing across the roof like that, he looked as if he had had some transcending vision or had just seen a ghost. Abruptly he jerked his head aside and Wexford was astonished to see his enraptured expression. What had produced that?

His wife was showing family snapshots to Mrs Baumann. 'We've four children, three sons and a daughter, and four simply adorable grandchildren with another on the way.'

Mrs Baumann was beginning an appropriate comment when Knighton spoke. He seemed to be addressing no one in particular. He looked at the view, at the stars, and said:

' "I had gone aboard and was minded to depart,
   When I heard from the shore your song with tap of foot.
   The pool of peach blossom is a thousand feet deep
   But not so deep as the love in your farewell to me." '

The Baumanns looked extremely embarrassed. A sheepish smile lingered on Vinald's face. Mrs Knighton looked at her friend and her friend looked at her. Then Mrs Knighton very slightly cast up her eyes.

'The work of Li Po,' said Knighton in his more usual cold and dry tone. 'The famous eighth-century Chinese poet.'

'I don't know about you, Irene,' said Mrs Knighton, 'but I feel like going up to my room.'

'Down,' said her friend.

'I mean down. Don't be late,' she said to her husband. 'You've had a long day.' She achieved, like someone doing facial exercises, a broad smile and said briskly, 'Good night, everyone.'

Knighton got to his feet with the air of someone following a weary old rule of politeness. But when the women had gone and the elder Baumanns had gathered up their things and started to follow them, instead of sitting down again, he walked away from the table to a distant part of the roof, leaned over the parapet and gazed at the moonlit landscape.

Wexford was left to play gooseberry to the lovers. He

said good night to Margery, went down to his room and made himself a cup of tea. The old woman with the bound feet had departed to wherever such materializations go when off-duty. Settled down with Poe's 'The Tell-tale Heart', he waited for Vinald's footfall in the corridor—unless, of course, he should forget his appointment and his footfall sound tonight in the corridor below, where Margery's room was.

But no more than half an hour had passed before he heard Vinald's light switch go on. Wexford collected his pieces of jade and knocked at the antique dealer's door.

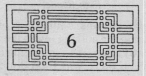

6

TREASURES SET ABOUT THE AUSTERE CHINESE HOTEL BEDROOM had transformed it into something resembling a corner of a museum in the Forbidden City. There were dishes of *famille jaune*, pieces of blue and white ware, a magnificent tall pearl-coloured vase with a design on it of birds and ripe peaches on a peach tree, lacquer trays, boxes of chops in jade and carnelian and soapstone, three or four plain pale bowls of exquisite shape, a pair of carved jade vases with lids, and everywhere a scattering of tiny pieces of carved jade, of snuff bottles, seals and metal scent bottles.

'I confess to liking the gorgeous stuff best,' said Wexford. 'Does that prove me ignorant and undiscriminating?'

Vinald laughed. 'Not really. That vase is a lovely piece. I'm lucky to have found it. There are a pair just like it that were made for the Dowager Empress.'

'It's not so very old then?' Wexford knew that much.

'Under a hundred years.' Vinald handed his purchases back to him. 'Your jade's OK. Frankly, I'd be surprised if it wasn't. Can I offer you a cup of tea?' When it was poured he began tidying the room. 'We're off again tomorrow, a ghastly roundabout journey since there's no direct route from Kweilin to Canton. It seems that the mountains get in the way.' He was thrusting items from the desk into a hand case, a ball-point pen, a stick of red sealing wax, a note book, the hotel writing paper out of the blotter. Wexford was amused. How people loved acquiring something for nothing, even the wealthiest! Here was this evidently rich man pinching three sheets of writing paper when there was little doubt he could have bought up all the notepaper stocks in Kweilin and given it back again without much noticing the loss.

Vinald took a drink of tea. 'I didn't exactly come to China to buy antiquities,' he said. 'I was in need of a holiday. I was literally dying on my feet for a holiday. But I had every intention of buying antiquities when I got here. I knew what a hoard China has, you see.'

Wexford raised his eyebrows enquiringly.

'Oh, yes. You can imagine the stuff that got pinched at the time of what they call Liberation, can't you? Not to mention the Cultural Revolution. They claim it has all passed through Government hands but the fact is they simply stole it from its rightful owners, and murdered them too if the truth were known.'

'The truth never really is known about China,' said Wexford. 'And that's not new, it's always been so.'

Vinald passed over the interruption with a slight impatient wave of his hand. 'I can tell you that if China chose to let loose what she's got on the world the bottom would fall slap bang out of the antiques market.'

'Which would hardly suit you, I suppose.'

'You're right there. I've helped myself to a few unconsidered trifles.' Vinald pulled tissue paper out of a drawer and started wrapping things up, packing them into boxes, some of which were padded with straw. 'Tell me,' he said, speaking rather abruptly, 'do you think it's wrong to buy something for fifty *yuan*—say fifteen pounds— when you know perfectly well its real worth would be five hundred pounds?'

'If by wrong you mean illegal, I shouldn't think that's illegal anywhere in the world. No doubt it's unethical; some would say it's taking advantage of innocence. Why? Have you done much of that sort of thing?'

'A bit,' said Vinald. 'They're so ignorant they don't know what they're offering you half the time. It might be unethical in some places. I don't think it is here. You can't think of yourself as taking an unfair advantage of the Chinese government, can you? It's not as if it were some individual trying to make a living.'

'How about a nation trying to make a living?' Vinald looked uncomprehending so Wexford turned aslant of the subject. 'I don't envy you carrying that lot home.'

'Most of it'll go in my suitcase.' Vinald packed the blue and white dishes, an ikon, a gleaming white bowl. 'I brought the minimum of clothes because I knew I'd want to fill up this end.'

'You don't anticipate trouble with the Customs?'

'I shan't fall foul of them. As long as you don't take anything out of China that's more than a hundred and twenty years old you're OK.'

Wexford thanked him for his opinion and his tea and left him wrapping up and packing a blue, crimson and gold ikon. In his own room, standing in the corner by the air conditioner, was the old woman with the bound feet. He stared and she changed into the wooden coat stand over which he had hung his jacket.

Her shadow flitted across the window blind. He knew she wasn't real now and because of something that had happened to his eyes or his mind he was imagining her. In the book of supernatural stories he was reading was one by Somerset Maugham called 'The End of the Flight', which had nothing to do with aircraft but was about a man in the Far East who had done some sort of injury to an Achinese and thereafter, no matter where he fled to, was haunted by this Achinese or his spirit or ghost. He, Wexford, had of course never done any sort of injury to an old Chinese woman.

The room was empty again, not a trace of her. The air-conditioning made it rather too cool. He went to bed, pulling the quilt up over his head. It was impossible to sleep, so in the middle of the night he got up again and made tea. There was no sign of the old woman but still he couldn't sleep, and to keep sleep still further at bay, at about four in the morning the drone of the air conditioner was augmented by a rushing roaring sound. It was raining.

When it began to get light he got out of bed and looked at the rain. He could see the rain crashing against the windows and that was about all he could see, the lake, the city roofs, the mountains were all blotted out by dense white fog.

It was absurd to attempt to go out unless one had to. The train party had to. They were embarking on a journey to Canton that was only about two hundred miles as the crow flies but which would take two days in a train. Their luggage was piled in the hotel lobby. In twos and threes they came down in the lift to await Mr T'chung and the bus.

Wexford sat in the rattan chair, reading Maugham's story about the ghost of the Achinese. The Knightons came first with their friend, who was wearing her dark blue trouser suit but not looking much like the old woman with the bound feet. The bus had drawn up outside. Lois Knox came out of the lift with Hilda Avory behind her.

'I suppose we must say goodbye,' Lois said with a meaning look as if she and he had been on intimate terms.

Wexford shook hands with her, then with Hilda and Vinald. 'Have a good journey.'

'And you,' said Vinald. 'Flying off in a nice little Fokker Friendship aren't you? We should be so lucky.'

The Baumanns and Margery waved to him. Fanning got out of the lift with Mr T'chung. 'So help me God,' whispered Fanning to Wexford, 'but once I get home the furthest bloody abroad I'm going ever again will be the Isle of Wight.'

Under umbrellas held up by their guides they filed out to the bus, joined at the last moment by the two women from New Zealand. The beautiful Pandora was in tight yellow trousers and a yellow tee shirt and Wexford saw Lois give her a glare of dislike.

The rain swallowed the bus as it went splashing off

towards the railway station. Wexford drank some tea, tried to sleep, read a story by M. R. James about a man dogged by the ghost of a Swedish nobleman whom he had inadvertently released from a tomb. He didn't finish it. He had seen the old woman with the bound feet cross the lobby just after the bus had left and now he could see her most of the time hovering on the edge of his sight. When he stared hard she would disappear and then, as he looked away, he would be dimly aware of her waiting, so to speak, in the wings of his vision.

It was useless to worry about it. When he got home he would get Dr Crocker to send him to an oculist or specialist in allergies or maybe, if it had to be, a psychiatrist. Instead of worrying, or instead of worrying more than he could help, he began to wonder if he ought to go and call on the local police. After all, he had originally come to China because he was a policeman, he had come at the express invitation of the Ministry of Internal Affairs. Having actually been on the boat at the time of Wong's fatal accident, should he not go and inform them of this fact? Rather glumly he thought about it. With his lack of Chinese and their undoubted lack of English? With Mr Sung as his interpreter? And what help could he be? He had been asleep at the time.

No, he wouldn't go. Such an action would smack of 'putting himself forward', of showing off his greater sophistication and that of the nation he came from. Besides, he could do nothing, tell them nothing, beyond revealing himself as possibly the least effective witness on the boat.

It rained all day. But twenty-four hours later, when he was starting to think his flight would be cancelled because of the bad weather, the sky cleared, the sun came back and the looped mountains stood out so sharply against the translucent blue that it seemed one could pick out every tree on their slopes. Mr Sung escorted him to the airport in a taxi.

'I like to say,' said Mr Sung, 'the very great pleasure

it has been to me to be your guide and I wish you good journey and pleasant stay in Guangzhou.'

This, Wexford knew, was what the Chinese called Canton, or perhaps it would be more correct to say that in trying to pronounce Guangzhou, Canton was the best those European merchants who had come there had been able to do.

'You will please convey best wishes to your friends and relations in UK and say they are welcome to China. All friends are welcome to China.'

The aircraft had no air-conditioning. Once they were airborne steam poured across the non-pressurized interior and the passengers fanned themselves with fans painted with the Kweilin mountains which the stewardess provided. Wexford was the only European on board. He knew that the stewardess walking up and down the aisle with fans and sweets on a tray was a young girl in her early twenties but for a moment he had seen her as an old woman with bound feet. Would he see her in Canton? In Hong Kong? Would he—like Maugham's man with the Achinese—would he see her in *England*?

At Canton he was met by his new guide, Lo Nan Chiao. Mr Lo shook hands and said he was welcome to Guangzhou and if he was agreeable, while his luggage went on to the hotel, they would proceed straight to Martyrs' Mausoleum.

The old woman with the bound feet was there waiting for him. He closed his eyes and opened them and she had changed back into the uniformed attendant. She emerged from the doors of the Sun Yat-sen Monument and came across the bridge from Sha Mian to meet him. By that time he would have been convinced of his own madness if Mr Lo hadn't gone up to speak to her, remarking afterwards to Wexford that she was an acquaintance of his mother's.

Wexford sweated. She wasn't *always* an acquaintance of Mr Lo's mother. It was even hotter here and the humidity was intense. When he tried to make tea he found the water in his thermos flask was only lukewarm and repeated requests to the hotel staff failed to produce boiling water. But at dinner he discovered a new brand of Lao Shan, the coldest and best mineral water he had so far tasted, and he bought a dozen bottles to the amazement of the waitress to whom such extravagance perhaps represented a week's wages. The food was good too and the coffee was drinkable.

He dozed in his bedroom and this time it might have been a dream and not a vision he had. He never knew. But he took the traditional action honoured in ghost stories. He threw something. Almost anywhere else in the world a holy book would have been provided in an hotel bedroom, the Bible or the Koran or the Gita, but here he had to make do with *Masterpieces of the Supernatural*. The old woman disappeared. Wexford felt worn out. He was sure he wouldn't sleep and he prepared for another white night, only to fall into a heavy dreamless slumber he didn't come out of until six when the phone rang.

'Good morning. Time to get up,' said a chirpy voice, habituated to the rhythms of Cantonese.

Wexford felt much better. The sun was shining on the green wooded mountains that he could see from his window. Breakfast and then off to the porcelain factory with Mr Lo, to the factory at Fu-shan where all the great Chinese porcelain of the past was made and from where it had been exported to Europe, where the peach-blossom vase acquired by Gordon Vinald certainly had been shaped and painted and glazed.

It was while he was having dinner back once more at the Bai-yun Hotel that he realized he hadn't seen the old woman once she had scuttled out of sight at the factory behind a group of girls modelling figurines. She didn't appear in his room that evening nor next day in Tung Shan Park nor was she anywhere around to spoil the beauty of the orchid garden.

Mr Lo came with Wexford's exit visa and a packed lunch to eat on the train to Kowloon. They went to the station and the old woman wasn't there. She wasn't waiting for him in his carriage either. The train had dun-coloured cotton covers with pleated valances on the seats and net curtains and pale blue velvet curtains at the windows. There was closed-circuit television on which sometimes a girl announcer appeared and sometimes acrobats gyrated. Wexford couldn't yet believe the old woman had gone and he even tried to catch glimpses of her round the edges of his vision but he achieved nothing by this beyond a headache.

He was leaving China. Quietly, without pause or frontier fuss, the train crossed the border into the Hong Kong New Territories at Sum-chun. By now Wexford had a feeling of complete certainty he would never again see the old woman with the bound feet. Ghost or hallucination, for some reason she had come to him in Shao-shan and, equally inexplicably, left him in Canton. He felt tired, shaky, with relief. The cool airy train raced pleasantly along towards the Crown Colony, back to luxury, ordinariness, a 'too high' standard of living, soft beds, capitalism.

Dora was there to meet him on the platform at Kowloon Station. She had missed her husband and guessed he had missed her but they had been married, after all, for more than thirty years and so she was a little surprised by the ardour of his embrace.

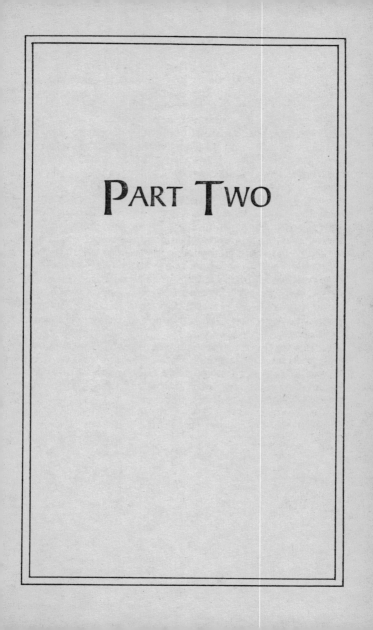

PART TWO

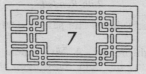

7

THATTO HALL FARM STANDS ABOUT A MILE OUTSIDE THE SMALL town of Sewingbury in pleasant hilly wooded country. The Hall itself was pulled down many years ago and the smaller house, which was bought by a London couple in 1965 and converted for use as a weekend residence, is now the only dwelling in Thatto Vale. Paunceley is the nearest village, a collection of cottages and a small council estate linked to Sewingbury by a B-class road and a system of footpaths that run close by the farmhouse.

It is a long low brick house, about a hundred and sixty years old, comprising six rooms, two bathrooms, a small washroom and a kitchen. The gardens have been well kept and the house has acquired a tended, even luxurious appearance. In October the Virginia Creeper which covers half the front of the house turns to a blaze of crimson and the two circular flowerbeds in the two front lawns are filled with dwarf Michaelmas daisies in shades of purple, rose and deep blue.

It was on a morning in October that Mrs Renie Thompson, the cleaner at Thatto Hall Farm, arrived at nine to find her employer lying dead on the dining room floor.

Wexford got to work half an hour later and that was the first thing they told him. The name rang a bell and so did the address.

'*Who* is it that's dead?' he said to Detective Sergeant Martin.

'A Mrs Knighton, sir. A Mrs Adela Knighton. The woman who found her said she'd been shot.'

'And Inspector Burden's gone over there, has he, with the doctor and Murdoch? I think we'll go too.'

It was a fine sunny day, a little morning mist still lingering. The leaves had not yet begun to fall. Where the footpath met the road, just before the farmhouse, a man came over the stile, carrying a shotgun and with two dead rabbits slung over his shoulder. Thatto Hall Farm lay in a misty golden haze. On its well-trimmed dewy lawns lay a scattering of red and yellow fruit from crab apple trees. The front door was open and Wexford walked in.

Murdoch, the Scene-of-Crimes Officer, was in the dining room with Dr Crocker and the body. Naughton, the fingerprint man, was busy in the hall. At the kitchen table with Burden opposite her, drinking strong tea, sat Renie Thompson. She was much the same age as her dead employer had been, somewhere in the middle sixties, a big gaunt woman with dyed brown hair in a hairnet and wearing a skirt and jumper covered by a mauve flowered overall.

'Where is Mr Knighton?' Wexford asked.

'Don't ask me.' Mrs Thompson kept up a bold and truculent manner even while in shock. 'I always come in nine sharp Mondays, Wednesdays and Fridays and this is the first time I've known him not be here as well as her. I went upstairs and looked. I mean he might have been dead and laying up there too for all I knew. They had twin beds and his wasn't slept in. I've never known that before, not all the time I've worked here and that's donkey's years.'

Wexford went upstairs. The staircase was of polished oak, uncarpeted, and, though the bedrooms were carpeted, the spacious upper hall had a polished floor on which lay blue and silvery grey rugs. The principal bedroom, with its made bed and its unmade bed, was done in shades of rose, the other three in blue, green and gold respectively. Victorian furniture, chintz curtains pinch-pleated or on rings, Arthur Rackham drawings in narrow silver-coloured frames, on a console table a bunch of everlasting flowers in a Bing and Grondahl bowl, and in every bedroom a jar of potpourri. All very correct and tasteful. Wexford looked in all the cupboards, he even looked under the beds. He went downstairs and looked in the large, similarly conventionally furnished living room. Having looked in the bathrooms, he looked in the washroom where he noticed a pane of glass was missing from the window. Knighton, alive or dead, wasn't in the house.

Dr Crocker came out of the dining room and said, 'Old Tremlett's on his way. I managed to get him at home before he left for the infirmary.'

'Is it true she was shot?'

'Through the back of the head. He must have brought the barrel of the gun right up against the occipital itself. All her back hair was singed.'

'He shot her through the *back* of the head? Put the gun against the back of her head and shot her? The mind boggles a bit. What do you think, Sergeant, she heard a sound, came down to see what it was, he crept up behind her and shot her?'

'She might have heard glass breaking, sir. There's a piece of glass missing from the window in there.'

'Except that it was cut out. You can get together with Mrs Thompson and find out what sort of valuables they've got or had in this house.'

Wexford knelt down and looked at the body. It was cold and heavy to the touch and rigor was already established. What he had seen of Adela Knighton in China he hadn't cared for but he forgot that in a rush of pity. She was a sad sight and there was no dignity in her death. While alive and in health she had been a plain, stocky, rather aggressive, no-nonsense sort of woman. Now in death she lay as a flabby heap, her face having a look of half-melted wax, her grizzled sandy hair burned black at the nape of her neck and around the red, charred-edged hole the bullet had drilled there. She wore an expensive-looking nightgown of some thick, shiny, peach-coloured silky material with lace borders and lace insertions and over it a dressing gown of dark blue velour. On her feet were flat-heeled slippers of quilted black velvet. Her wedding ring, a chased platinum band worn down to the thinness of wire, was on her left hand.

'It doesn't look as if anything very alarming fetched her down,' said Wexford. 'There's a phone extension by her bed and the wires haven't been cut.'

A black Daimler drew up on the gravel drive. Sir Hilary Tremlett, the pathologist, had arrived. Wexford went into the washroom off the hall. It contained a lavatory pan with low flush cistern, a vanity table with bowl insert, a small round mirror on the wall above the bowl. The window was the sash kind divided into four panes, each about fifteen inches square, and from one of these the glass had been cut. Wexford decided there was no way he himself could have squeezed through the aperture thus obtained but he was a large man with a big frame. Most women could have got through there and any average-sized man.

Directly below the window outside was a small narrow flowerbed in which pink sedum was blooming. Wexford knew there wouldn't be any footprints. He went out to look and there weren't, though someone had plainly kicked over the remains of what footprints there had been.

Mrs Thompson was telling Martin that the Knightons had never kept money in the house as far as she knew. Mrs Knighton, like a lot of well-off people, Renie Thompson implied, was always short of cash and as often as not would pay her with a cheque. No ornaments were missing, no attempt had been made to remove heavy equipment, television, record player or any kitchen machinery.

'Presumably she had some jewellery.'

'Must have done,' said Martin in a way that indicated he wouldn't have thought of it if his chief hadn't reminded him. 'How about jewellery, Mrs Thompson?'

'I only saw her in the mornings, didn't I? It's no good asking me what rings and whatnot she had.'

Wexford remembered, from China, a platinum watch and an engagement ring with, he thought, a square-cut stone. He mentioned those items to Mrs Thompson.

'If you say so. Don't ask me where she kept them.'

'Very well, we won't ask you,' said Wexford, irritated by her truculent huffy manner. 'We'll look. There are a limited number of places. She didn't keep them in the fridge or up a chimney.'

Sir Hilary had finished his preliminary examination and they were about to take the body away. Murdoch was still meticulously at work on table surfaces, banisters, door jambs. The doctor, about to leave, said to Wexford, 'Did she live here alone?'

'There's a husband,' said Wexford.

'Where is he then?'

'I wish I knew.'

Martin came downstairs. 'There's no jewellery or jewel case in her room or any of the bedrooms, sir.'

'Right.' He said to Mrs Thompson, remembering a table on a hotel roof, a yellow envelope of snapshots, 'She had children. Where do they live?'

'The daughter in Sewingbury, that I do know. Don't ask me where you'll find the sons, all off abroad somewhere, I daresay. There might be numbers in that book.'

A leather-bound directory lay on a table by the telephone. Wexford himself held his daughters' phone numbers in his head. He was justly and secretly proud of his memory, knowing it to be exceptional.

'What's the daughter's married name?'

'Her *surname*? That I wouldn't know. I'd no reason ever to be told that, had I? Jennifer, they call her. Mr Knighton could tell you.'

'Yes, I've no doubt he knows his own daughter's name,' said Wexford. 'You can go home now, Mrs Thompson, if you like. I expect we'll want to see you again. We'll let you know.'

'Don't I get a lift home then?'

'I beg your pardon?'

'I should think the least you could do is one of you run me home. I reported finding her, didn't I? I've helped you with your enquiries. It's usual to arrange for transport under the circumstances.'

Wexford was amused. 'Not in this neck of the sticks it isn't. Maybe in Y Division or Los Angeles. You've been watching too many crime serials.'

Renie Thompson stuck her chin in the air and flounced out. Wexford laughed.

'She only lives in Paunceley,' said Burden. 'You don't think she could have done it?'

'Come on. She couldn't tell a Beretta from a bottle opener. Have you finished, Murdoch? Better get back then. Martin, I want Knighton's daughter found—she lives somewhere in Sewingbury—and the sons too if possible. I want a house-to-house between here and Sewingbury and the other side of Thatto Vale through Paunceley. Luckily, or maybe unluckily, there aren't that many houses.'

'What are we looking for, sir?'

'Any suspicious happenings during the night, any strange cars seen, strangers on foot yesterday or in the night. Oh, and we're looking for Knighton. Very keenly are we looking for Knighton.'

When they had gone Wexford began telling Burden about China. Not about the trip in general—with restraint he had done that weeks before—but everything he could recall of Adam and Adela Knighton. It wasn't much. By a curious irony he had paid more attention to the other members of the train party than he had to the Knightons and their friend. Perhaps it was because the others had been rather thrust upon him and when, belatedly, he had made the Knightons' acquaintance it was at a time when he was being most bedevilled, haunted, plagued by that fantasy or hallucination or whatever you liked to call it. To the women he had hardly spoken a word, to Knighton . . . What could he remember of him? A tall, thin, silver-haired man in his sixties who had looked for a moment as if he had seen a vision and who had recited, for no apparent reason, a strange little piece of Chinese poetry. To Burden, now that he told all this—leaving out only the bit about his own visions—and delved in that excellent memory of his, he was able to reproduce, accurately, he was sure, every sentence he had heard Adam and Adela Knighton utter.

'It may be useful,' said Burden not very encouragingly.

Wexford retorted rather obscurely, though Burden understood. 'Well, it wasn't a burglar, was it? She didn't get up and go down for a burglar. A burglar didn't come up behind her and stick a gun in the back of her head. It wasn't like that. And where the hell is Knighton?'

'Murdered his wife and run off with her friend. No, but seriously, it looks as if he might have. Not run off with the friend, I don't mean that. Not at their ages. But had a row with her in the night and shot her and then got the hell out. Why not? It's the most likely thing. He could be out of the country by now, probably is. People in his position always have wealthy and influential friends.'

'You don't need wealthy and influential friends,' snapped Wexford. 'You just need to buy a plane ticket. On American Express. It's all made so damned easy these days. OK, I agree it's quite likely, though I'd have expected them to be upstairs having their row if she was in her nightdress, and I certainly wouldn't have expected an English gentleman like Knighton to shoot anyone, let alone his wife, through the *back* of the head.'

'That's going to bother you a lot, isn't it?'

'Of course.'

They were in the living room. Once three or four small rooms, now made into one, it was about thirty feet long with french windows at the back and casements giving on to the front lawns and the drive. A grandfather clock began chiming eleven with rich sonorous notes. Wexford heard another sound. He moved to one of the

77

windows and looked out. A car was coming up the drive, a large dark blue Ford.

'That's one of the Kingsmarkham station taxis,' said Burden.

'Yes.'

The car drew up. A man got out of the back of it, paid the driver and picked up a black leather suitcase of overnight bag size which he had set down on the gravel for a moment, and walked towards the front door where he was lost to their view.

'Knighton,' said Wexford.

His key turned in the lock. The two policemen stood absolutely still, waiting. The front door opened and closed, footsteps sounded across the hall and Knighton's voice called, 'Adela!'

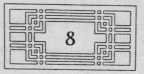

8

IT WAS TIME TO DECLARE THEMSELVES. WEXFORD COUGHED BUT perhaps Knighton didn't hear, for when he saw the two men emerge from his living room he gave a violent start.

'What on earth . . . !'

'Good morning, Mr Knighton,' Wexford said. 'Yes, we've met before. In China. I see you recognize me as I do you. Chief Inspector Wexford of Kingsmarkham CID. This is Inspector Burden.'

'Mr Wexford, yes. I do remember you, though I had no idea . . . What are you doing in my house? Has there been some sort of robbery or what . . . ?'

'That we don't yet know. However, something very serious has taken place. You must be prepared for . . .'

'Where's my wife?'

Wexford told him. All the colour went out of Knighton's face. He walked into the living room and sat down in an armchair.

'Shot?' he said. 'Adela—shot?'

'I'm afraid it's true, sir.'

'Shot by some intruder? She's dead?'

'Yes, it appears she was shot by someone who forced an entry to this house during the night.'

Knighton passed a hand across his face. 'And you— you're a policeman in Kingsmarkham? You came in here and found my wife dead?'

'I among others. Your cleaner notified us.'

'Good God. Good God in heaven!'

Burden had sat down and now Wexford sat down too. Knighton's face was still paper-white, his eyes glassy with shock. Wexford could have sworn it had been a shock. He noticed something that hadn't really struck him while they were in China—his wretched preoccupation with the old woman with bound feet, no doubt, had distracted him—he noticed how extraordinarily good-looking Knighton was. He was still good-looking now, though he looked ill with shock. What must he have been like when young? He still had a boy's figure, a young man's lithe carriage, and his features were of the classical sort, grown somewhat marble-like with age. His golden locks time had to silver turned. Adela Knighton, on the other hand, had been very plain, ugly even. And hers was the kind of ugliness not created by time but bred in the bone.

All that, of course, might be quite irrelevant. Wexford asked the classic requisite question that always made him feel like a character in a detective story.

'Where were you last night, sir?'

'Where was I? Staying with a friend in London. Why do you ask?'

'Routine.'

'Good God.' A sort of horrified understanding twisted Knighton's mouth. 'I thought you said a burglar . . .'

'If you could just tell us where you were last night, sir, the name of your friend and so on, we should be able to get through this painful business a good deal faster.'

'Oh, very well,' Knighton hesitated a fraction. 'An old friend of mine, Henry Lacey,' he said, 'was giving a dinner party at a club to which both he and I belong. The Palimpsest in St James's. It was to celebrate his fifty years at the bar, what it would be the fashion to call a Golden Jubilee, I suppose. I was invited. On such occasions I stay in London as I have never cared to fetch my wife out with the car at one o'clock in the morning. And the station taxi service is not available at that hour, as you doubtless know.'

'You stayed at the club?'

'No, with a friend who has a flat in Hyde Park Gardens.'

The phone rang. Knighton gave another violent start. Wexford was rather surprised that he glanced at him for the go-ahead before answering it. He nodded.

Knighton gave the number in a steady low voice. Whoever was at the other end, unless exceptionally insensitive, would have recognized it as the voice of one recently bereaved. A cruel estimate, Wexford thought, but just. Knighton was shocked but he was not unhappy—perhaps unhappiness would come hereafter.

'Oh, Jennifer . . .' It was the daughter. 'The police have told you? Have you talked to Rod? Yes, please do come . . .' He put the phone down, again touched his forehead with his hand. 'My son is coming and my daughter and son-in-law.'

'I understand you have four children?'

'A daughter and three sons. One is in America and one in Turkey.'

'While we're waiting for your son and Mr and Mrs . . . ?'

'Norris. My son-in-law is a solicitor with Symonds, O'Brien and Ames in Kingsmarkham.'

'While we're waiting for them, perhaps you'll give me the name of your friend in Hyde Park Gardens and the address of Mr Henry Lacey.'

Jennifer and Angus Norris got there first. She was a plain young woman, dumpy and freckled, who resembled her mother. She was also about seven months pregnant and Wexford remembered Adela Knighton speaking of another grandchild 'on the way.'

Her brother Roderick turned up soon afterwards in a yellow Triumph TR7, having driven very fast from London. He was handsome and tall like his father, though anxious-looking and a good deal older than his sister. A barrister also, Wexford gathered. The law was well represented in the Knighton family to whom this lawless thing had happened. The spry little son-in-law, no taller than his wife and with a shock of dark curly hair surrounding a bald spot, he had sometimes seen in the Magistrates' and Crown Courts.

Young Mrs Norris had a manner Wexford had met before in women of the upper middle class who have led indulged lives. She called her parents Mummy and Daddy and spoke of her family and its immediate circle as of an élite.

'It's so awful, I feel it just can't be happening to us. Daddy was at the criminal bar, you know, and I remember Mummy saying how that really brought home to one what a horrendous lot of murders there actually are. And Daddy used to say she needn't worry because only a fraction of those murders happened to people like us, they were nearly all confined to the lower classes. And now poor Mummy . . . I mean, it seems so unfair. You lead a decent life and try to keep up some sort of standard and then an appalling thing like this has to happen.'

No doubt she would have found the murder more comprehensible if Renie Thompson had been the victim. But for those remarks of hers Wexford might not have asked where she and her husband had been on the previous night.

'What sort of time had you in mind?' said Norris. 'What does "night" mean?' He spoke in the style he used when cross-examining nervous witnesses. 'What time did all this take place?'

'Let's just stick to "night" for the moment, Mr Norris.'

'I asked because it so happens I took my wife out for a while during the evening.'

Jennifer Norris made a sound which in the circumstances couldn't have been laughter but which came very near it, an unamused grim laugh. Her brother turned cold magisterial eyes on her.

'Yes, but really, Angus, *you* took *me* out! What he means, Rod, is that we walked down to the river and back and had a drink at the Millers', the usual extent of our wining and dining these days . . .'

Wexford coughed.

'Yes, well, Chief Inspector,' began Norris who had gone rather pink, 'we went to bed early, we . . .'

'Oh, Angus, let me tell him. My doctor gives me a mild sedative and the result is I sleep like a log. And lately we've been taking the phone off the hook, so if poor Mummy had tried to get through . . .' It was plain to Wexford that she couldn't for a moment imagine she or her husband might come under suspicion. This was murder in the course of robbery. This was a 'lower class' crime. 'We live in Springhill Lane, actually,' she volunteered. 'In one of the *old* houses.' This was a facet of local snobbism Wexford had encountered once or twice before. People living in this prestigious district of Sewingbury had an edge on their neighbours if they possessed one of the original seventeenth-century houses. There were perhaps half a dozen of these, around and among which new building had taken place during the past twenty years.

'Mummy can't have heard that glass breaking. She had a phone by her bed and even if she couldn't get through to us she'd have tried to phone the police. I mean, how could she have hoped to deal with some rough type like that?'

'He forced an entry by breaking a window?' asked Norris.

'Not exactly, Mr Norris. Rather let's say a pane of glass was cut out from a window. And what were your movements last night, Mr Knighton?'

Roderick Knighton had a breezy manner. He glanced frequently at his watch. Already he had made several phone calls, declaring during the intervals between them that he didn't know what use he could be here but if there was anything he could do his father, sister and the Chief Inspector had only to ask. He yawned, looked once more at his watch and replied to Wexford that he had hardly slept a wink on the previous night, he and his wife and the au pair having been up for most of it with the youngest child who was ill.

'Mumps, actually,' he said. 'Poor little scrap.'

Jennifer Norris had put her feet up. Her husband was standing by one of the windows, looking thoughtful. He seemed worried or puzzled, perhaps only concerned that a man in his position—as he would doubtless refer to himself—could suddenly find himself involved in so unsavoury a business. And Wexford's next remark made him turn slowly round to exchange with his wife a glance of dismay or possibly incredulity.

'I'd like to see what we can do by way of making an inventory of Mrs Knighton's missing jewellery.'

For Knighton this was a hopeless task. He now seemed stunned or bemused by what had happened and his face was drained of all colour and animation. He sat limply in an armchair, gazing at a fixed point and occasionally shaking himself out of his reverie with a shiver. Wexford's suggestion fetched from him a vague shake of the head. Roderick was on the phone again, whispering discreetly, sometimes cupping his hand round the mouthpiece.

'Is any jewellery actually missing?' asked Norris in his courtroom drawl.

'One would suppose so. There's none in the house.' Wexford said dryly, 'I'm assuming Mrs Knighton possessed jewellery apart from her wedding ring.'

'Of course she did,' said Jennifer very sharply. Wexford wondered how much of that steel-trap snapping Norris had to put up with. 'There was a gold bracelet that had been my grandmother's,' she said, and added with a resounding lack of discretion, 'that she always said would be mine one day.' Norris closed his eyes and winced. 'And her pearls, of course. A few rings and brooches, a couple of watches. We aren't the sort of people who decorate ourselves like Christmas trees. Mummy thought it dreadfully vulgar to have your ears pierced.'

'I'd like you to do your best to make a list, Mrs Norris. No doubt your father gave her presents of jewellery over the years?'

Knighton said nothing. Wexford suddenly noticed the

large, square-cut diamond on the daughter's small red left hand. 'I don't actually think he did much,' she said.

Dr Moss, who was Crocker's partner and Adam Knighton's GP, arrived at one and offered Knighton sleeping pills, tranquillizers and restrained sympathy. Roderick said he would be off but if there was anything he could do they had only to ring him. He left a string of phone numbers. Jennifer Norris remarked to her husband that they could phone her brother in Washington now, it would be eight in the morning in Washington. To her brother in Ankara she had sent a cable.

Wexford went back to the police station.

The house-to-house had produced nothing. Wexford hadn't thought it would. Thatto Hall Farm was too isolated. Pending Sir Hilary Tremlett's report, Crocker had volunteered that death had taken place approximately between two and four a.m. It would be at least tomorrow before they knew more: the type of gun used, the precise cause of death, other injuries, if any, to the body.

'It wasn't a burglary, was it?' asked Burden. 'It was a clumsy half-hearted attempt to make it look like a burglary.'

Wexford nodded. 'Possibly not even what Jennifer Norris calls a "rough type".'

'Knighton,' said Burden cautiously, 'is not what anyone would call a rough type.'

Wexford's eyebrows went up.

Burden sat down in the only other seat apart from Wexford's swivel one that might remotely be called an armchair. 'He's fixed himself up a wonderful alibi for an innocent man. Going up to London, dining in St James's, staying in Hyde Park Gardens. He hardly ever spends a night away from home but the very night he does his wife gets murdered. Would you have reckoned when you met him in China that he was—well, fond of his wife? I mean, was it a happy marriage?'

'Marriage is a funny old carry-on altogether, isn't it? Hard to say. I couldn't say.'

'Helpful. I really came to say do you feel like a spot of lunch? The Pearl of Africa? Oh, God, I can see it in your face, you want to go Chinese again. The day is coming when I shan't be able to face another crispy noodle.'

'I can't resist impressing people with my dazzling virtuosity with the chopsticks,' said Wexford as they walked down Queen Street towards the Many-Splendoured Dragon. 'D'you know, Mike, I wish I'd paid more attention to the Knightons in China. I've a feeling it would have been profitable. But all I can really remember is Knighton sitting at a table and suddenly looking as if he'd seen a ghost. Or maybe not a ghost.' He paused thoughtfully. 'Maybe the Holy Grail or the City of God or, if he were Dante, Beatrice.'

9

LODGED IN THE DEAD WOMAN'S SKULL, EGRESS STOPPED BY THE frontal bone, was a bullet from a Walther PPK 9 mm automatic. She had been shot at the closest possible range, the barrel of the gun having been in contact with the back of her head.

Sir Hilary Tremlett's more precise assessment narrowed down the time of death to between 2.15 and 3.45 a.m. Adela Knighton had been a normal healthy woman of about sixty-five, somewhat overweight, who had borne several children and at several times in her life had undergone surgery. For mastoid, for varicose veins, appendicitis and, within the past four or five years, a hysterectomy. There was a mild degree of bruising on the upper left arm.

The fingerprints in Thatto Hall Farm proved to be those of the dead woman herself, Adam Knighton, Renie Thompson, Jennifer Norris and Angus Norris. On the evening of the day of her mother's death, Mrs Norris had provided Wexford with a list of all the jewellery she believed her mother had possessed. But by that time Wexford's officers, combing the grounds of Thatto Hall Farm, had found a green leather jewel case under the hedge by the front gates. Items from it also came to light, scattered haphazardly with no apparent attempt at concealment, in flowerbeds, under the same hedge, on the bank that bordered the road. Two watches, a gold bracelet, a string of pearls, two diamond and ruby rings in old-fashioned settings. Mrs Norris identified it all as having belonged to her mother and told Wexford that nothing was missing.

He saw clearly what had happened. This was no burglar who had come into Thatto Hall Farm during the small hours. Whoever it was had taken the jewel case, having at the time the intention of making the intrusion look like robbery. Later, abandoning this idea as likely to deceive no one and not wishing to be encumbered with some not very valuable jewellery, he had thrown it away, item by item, as he fled from the house.

He had known the house, he had known about that window. He had known Mrs Knighton would be alone. He had cut out that pane of glass and rested the cut-out pieces neatly up against the wall, entered silently, gone upstairs and awakened the sleeping woman. She had been forced to get up and walk downstairs ahead of him at gunpoint. The gun had been pressed against the back of her skull and she had been gripped by the upper arm. There, in the dining room—because she had refused to show him something, tell him something, lead him somewhere, promise, betray, give?—he had pressed the trigger and she had fallen forward, dead on the floor.

That was what he thought had happened. It would do as a working hypothesis.

'Knighton,' said Wexford, 'says he left home at three on Tuesday afternoon, having phoned for a car to take him to Kingsmarkham station, and caught the three-twenty-seven train. He has a car, a Volvo estate, but he says his wife wanted to use it and if he had let her drive him to Kingsmarkham it would have delayed her.'

'Where was she going?' Burden asked. They were in the car, being driven to London.

'Shopping in Myringham. A regular Tuesday afternoon exercise, apparently. Knighton got to Victoria at four-fifteen and from there he went by tube to Lancaster Gate and walked the short distance to the flat of a friend of his called Adrian Dobson-Flint in Hyde Park Gardens,

Dobson-Flint having arrived home a little earlier than usual to let him in.

'This dinner at the Palimpsest Club was at seven for seven-thirty. He and Dobson-Flint left Hyde Park Gardens in a cab at ten to seven, remained at the club having their dinner and generally merry-making until eleven-thirty, at which time they left and walked home. There they had something to drink and went to bed at about half-past midnight. Dobson-Flint had to be in the Old Bailey by ten in the morning, so they were both up by eight. Dobson-Flint left soon after nine and Knighton about nine-twenty, catching the nine-forty train to Kingsmarkham from Victoria.'

'You suspect him,' said Burden.

'Not really. Only I don't know who else to suspect. Early days, I daresay. She left a will, by the way. Angus Norris told me all about it without waiting to be asked. His firm were her solicitors. Adela Knighton had quite a bit of money of her own, a few thousand inherited from an aunt, another few from an uncle, parents' property, as like as not some share in a family trust. Anyway, there was two hundred thousand and she left it equally between her four kids.

'Julian, the son in Washington, is married to an American woman whose father is some sort of millionaire. Roderick has a thriving law practice and his wife's got her own employment agency. Colum, the youngest—he's thirty—is an attaché at the British Embassy in Ankara and whether or not he was looking to his inheritance there's no doubt he was in Turkey at three on Wednesday morning.

'I jib a bit at the idea of a woman seven months pregnant killing her own mother. On the other hand, she wouldn't have had to get in the window. She, apart from Knighton himself and Mrs Thompson, was the only person to have a key to the house. She would certainly have known her father was going to be away for the night and her mother would be alone. But where's her motive? The fifty grand she would inherit? Norris is only an assistant solicitor but he's obviously no fool and likely to be a partner one day. They live in Springhill Lane which is hardly a milieu for people short of the ready. We can put them on one side for the moment. Julian and his wife were in Washington, Colum, as I said, in Ankara and Roderick is alibi'd—if he needs an alibi—by his wife, his au pair, his unfortunate GP and no doubt would be by his mumps-stricken daughter if we asked her.'

The chambers of which Adrian Dobson-Flint was a member were those to which Adam Knighton had formerly belonged. It was the death, and such a death, of Knighton's wife which was presumably responsible for the expression of discreet woe on the face of the Clerk to Chambers, a man called Brownrigg, who showed Wexford and Burden into Dobson-Flint's room.

Adam Knighton's friend was some seven or eight years younger than he, a man who must have been improved by his barrister's wig, for he was almost totally hairless. Since his face was unlined, pink and youthful-looking, this gave him something of the appearance of a skinhead. His room too was untypical, neither dusty and dark nor a litter of books, but a coolly, creamily painted office with fawn carpet and mahogany furniture, a view of a little enclosed garden and a window that let in sunlight.

'In what way can I be of assistance to you gentlemen?'

The skinhead image was quickly dispelled by Dobson-Flint's gracious, modulated voice. It too held the requisite, muted note of sorrow. The baby face contorted into a twist of petulant distress.

'I must say this is really the most shocking and appalling thing I ever heard.'

Which, if it were true, would give a very curious slant to the man's courtroom activities over the past quarter of a century or so. Wexford asked him for an account of Tuesday evening. In discussing alibis, times, reasons why persons should be in such and such a place rather than in another, Dobson-Flint was very much at home. And in spite of having heard his voice raised in public almost every day for many years, he was still fond of the sound of it. He discoursed lucidly, mellifluously, on the dinner party, the date some weeks previously on which invitations to it had been received, the time of Knighton's arrival at his flat, the time of their departure for and arrival at the Palimpsest. There was a note of faint amusement, such as would have been present had he been playing with a witness like a fly fisherman tickling a salmon. Underlying it seemed to be the unspoken question: Are you so obtuse that you can even remotely consider my old friend Adam Knighton under suspicion of murder?

His distress at the death of his friend's wife, if he had ever felt it, now seemed forgotten. His pale blue eyes twinkled. He sat back in his chair with his legs crossed at the knees, one arm resting negligently on the arm of the chair, the other hand supporting his chin.

'It being a fine clear night,' he said, 'we resolved not to indulge ourselves with a cab but instead, in short, to walk it. We arrived on my doorstep at precisely two minutes to midnight. And now, Chief Inspector, you will ask me in time-honoured fashion how I can be so sure of the time, will you not? And my answer will be to you that as I raised my hand to insert my latchkey in the lock Mr Knighton informed me of the time, remarking that twenty-eight minutes from St James's to the Bayswater Road was not bad for two men no longer in their first or indeed second youth.'

With people of Dobson-Flint's kind Wexford generally allowed his own manner to become dull and dead-sounding, and it was in a leaden voice that he asked, 'You live alone, sir?'

'Oh, yes, and have done these twenty years since my wife and I reached an amicable agreement to part.'

Wexford made no comment on this marital revelation. Dobson-Flint said, 'Shall I proceed? Mr Knighton and I each took a glass of Chivas Regal whisky and retired to our beds at approximately twenty past twelve. I say ''approximately'' because this time Mr Knighton did not happen to make any remark upon the time. At seven forty-five or thereabouts in the morning I rose up, took my bath, girded my loins and was about to enter Mr Knighton's room with a cup of China tea when he appeared, fully-dressed, and announcing his kind intention of taking breakfast with me. At nine-ten, as is my wont, I departed to win my bread, leaving Mr Knighton to go on his way rejoicing, though in point of fact it was rather to a weeping, a wailing and a gnashing of teeth.'

'Yes, sir. Did Mr Knighton often stay with you?'

'Often is an imprecise adverb,' said Dobson-Flint in his best Central Criminal Court manner. 'A man might say "I often go abroad", implying he leaves the country three or four times a year, but he may equally aver, "I often visit a cinema," meaning in this case that he attends a picture palace twice a week.' He smiled.

'And which would be true of Mr Knighton's overnight stays with you?'

'Neither!' said Dobson-Flint triumphantly. 'It would probably be true to say that, in the three years since his retirement and removal to the country, he has stayed with me on an average one and a half times per year.'

Wexford got up. 'I expect you'll be having a lunch-time break now, sir?'

'If you will excuse me, Chief Inspector.'

'I didn't quite mean that, Mr Dobson-Flint. I meant that since you'll no doubt be free for the next hour or so, we might use the time in having a look at this flat of yours.'

'Oh, come, is that necessary?'

In the same deadening voice Wexford said, 'It's essential. I have a car. You won't be much inconvenienced.'

Hyde Park Gardens, the mid-nineteenth-century terrace which faces the Bayswater Road and Hyde Park at the Lancaster Gate, is divided by Brook Street into two sections. The eastern part is older, larger and rather grander. Here the Sri Lankans have their embassy, and from a house once owned by the mysterious Duke of

Portland (who went about always in a black veil) legend has it a secret passage runs underground to Baker Street. However, it was in the western terrace of Hyde Park Gardens that Adrian Dobson-Flint had his flat. Wexford had been into the block once before, years ago, and then had gone in through the front entrance, up the steps, through double doors, past the porters' office and up the wide curving staircase. He expected to do so again but Dobson-Flint directed the taxi into Stanhope Place which runs along the back of Hyde Park Gardens and led them up to the front door of a flat which though on the ground floor at the back would have to be designated 'basement' or 'lower ground floor' at the front. It took Wexford no more than a few seconds to realize that it was only from these flats which had access to Stanhope Place that occupants of Hyde Park Gardens could come and go without passing through the front entrance or chancing an encounter with porters.

On the doorstep Wexford said, 'What time did Mr Knighton get here on Tuesday afternoon?'

'I was back here by five,' said Dobson-Flint. 'Shall we say ten past? Yes, I should say about ten past.'

They went inside. There were two bedrooms, the spare one being the nearer to the front door. Dobson-Flint had dropped his keys into a shallow pewter dish which stood on a console table and which already contained another bunch of keys and car keys attached to a fob.

'Are you a heavy sleeper, Mr Dobson-Flint?' Burden asked.

'I succeed in sleeping through some of the worst traffic noise in London, so I should say yes, I am.'

There was nothing else of interest to see. Wexford said, 'I suppose Mr and Mrs Knighton were a happy couple?'

He didn't expect a frank answer but he wanted to see just what sort of answer he would get. Dobson-Flint replied with a kind of forced impatient enthusiasm.

'Oh, absolutely devoted. They simply adored each other. The Knightons were what is generally called a very united family. Until this fearful tragedy struck them Mr and Mrs Knighton lived for each other. I can't imagine either of them ever having had eyes for anyone else.'

He refused Wexford's offer of a lift back and departed in a taxi, leaving them in the street outside his front door.

Wexford said thoughtfully, 'He doth protest too much.'

'About the Knightons' mutual devotion, do you mean?' asked Burden.

'That was a strange remark. "I can't imagine either of them ever having had eyes for anyone else." It's not the sort of thing that would come to mind at all when considering the domestic happiness or otherwise of people in their sixties. Why did he mention it? It's a funny thing, Mike, but I keep having this feeling that what's happened in this case, and maybe is happening, ought to be to people thirty years younger than the Knightons. I've got a feeling this was a crime of passion, yet any less likely candidate for passion than Mrs Knighton I've yet to see.'

'And that bald-headed stuffed shirt feels it too?'

'Harsh words, Mike. But maybe, yes, I think he does. Knighton could have gone back to Sussex during the night, shot his wife and returned here hours before Dobson-Flint started fiddling about with his Lapsang-Souchong.'

'How? There's no train between the twelve fifty-five and the six-forty.'

'It doesn't have to be by train. In fact, the train would have been no use to him since he couldn't have got from Kingsmarkham to Sewingbury at the other end. But he could have done it by car.'

'We know he didn't. His car was in the garage at Thatto Hall Farm.'

'Listen, Mike. What was he doing between getting to Victoria at four-fifteen and arriving at Hyde Park Gardens at ten past five? Fifty-five minutes to get from Victoria to Lancaster Gate? There's something he could have been doing. He could have been in a local car hire place, renting a car, and returning it next morning.

'All he had to do was book himself a car by phone and turn up to collect it at four forty-five, drive it here and leave it on a meter. It looks to me as if the whole of this area is metered, I noticed as we were coming along. Metering ends at six-thirty so he'd only have to put his money in for an hour and a half. After Dobson-Flint's gone to bed he leaves the flat, helping himself to a key out of that pewter plate thing, retrieves his hired car and drives to Sewingbury—an hour's drive at that time of night. He lets himself in by the front door, awakens Adela and shoots her, takes her jewel case. Then he cuts the pane out of the loo window. On his way back to the road where he has left the car parked on the verge he discards the jewellery and the case. An hour later he's back in Hyde Park Gardens and it's still only three-thirty. How about that?'

'He was taking a hell of a risk,' said Burden. 'Suppose Dobson-Flint had gone into his room?'

'Never! Can you imagine it? Not those sort of people, they never would. Their sons might, yes, but never those two. Dobson-Flint would have gone in there only if Knighton had cried out and even then he'd have hesitated.'

'By the way,' said Burden as they got back into the car, 'his son lives in London. Why couldn't he stay with him?'

'Roderick Knighton and his wife live in Mill Hill, quite a way out. Too far out if you're depending on public transport and taxis. Or I think that's what Knighton would say. The truth may of course be that if he was planning a small hours murder trip the Bayswater Road is a good deal nearer to Sussex.'

Men were searching for the weapon in the grass verges, the hedges, the fields, the footpaths, even wading in the Kingsbrook itself where it flowed through Thatto Vale. Wexford asked himself if the gun had belonged to Knighton. A retired counsel who had been at the criminal bar might well know where to acquire an automatic.

The little gun, it had been discovered from a hairline scratch on the bullet that had killed Adela Knighton, had a tiny pinhead-sized protuberance, a minute wart-like flaw, on the inside of its barrel.

It was a damp chilly day, rather colder than usual for the time of year and darker than usual for the time of day. The surrounding hills and woodland were blanketed in grey mist. The gun might be hidden anywhere in there, a tiny metal tube in innumerable tons of earth, leaf mould and water. Or it might be cleaned and polished, folded in a soft cloth, put away in a drawer. He went up the drive to Thatto Hall Farm.

Julian Knighton with his wife Barbara had arrived that morning from America. Julian was shortish, thick-set like his mother, moon-faced like his mother, perhaps forty years old. The Knightons had evidently belonged in that category of couples who, like the Queen, had had two families. The first pair, the two older sons, must surely have been about ten and eight years old before Jennifer was born, and then they had had another son two or three years later, the still absent Colum.

Adam Knighton looked ill, stricken with suffering. His face was drawn in under the cheekbones. Wexford remembered how astounded he had been, how disbelieving, when first told of his wife's death. Only a brilliant actor could have feigned that. He looked at the Chief Inspector with sunken haunted eyes. The pregnant Mrs Norris reclined in an armchair with her feet up. Barbara Knighton was drinking something from a glass that might have been iced tea or heavily diluted whisky. Her husband presented Wexford with a theory.

'It strikes me as being highly probable he expected to find a safe, Chief Inspector. My father did in fact have a safe in this house at one time but when break-ins became so frequent in Sewingbury he had it taken out. Its presence did seem to advertise that one had rather special things to protect.'

'It was while we were still using this house as a weekend retreat,' said his father. 'On a Sunday night before we left to go back to Hampstead I used to put our few valuables in the safe. Could he have been looking for that? Is that at all feasible? Do you think it conceivable my wife was shot by accident? That this man threatened her with the gun if she refused to reveal the whereabouts of the safe to him and when she did refuse the gun went off by accident? Is that at all a useful theory?'

The man had been a distinguished, even brilliant, counsel. It was hard to believe it in the face of this nonsense. Wexford remembered reading of him in the newspapers, 'Mr Adam Knighton, defending . . .' 'Mr Adam Knighton's masterly presentation of the prosecution's case . . .' Something soft and weak had come into the hard aquiline face. When they were in China it had been like the face of some noble bird of prey but now it was as if those features had been made of wax and a warm hand had passed, smudging, across them. There had been a pathetic loosening of the muscles around the mouth. The uncomfortable thought came to Wexford, became a conviction, that when he was alone, when he went to his bedroom and shut the door on all those sympathizing considerate children, he wept. His face was the face of a man who has soaked it with tears.

'Have you ever possessed a gun, sir?' The question was addressed to Julian Knighton who exclaimed, 'Good God, no! Certainly not!'

Wexford's eyes rested on Adam Knighton.

'When I first came here and fancied myself a weekend country gentleman I had a shotgun. I sold it five years ago.'

Jennifer Norris whispered something to her sister-in-law. They both looked truculently at Wexford.

'I should like to have another look over the house, if I may,' he said.

'I thought my brother made it plain the safe isn't here any more,' said Jennifer Norris in the tone of a nineteenth-century chatelaine addressing a bailiff.

'Quite plain, thank you.' Wexford looked at Adam Knighton.

'You must do as you please, Chief Inspector.'

Wexford closed the living room door after him and went upstairs to the bedroom where Adela Knighton had slept alone that Tuesday night and from where she had been peremptorily and terrifyingly summoned. Since his last visit the bed had been made. There was nothing to be learned from a perusal of Mrs Knighton's clothes. Their pockets, as were her handbags, were empty. On the windowsill, between looped-up rose-printed curtains, stood a china candlestick, a pomander and bookends encompassing the reading matter of someone who stopped reading when she was in her teens: two or three Jeffery Farnols, *Precious Bane, The Story of an African Farm*, C.S. Lewis's *Mere Christianity*, Mrs Gaskell's *Cranford*. Wexford was looking for something he hadn't been consciously looking for when, two days before, he had searched the desk downstairs.

The dressing table had only one drawer. He opened it. Handkerchiefs, a box of tissues, a card of hairclips, two unused face flannels, a cardboard carton of cotton wool. Mahogany bedside cabinets supported pink porcelain lamps with pink tulle shades. Each cabinet had a drawer. In Mrs Knighton's were a bottle of aspirin, two more handkerchiefs, an old-fashioned silver-handled manicure set, nasal drops, a pair of glasses in a case; in Knighton's a pair of glasses in a case, two ballpoint pens, a scribbling pad, a tube of throat pastilles and a battery shaver in a leather case. Each cabinet had a cupboard under its drawer. Mrs Knighton's held a pair of black corded velvet bedroom slippers and a brown leather photograph album, Knighton's a stack of books, evidently his reading-in-bed for some weeks or months past, for the present and possibly the immediate future. They were, to Wexford, an unexpected collection.

Han Suyin's *A Mortal Flower* and a book of linguistics called *About Chinese*. Understandable inclusions, those two. The man had recently been in China. *Anna Karenina, The Return of the Native*, Elizabeth Barrett's *Sonnets from the Portuguese* and *The Browning Love*

Letters. Wexford looked at them, intrigued. 'Romantic' was the word that had come into his mind. With the exception of that linguistics book they were all voluptuously romantic. They seemed highly unlikely reading matter for that white-haired, dried-up, unhappy old lawyer downstairs. Yet they must be there because he had read them, was reading them now or had at any rate intended to read them.

He opened *Sonnets from the Portuguese* where the place ('If thou must love me, let it be for naught Except for love's sake only . . .') was kept by a marker. The marker was a scrap of paper torn from the scribbling pad and on it, in Knighton's stylized 'ronde' handwriting, were written a few lines of verse. Not Elizabeth Barrett, nor the piece Knighton had quoted leaning over the parapet in Kweilin, but a fragment that was also, unmistakably, Chinese poetry:

> 'Shoot not the wild geese from the south;
> Let them northward fly.
> When you do shoot, shoot the pair of them,
> So that the two may not be put asunder.'

Very curious indeed. Of course it might be assumed that Knighton had written that down after his wife's death, after someone had in fact shot her and put the two of them asunder. Somehow Wexford didn't think so. Those words hadn't been written since Tuesday. The paper was creased from many usings, many insertions into that volume of sonnets. And when he went out on to the landing again and looked through the open doorway of the 'green' bedroom opposite, he saw the bedcover turned down and a brown plaid dressing gown lying over a chair. Temporarily, the widower had removed himself from the room he had shared with his wife.

They were still in the living room, all four of them. Jennifer Norris still reclined with her feet up. She and her father were drinking tea. Barbara Knighton was arranging the last roses of summer in a copper bowl, October blooms from a second or third flowering. They were a little pale and worn, those roses, with a papery look.

'Just one thing, Mr Knighton. What has become of the photographs you and Mrs Knighton took while you were on holiday?'

'Photographs?'

'They aren't in the album I found in Mrs Knighton's bedside table, though pictures from your previous holidays are.'

'Probably you didn't take any this time, did you, Father?'

Knighton hesitated. Wexford guessed he might clutch at the straw Julian offered him and to prevent this said firmly, 'I don't think there's much doubt that both you and Mrs Knighton took photographs, do you?'

Their eyes met. Wexford wondered if he was reading the other man's expression accurately. Or was he imagining the reaction that nothing could have been less fortunate than that he and this policeman had happened to encounter each other on that Chinese holiday? 'We did take a few snaps, yes,' he said languidly. 'If they came out, if they were ever developed, no doubt they're somewhere about the house.'

But they were not.

Wexford said no more about it. He pondered on Adam Knighton, his wistful predilection for romance, his listless, sometimes hag-ridden or haunted look, the possibility that he who loved poetry and the great love stories had held a gun to his wife's scalp and sent a bullet into her brain.

The inquest was on Monday morning, the funeral the following day at All Saints, Sewingbury. By that time it had been established that no car hire company within a three-mile radius of Adrian Dobson-Flint's home had hired a car to a man answering Adam Knighton's description. By then the search for the gun in the vicinity of Thatto Vale had been called off.

Sewingbury has about four thousand inhabitants, a golf course, a convent and girls' school, a disused mill on the Kingsbrook and a huge market square, usually packed tight with parked cars. The church is halfway down the hill that leads to the river and the new 'weir'. Wexford's driver took the route along Springhill Lane, over the newly built bridge, along the river bank past where the footpath from Thatto Vale comes out and up River Street.

All the Knighton family were assembled: Adam, lean, gaunt, bareheaded, wearing a waisted black overcoat; Roderick in a dark suit with a black tie, and Roderick's wife Caroline in a tight black suit and high-heeled black patent shoes. Julian and his wife were in light colours, grey and green respectively, but wore the most doleful expressions, perhaps to compensate. The fair young man with the beaky nose and the thin dark Greek-looking girl Wexford decided must be Colum and his wife. Only Jennifer was absent, though represented by her husband who arrived late and on foot.

Leaving the church when it was all over, after the family had filed out, Wexford, who had been sitting in the very back row, happened to look over his shoulder along the aisle. The small elderly woman he remembered from China as Adela Knighton's friend was walking towards him from where she had been sitting in one of the front pews. He had forgotten all about her until now.

He could tell she was astounded at seeing him. She looked at him as he must have looked when he saw his persecutor with the bound feet. And then her eyes turned sharply away.

Wexford went out and waited for her in the porch.

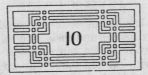

10

'MY NAME IS IRENE BELL. I DON'T BELIEVE WE WERE EVER introduced in China.'

'Chief Inspector Wexford of Kingsmarkham CID. How do you do, Miss Bell?'

'So you're a policeman and living here. How very odd! That must have been quite a shock for poor Adam on top of everything else. He's very cut up, isn't he? Well, we all are. Adela and I were at school together, we'd known each other nearly all our lives. I suppose we'd been friends for something like half a century.'

'It's a long time,' said Wexford. 'Can you and I have a talk, Miss Bell?'

'Now, d'you mean? I suppose so. I wouldn't go back to the house anyway. I don't care for all this eating and drinking at funerals. People don't mean to be irreverent but somehow they forget what they're there for, someone starts laughing and before you know where you are it's turned into a party. I call that very bad taste.'

Wexford nodded in agreement. She seemed a woman of character. 'I'll see you get to Kingsmarkham station afterwards. You wouldn't think a cup of tea irreverent, would you?'

'I could do with a cup of good hot tea,' said Miss Bell.

She was short and sturdily built, though not fat, with a round sharp-featured face and dark hair that still hadn't much grey in it and was crisply permed. The blue trouser suit would have been unsuitable for today and in any case too light in weight, for the previous night had seen the first frost of the winter and a little white frost still lay in shady places. She had on a dark grey tweed suit, beige silk blouse and black court shoes that were nevertheless 'sensible' ones. Up until three years before, she told Wexford, she had been the manager of a travel agency at Swiss Cottage near where she lived. In fact it was this agency that had arranged the trans-Asia trip for her and the Knightons. It wasn't the first time the three of them had been away together. She had gone with them to Egypt as well as on various European holidays. It was company for Adela, she said, which Wexford thought an interesting remark.

Back in Kingsmarkham Wexford took her into the Willow Pattern, a café in the High Street, and ordered tea for two. Irene Bell refused food, perhaps once again on the grounds of the unsuitability of eating just after one has buried one's best friend. For this was what Mrs Knighton had evidently been, a devoted dear friend, as close as a sister, and when Miss Bell referred to her in this way a look of heavy bitter sadness came into her sharp face. She was, she said, godmother to Jennifer, 'Aunt Irene' to all the young Knightons, as nearly a member of the family as one could be who was not allied by blood. Wexford let her talk for a while about her long friendship with the dead woman, noting that though she referred to all Mrs Knighton's children by name and spoke of their children, Adam Knighton was never mentioned. He interrupted her by reverting to what she had said in the car.

'You said you were company for Mrs Knighton. Wasn't her husband company enough for her?'

She lifted her shoulders and gave a half-smile.

'Was it a happy marriage, Miss Bell?'

'Someone said the state of marriage is unhappy only insofar as life itself is unhappy.'

'Samuel Johnson said it. What do you say?'

'In general, Mr Wexford, I don't think much of it. It goes on too long. If it could be for five years, say, I

103

think it would be an excellent institution. Who can stand the same person morning, noon and night for forty years? People think a single woman of my age hasn't married because she hasn't had the chance. That's not so of course.' Irene Bell chuckled. It was a grim chuckle that hadn't much to do with amusement or pleasure. 'I'm not much to look at and never have been but neither are most of the married women you see around you. If folks only got married because they were pretty or charming it'd be a world of singles. No, I never fancied marriage myself. I don't much like sharing. I don't like cooking or housework or babies or sex. Oh, yes, I've tried sex. I tried it three times forty years ago and those three times were enough for a lifetime in my opinion.

'But those are my views. That's marriage in general. In particular, which is what you're asking, I daresay the Knightons were as happy as most people. She was very fond of *him,* poor Adela. She made her choice and she stuck to it and she was a good wife, no one could have had a better wife.'

You don't like him, Wexford thought to himself. Or is it more complex than that? Is it that once you liked him too much?

'They never had much to say to each other. That's partly what I mean when I say I don't think much of marriage. How else do we communicate but in words when all's said and done? You hear a lot of nonsense about the language of the eyes, the language of love, silent communion, all that kind of thing. There wasn't anything of that sort with Adela and Adam, I can tell you. Adela wasn't that sort of woman anyway. Adam— well, it always seems a funny thing to me, a man who reads poetry.'

'Most of it was written by men.'

'That's different,' said Miss Bell. 'Don't confuse me. I mean it's not very robust, it's affected, if you ask me, a man reading—what d'you call 'em?—sonnets.'

Wexford said abruptly, 'Was he unfaithful to her? Did he have love affairs with other women?'

She was taken aback. She had been raising her teacup to her lips. The motion was arrested in mid-air, then slowly she restored the cup to the saucer. 'Good God, no. What an extraordinary idea! He was sixty-three.'

'He wasn't always sixty-three. In any case he's a very handsome man, with what I'd call an attractive presence.' Wexford paused. How intimate they had become, how frank, in ten minutes over the teacups! It seemed at that moment as if there were nothing they couldn't have said to each other. It was a pity she hadn't more to say. 'There's many a man of sixty-three,' he said, 'would be horrified at a suggestion his emotional life was over.'

She gave a short, rather harsh cackle. 'See the day looming yourself, can you? No, there was nothing like that with Adam, you can forget that. Who would he carry on with? Never saw a woman but the vicar's wife. If you're thinking he shot poor Adela to take up with someone else, you're cold like they say in "hunt the thimble", you're stone cold. Adam wouldn't point a gun at anyone, let alone fire it. He gave up shooting pigeons because he said it wasn't ethical. I once saw him get stung by a wasp trying to put it out of the window because he wouldn't kill it.' She laughed again, then set down her cup with a rattle. 'I knew it!' she said. 'This is turning into a party, a beanfeast, and I'm not having it. I call it very bad taste. It was good of you to give me tea but now you'll take me to the station, please.'

Wexford pleaded, 'Five more minutes, Miss Bell, and I promise I will. I want to ask you something about China. Do you remember when we were all sitting in that bar on the hotel roof in Kweilin?'

She was putting on her gloves. 'The temperature was ninety and they were playing "White Christmas". Of course I remember.'

'Mr Knighton had a shock. He went white. He saw something or someone and he was absolutely astounded by what he saw. Did you notice that?'

'I can't say I did.'

'A minute or two later Mrs Knighton said she thought she would go to bed and you and she got up to leave.'

'Maybe, but I don't remember.'

'And the next day he didn't mention it to you? Or to Mrs Knighton in your presence? I mean, he didn't say, "Something I saw on the roof last night amazed me"?'

'No, he didn't. Why don't you ask *him*?'

'I will. You took a lot of photographs. So did Mrs Knighton. Did she show you the ones she took?'

'Weeks ago,' said Irene Bell. 'She came up to town. She always had lunch with me when she did that. We had lunch and we looked at each other's snaps.'

'What did she do with hers?'

'Took them away, of course. She was going to put them in an album she'd got.'

Up in his office on the second floor of the police station he found Burden and Dr Crocker talking about guns. Burden even had a replica of a Walther PPK 9 mm, one which they had taken off a young tearaway who had threatened a visiting pop star with it and which, after the case was over, had unaccountably got into Wexford's desk drawer and remained there ever since.

'I feel more at home with a scalpel,' said the doctor. 'Had a nice funeral, Reg? It beats me why people who aren't religious have funerals. Boring, embarrassing, awkward affairs with no grace or beauty to them now the old prayer book's more or less gone.'

'You have to have a funeral, don't you?' said Burden.

'If you mean by law, certainly not. People have them because they think they've got to but they haven't. You can just get your undertaker to do a quiet little disposal when the crematorium's not busy. Nothing to it. Mind you, it'll cost you much the same. Five hundred quid give or take a little, that's what a funeral comes to these days.'

Wexford, who had been silent, sat down at his desk and, taking the replica gun, turned it slowly over and over in his hands, saying, 'He was sitting on that roof, drinking cassia wine, and suddenly he saw something that utterly astounded him. Not something unpleasant, mark you, rather the reverse. I could almost hazard a guess he saw something wonderful. But what did he see?'

'A pretty girl,' said the doctor.

'Oh, come on. You'd only look like that when you saw a pretty girl if you'd been shut up in solitary confinement for the past twenty years.'

'An old friend?' said Burden. 'Someone maybe he'd defended in court years ago and thought he'd never see again?'

'In that case why didn't he immediately get up and go and speak to him? Why did he go and lean over the parapet and start muttering Chinese poetry?'

'You'd better ask him.'

'I will, but I'm sure he'll lie about it. One of the things we have to do is find out just who knew he was going to be away last Tuesday night. We haven't done much about that but it's on the cards a good many people did know. Everyone at that Golden Jubilee party at the Palimpsest Club for a start. Probably most of Mrs Knighton's acquaintances in Sewingbury. Friends or relations she may have written to or talked to on the phone.'

'You mean,' said the doctor, 'it's a bit fishy it happened that night. I mean here's a chap stays away from his home once a year and on the very night he's away his wife gets murdered.'

'At any rate it teaches us that it was planned. It may have been planned by one of those people who knew he'd be away or it may have been planned by Knighton himself in collusion with someone else or Knighton may have done it alone.'

'Everyone in Hyde Park Gardens,' said Burden, 'is being questioned as to the possibility of their having seen Knighton that night.' He hesitated, said in a rather embarrassed way, 'You may think this very far-fetched . . .'

Wexford countered, 'I'm the one that gets accused of that.'

'Maybe it's infectious. Maybe it's because I—well, I sort of read more than I used.' It was well known that Burden's cultured wife was in the habit of recommending books to him, was one of those rare people who like being read to and had discovered in her husband an unexpected histrionic talent for reading aloud. Burden's face had become a little pink. 'Fiction, you know. I must admit to having read only novels lately.'

Wexford exploded into a quotation from Jane Austen.

'Only novels! Only some work in which the most thorough knowledge of human nature, the happiest delineation of its varieties, the liveliest effusions of wit and humour are conveyed to the world in the best chosen language!'

'OK, let him tell us his idea,' said Crocker.

'It's just that—well, it sounds like something out of Conan Doyle really. On the other hand, you do read in the papers sometimes . . .' Seeing Wexford's eyes sharpening with rage, Burden went on hurriedly, 'You hear of old lags, or any villains really, getting sent down by a judge and swearing to get back at him later. Right? And I'm pretty sure I've come across actual cases—attempts anyway. It did strike me it might be something like that which had happened here.'

'Knighton wasn't a judge.'

'No, but someone accused of a crime in a case where he was prosecuting might feel much the same towards him as towards the judge. He might easily feel that Knighton's presentation of the evidence against him had more effect on the jury than the judge's summing up. Say that because of what Knighton said for the prosecution some guy either got convicted when he expected to be acquitted or got sent down for twice as long as he anticipated. Mightn't he then resolve to get back at Knighton when he came out? And I reckon Knighton's prosecuted in dozens of possible cases. His name was always in the papers.'

'You mean this chap shot Mrs Knighton to get revenge on her husband?' Wexford was interested. He didn't dislike the idea. 'It's a possibility, especially if as you say Knighton got him put away for ten years instead of four or five. Wouldn't he shoot Knighton, though?'

'There's many a married man,' said Burden, 'whose life wouldn't be worth living without his wife.' He gave the doctor an uneasy look as if he expected to be laughed at. 'I know I felt that way when Jean died and if it doesn't sound too ridiculous I'd feel it now about Jenny.' The others didn't laugh but Burden himself did in a high embarrassed sort of way.

'Knighton had been married a very long time too,' said Crocker. 'If you believe the funny postcards and the cartoons and whatever, you'd think that made people less fond. But it doesn't. The long habit of the years, the shared things, the curious kind of oneness—my God! You haven't had a chance yet, young Mike. You don't know the half of it.'

And nor did Irene Bell, thought Wexford. He quoted:

> 'Shoot not the wild geese from the south;
> Let them northward fly.
> When you do shoot, shoot the pair of them,
> So that the two may not be put asunder.'

'Where did you get that from?'

Wexford told them. 'I got the library here to trace it for me. It's a Chinese poem from a collection of T'ang verse, ninth century. The poet was called Shen Hsun and a curious note to it is that he and his wife were murdered by a slave.

'We keep coming back to China, don't we? I've got a feeling, I've had it almost since the murder really, that the key to all this was in China.'

'You can't very well go back there,' said the doctor.

'No, but I can at least see the people Adela Knighton travelled across Asia with. I met them too, remember. There were some strange things . . .' He told them about the two men who hadn't spoken to each other from Irkutsk to Kweilin, about Wong who had drowned. 'She and he took photographs in China, they were always making with the camera. What's happened to those photographs? Why aren't they in her album or sculling about the house in packets? No, I'm more and more sure it's to China and what happened there that we have to look. I just wish I'd taken more notice. I wasn't to know, of course, but usually I like watching people, seeing how they behave. I was too damned preoccupied with that woman with the bound feet.'

Crocker looked at him. 'What woman?'

Diffidently Wexford told him. He had often felt he should have told him long before but he never had. When the symptoms disappear who cares about the cause of the disease? Crocker, who hadn't even smiled at Burden's marital confidings, now burst out laughing.

'What had you been reading?'

'OK, I know, something called *Masterpieces of the Supernatural* and I never finished it.'

'I wouldn't have your imagination for all the tea in China.'

'Sure, but all hallucinations are from the imagination. That doesn't make them any less real to the hallucinator. D'you think it was just that book and lack of sleep?'

'And getting dehydrated and drinking that filthy Maotai you brought home a bottle of.'

'Start getting worried,' said Burden, 'when you see the lady tottering over the Kingsbrook Bridge.'

Wexford gave him a bland look. 'We mustn't risk not investigating the possibilities of this revenge motive, so you can make it your business to inquire into the present circumstances of every villain Knighton prosecuted in, say, the fifteen years prior to his retirement. And for good measure into those of every villain he failed successfully to defend. That should keep you busy for a bit.

'As for me, I shall "fire a mine in China here with sympathetic gunpowder".'

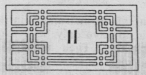

11

DONALDSON WENT OFF TO FIND SOMEWHERE TO PARK THE CAR
and Wexford crossed Kensington Church Street to the
shop above whose window in gilt Times Roman was the
single name 'Vinald'. In the window itself, in solitary
splendour, stood a vase. Not one of those Vinald had
collected in China, but a vessel as tall as a small man
and of dully gleaming black porcelain with a design on it
of a blood-red gilt-clawed dragon.

Inside, deep soft black carpet like cat's fur. The place
was discreetly lit by wall lights in gilt rococo brackets
and by a single spot that fell upon a spinet or harpsi-
chord or some such thing. A few other *objets d'antiquité*
were set about the long room, wax fruit under a glass
bell, a china clock around whose face a Chelsea china
Eros and Psyche sported, a tall slender glass jug, and on
a console table a book of Audubon prints open at a
picture of green and yellow birds.

Wexford introduced himself to the woman in charge
and asked for Gordon Vinald. She was afraid Mr Vinald
was at a sale and not expected back until late afternoon.
Was it very important? Wexford said yes but he would
come back.

'Would it help to see Mrs Vinald? I know she's in.
She phoned just a couple of minutes ago.'

Surely he hadn't been married when Wexford had last
seen him? 'I didn't know there was a Mrs Vinald.'

She smiled in the way people do who find something

111

sweet or touching about matrimony in its early stages. 'Mr and Mrs Vinald have only been married a month. Shall I give her a ring? Their house is just round the corner in Searle Villas.'

He realized what had happened. Hadn't he foreseen it? Vinald had married Margery Baumann.

'Mrs Vinald says if you'd like to go straight over, Mr Wexford, she'll be happy to see you.'

Searle Villas was indeed just round the corner. The garden of number sixteen must have backed on to the shop. It was a house in a Victorian terrace that no one would have looked at twice in Kingsmarkham but here was no doubt worth about half a million. He was admitted by a young black woman in jeans with a duster in her hand. She pushed a door open and said to him indifferently, 'She's in there.'

The room was a museum, seemingly furnished with overflow from the shop. In the middle of the Chinese carpet sat a very large stout lushly-furred tabby cat which ceased washing itself to stare at him with glittering zircon eyes. Standing by the marble fireplace, one white arm extended along the mantel, was the beautiful black-haired Pandora.

She didn't recognize him. Probably she hadn't even noticed him on that previous occasion. While a man of Wexford's age will inevitably notice and remember such a woman, to her he may be invisible.

Her hair was longer, cut now with a fringe that curved symmetrically down into a page-boy, the Egyptian queen look. Her mouth was as red as cinnabar and her eyelids painted jade. Wexford felt that either he had seen her before—and he meant before the encounter on the hotel roof—or that she reminded him strikingly of some famous beauty. A film star from when he was young? Hedy Lamarr? Lupe Velez? She wore a clinging black silk jersey and a skirt of black and red printed velvet and her legs were the best he had ever seen, better even, he thought disloyally, than his daughter Sheila's.

'I think you've come to talk about the late Mrs Knighton. Am I right?'

He was surprised and his eyebrows went up.

'What else could it be?' Her twang brought her down to earth, made her less of a goddess. 'I travelled with her to Hong Kong. Well, all the way to England, if you count being in the airplane. Don't you care to sit down?'

The cat leapt—gracefully for one of her girth—up on to the chair before he could sit in it.

'Oh, get out, Selima.' She picked it up and dumped it on to a chaise longue. 'She's called the Pensive Selima for some reason known to my husband, some poem.'

'Demurest of the tabby kind,' said Wexford.

'Maybe. I'm not poetical myself.' In a way she was, though. Any man would have wanted to write a poem to her or about her. But with a faint feeling of disappointment he saw what she meant. Despite her looks, the Hollywood profile, she was of the earth, earthy. 'So what can I do for you?'

'I don't know, Mrs Vinald, I'm a bit in the dark. You didn't travel on that train across Asia, did you?'

She shook her head. 'We met up with the train party in a place called Kweilin. I first met my husband in the hotel there. I was doing a kind of world tour. We'd come from Auckland to Jakarta, Jakarta to Singapore, Singapore to Peking. It was going to be Bombay after Hong Kong but—well, London suddenly seemed that much more attractive! But I have to tell you, I don't think I spoke one single word to that poor Mrs Knighton. I only know her name because Gordon said who she was after we saw in the papers about her getting murdered.'

Wexford thought it was time he explained that he too had been in China. She was astonished and then confused. Had he been there tailing Mrs Knighton, watching her or what? No, she couldn't follow it. He'd actually seen her, Pandora Vinald, before? It is always hard to understand that someone very beautiful, particularly someone with a sensitive face and a sweet expression, may be quite stupid. Pandora Vinald, he decided, was—to put it as kindly as possible—not very intelligent. Not a patch really—except in one vital way—on Margery Baumann.

'Have you seen any of the train party people since you came here?' he asked.

'No, we haven't. Gordon says holiday friendships are a dead loss, they never lead to anything.'

'Unlike holiday romances.'

It took her a moment to understand but when she did she broke into merry gratified laughter. The Pensive Selima sat up and began frantically washing her face in the way cats do, as if they have suddenly been warned by some inner voice of a disfiguring smut. Pandora Vinald said, 'We did have a photo sent us by a Mrs Knox. I mean Gordon did. We were in it, you see, and a lot of other people. You couldn't see us very well, it wasn't very good. Gordon said not to answer, it would only encourage her, but I didn't think that was very kind, I thought of how *she'd* feel, you see.' She smiled and said naively, 'So I wrote back and thanked her and said it was very nice, though it wasn't, and mentioned we were getting married.'

'Do you still have her address?'

The cat jumped off the chaise longue, stalked to the door and emitted a shrill impatient mew. Because the mew wasn't attended to she followed it up with a series of near-screams.

'Oh, Selima, you noisy beast. She's a terribly spoilt cat. Gordon's ex-wife let her do anything she wanted, scrape her claws down some practically priceless old pieces, just awful.' The door was opened and the cat went out with a slowness that was insolent. 'Address, did you say? I've got all their addresses, as a matter of fact. The tour company sent Gordon a list of the people going, with their addresses, before he went, and it's right here in the top of the desk. Would that be of use to you?'

There they all were in alphabetical order:

Mrs H. Avory, 19 Oswestry Place, Rosia Bay, Gibraltar.

Dr and Mrs C. Baumann, Four Winds, Southwood Hill, Purley, Surrey.

Dr M. Baumann, 2 Crestleigh Drive, Guildford, Surrey.

Miss I.M. Bell, Flat 6, Meleager Court, Queen Charlotte Road, London NW3.

Mr L. Fanning (tour leader), 105a Kingsland House, New King's Road, London SW6.

Mr and Mrs A.D. Knighton, Thatto Hall Farm, Myring-ham Road, Sewingbury, Sussex.

Mrs L. Knox, 26 Redvers Lodge, Redvers Road, Rosia Bay, Gibraltar.

Mr A.H. Purbank, 10 Fairmead Farm Court, Disraeli Road, Buckhurst Hill, Essex.

Mr G.W.M. Vinald, 16 Searle Villas, London, W8.

He thanked Mrs Vinald and said goodbye to her. Outside, ornamenting the top of one of the columns that flanked the gate, sat Selima like a sphynx. Unwisely Wexford put out a hand to stroke her and got a scratch that made the blood run.

Only Lewis Fanning's wife was at home in the mansion flat down below the World's End; a stringy woman with grey roots showing in her henna'd hair. She was short with Wexford and indifferent. Her husband was away again, shepherding a party round the Aegean, and wouldn't be back till the end of the month.

Purley, where the Baumanns lived, would be passed through on the homeward journey; it was on the route of the Brighton Road. Before that Wexford thought he might take a look at what had been the Knighton's home before their permanent removal to Sussex. He told Donaldson to take him up to Hampstead.

His knowledge of London was better than Burden's but it was still full of gaps. It was only seeing a sign to Swiss Cottage which reminded him that Irene Bell had said she lived there, though to him the postal address looked like Hampstead.

'See if you can find Queen Charlotte Road.'

115

But Donaldson who, long before he joined the force, had thought of being a London taxi driver and had gone so far as to ride round on a bicycle to acquire the 'knowledge', knew where it was without a map. Meleager Court was a block that seemed to be composed entirely of red brick balconies set among plane trees. Irene Bell looked more the way he remembered her today, in a grey trousered garment which, when he was young in the forties, had been called a 'siren suit'. She showed no great surprise at seeing him.

'I've just made a pot of our favourite poison, Chief Inspector. Come in. Mind the step. It takes a true-born Englishman to fancy tea at one pip emma, that's what I say. I've made a sandwich too or have you had lunch?'

'I was thinking of having it at my daughter's. She lives up the hill in Keats Grove, only I've just remembered it's Thursday and she's got a matinee.'

'Sheila Wexford,' said Miss Bell. 'That's who you are, her father. I mean apart from what else you are. *Sluttish Time* still running, is it? Not my kind of play but I loved her in it, she's a joy to look at.'

Wexford felt that he really liked Irene Bell very much. He accepted tea and a ham sandwich. Perhaps she could tell him, he said, whereabouts in Hampstead the Knightons had lived. She told him, pouring a second cup for both of them.

'I should have been more forthcoming the other day,' she said. 'I was upset and it didn't seem right. But there's quite a bit more to say, though I don't know if it's the kind of thing you want to hear.'

'I want to hear everything.'

'Old stuff from years ago?' She frowned, thinking back. Then she said, 'I'd like you to find who killed Adela and I'd like him to get his just desserts. Not that that'll be much these days—five years inside doing an Open University degree, I daresay, and then let him out with a new suit and fifty quid out of the poor box.'

'Not quite that,' said Wexford who couldn't help smiling.

She said abruptly, 'They had to get married, you know.'

'I beg your pardon?'

'Adam and Adela. You know what the expression means, I suppose? They used it in your young days as well as mine. Don't any more of course. Girls have babies or abortions and as often as not from what I hear it's the boys who beg the girls to marry *them*. Adela fell in love with Adam the first moment she saw him. His sister had been at school with us too and she asked us to be her bridesmaids and that's how we came to meet Adam. We were all twenty-four and Adam was twenty-one. He was up at Oxford. Well, I've never been much for men as I think I said the other day but Adam was something else again as the young folks say. He wasn't handsome, he was beautiful. You hear people talk about 'tall, dark and handsome' but to my mind there's nothing to beat a really good-looking *fair* man. Sound soppy, don't I, but he was like a god in a painting.

'I was very fond of Adela, very. Anyway I think she'd have been the first to agree with me she was never much to look at. Mind you, she came from a very good family. The Aylhursts, you know. They're a cadet branch of the Staffordshire Aylhursts, nothing wrong there.' She hesitated. Wexford hadn't guessed her a snob and was surprised to find such frank snobbery in her. But there, she had been Mrs Knighton's closest friend. . . 'Gerald Aylhurst was her father. He was the Recorder of Salop. I can't tell you how Adam came to be interested in her. I don't know. Perhaps he was flattered because she was older or something. I've heard men of my generation say they used to suffer from terrible sex frustration when they were young—far cry from these days, eh?—so maybe it was that. Adela didn't say no, though you'll no doubt recall that nice girls usually did say no in 1939. Anyway she got pregnant and of course there were no two ways about it, Adam had to marry her. I don't think he ever questioned that he had to marry her but he told his sister and his sister told me that when they sort of first made it

117

clear to him he decided he'd rather die. He said he was
in love with someone else and he'd kill himself before he
married Adela.'

'Who was the someone else?'

'Don't ask me. You needn't look like that. It wasn't
me. Come on, Adam Knighton wouldn't have looked
twice at me. I don't know who it was, some girl at
Oxford, and it can't matter now, not after forty years.'

Wexford agreed that it couldn't matter now. Irene
Bell went on, 'He didn't kill himself as we know. The
Aylhursts fixed up a big white wedding at their village
church. Very bad taste, with Adela four months gone
and showing it. Adam went back to Oxford and took his
finals, and got himself a First incidentally, and in September Julian was born.

'They must have got on well enough because the next
year, in the November, Adela had Roderick. That was
1941 and Adam had to go off with his regiment to the
Far East somewhere, Burma, I think it was. He was
away four years. When he came home he went back to
reading for the bar and he was called and everything and
he made quite a success for himself, as we all know. I
used to see quite a bit of them. I was sharing a flat with
another girl in Maitland Park and they were living in one
of those roads off Haverstock Hill near Belsize Park
station. He had a funny way of treating her, sort of
tolerant exasperated patience. I don't know if I make
myself clear? These days they'd say he was always
putting her down. I remember once—they'd just got
their first TV set—he said he was going to watch *The
Brothers Karamazov* and Adela said, "Is that from the
London Palladium, darling?" Well, I happened to know
it was a famous sort of Russian novel, though I'd never
read it, but it was the kind of mistake anyone might
make. It does sound like acrobats, doesn't it? Adam
called the boys in and said, "Come and hear what your
intellectual mama's just said," and then when that pansy
phoned, that Dobson-Flint, he repeated it to him.

'Adela had the other two children. I think she did that

to keep a hold on Adam. I don't know for sure but that's what I think.'

'You mean he was straying?'

'I don't know. It got so that he was never at home. Working, he used to say, and perhaps he was. He had to do a lot of entertaining too, he said, though Adela always entertained well at home for him. She was a good wife, like I said, she cared, she went to a lot of trouble. Anyway she had Jennifer and Colum but that didn't seem to have much effect on Adam. He slept at home, they'd moved to Fitzjohn's Avenue, and that's about all you can say. It'd be true that for—what? Five years? —anyway for years after Colum was born Adela had a husband insofar as there was a man sleeping in the other bed in her room.

'And then, suddenly, I remember it well, some time in the late fifties it must have been, he came back. He lived at home, he had his meals there, he started taking Adela out—the lot. It was as if he'd had a shock and come to his senses. It's my belief she threatened to leave him and take the children with her, take them away from him. He was fond of his kids all right. Anyway back he came and there he stayed. They were quite a model couple after that except that they never had anything to say to each other. All the old Adam had gone out of Adam, that's for sure. He was bored stiff but he was resigned. And poor old Adela, she went on beavering away at being a good loving wife, but she had to take me on holiday with her, there are limits to how much you can stand of a man who doesn't say two words to you for hours on end.

'Good God,' said Irene Bell, 'do you wonder I don't think much of marriage when that was the marriage I saw at close quarters?'

A fine house of many rooms, rose madder brick, Edwardian probably, with the gables and diamond panes the Edwardians loved. It stood about half-way up the big hill to Hampstead on the right-hand side. Its garden was a shrubbery of rhododendrons, an ilex, in the oval lawn a monkey puzzle. As Wexford looked from the car at the house where the Knightons had lived in such sad contiguity, a hook-nosed man in a burnous came out of the front door. Only an Arab could have afforded to buy the house and live there now.

'Marriage,' murmured Wexford, as if to himself, 'is a desperate thing. The frogs in Aesop were extreme wise. They had a great mind to some water but would not leap into the well because they could not get out again.'

Donaldson said nothing to this. But he remarked some time afterwards to Loring that life was full of surprises, he had always thought the Chief Inspector got on OK with Mrs Wexford.

'Purley now, sir?' he said after a minute or two.

'Purley it is and then Guildford.'

But from that particular journey across Surrey they were to be saved. Just as Wexford had been taken aback *not* to see Margery Baumann open Vinald's front door to him, so he was surprised to see her open this one. She recognized him at once and was herself as astonished as anyone would be to find a man she had encountered by chance in China three months before standing on her parents' front doorstep.

He explained who he was and why he had come. Margery Baumann understood more readily than Pandora Vinald had done. Since she had no late surgery on Fridays, she said, she always spent those evenings with her father and mother. By that time they had passed through the panelled hall of the Baumanns' rather opulent thirties house and entered a living room where the Baumanns were having a thirties tea. Cucumber sandwiches, bread and butter, strawberry jam, Victoria sponge and custard creams. Dr Baumann wore grey flannels, white shirt, college tie, sports jacket, his wife a flowered afternoon dress and pearls. She was in the act of pouring from a silver teapot. It looked exactly like a stage set for a piece from the vintage days of drawing room comedy, and but for the autumnal state of the garden and the grey of the sky, one would have expected at any moment the entry from the french windows of a young man in flannels holding a tennis racquet.

All this Wexford remarked while Margery went through the business of explaining to her parents his status and the reason for his visit. They seemed very little less puzzled when she had finished than when she began.

'Now you're here, do sit down and have a cup of tea,' said Mrs Baumann rather faintly.

'I expect he would like a piece of your splendid cake, Lilian.' Dr Baumann got up. 'I shall go and fetch him a plate. I can't say it's at all clear to me why he's here but he's not the man I take him for if he won't enjoy Mother's excellent cake.'

'Milk *and* sugar, Mr Wexford?'

'No sugar, thank you.'

'What exactly did you want us to tell you then?' Margery asked.

'For a start, everything you can remember about the Knightons. Oh, thank you, very kind of you.' Dr Baumann had returned with a tea plate and a small napkin with lace round it. Wexford, who was always more or less on a diet, was obliged to accept a large slice of yellow sponge cake with jam filling. 'You travelled in the train with them. I'd like to know whatever you can recall about them.'

'Aha,' said Dr Baumann, 'so that's what he wants. Well, my dear? Well, Margery? He'll be surprised to find what an observant couple of girls I've got, I daresay.' He barked at Wexford, 'How d'you find the cake?' It was the first time he had addressed him directly. Wexford had been beginning to think the doctor had acquired his habit of speaking in the third person from constant reference for the benefit of students to bedbound patients.

'Very nice. Do you think you could give me your impressions of the Knightons, Mrs Baumann?'

He had utterly floored her. 'I didn't have any impressions. They were just—well, quite nice, ordinary people. That's what we said, wasn't it, Cyril? At the time, I mean, when we were talking about the other people in the party, you know the way one does. I said to my husband that the Knightons seemed quite nice and that Miss Bell they were with, she seemed quite nice. Mr Knighton had been a lawyer, I remembered seeing his name in the papers. He was a very well-informed man, I thought.'

Margery said suddenly, 'She was anti-Semitic.'

A shadow passed across Mrs Baumann's face and was gone. Her husband smiled, a little too widely and tolerantly. It hadn't occurred to Wexford before that they were Jewish, but of course they were.

'That sort of thing is very nasty,' Margery said. 'It was embarrassing. *I* didn't like hearing somebody or other called a "Jewboy" and her call her husband an old Jew when he didn't want to spend money on something. But my mother lost all her family in the Holocaust—did Mrs Knighton consider how she must have felt?'

'That wasn't the first time your mother and I have had to put up with that kind of thing and it won't be the last.' Baumann took his wife's hand. 'He doesn't want to hear about that. He wants to hear about threats and blackmail and murder attempts. About revolvers fired at the dead of night and arsenic in the chop suey.'

'I hardly think . . .'

'Oh, good heavens, no. There was nothing of that. But I know what you chaps like, something to get your teeth into. He doesn't think I've ever read a detective story, Margery.'

Wexford suppressed a sigh. A light rain was falling now and the dusk was coming down. Margery switched on a couple of wall lights and a table lamp with a galleon painted on its parchment shade. 'We really didn't notice anything out of the ordinary about the Knightons, Mr Wexford.'

'Then let me ask you something else. Do you remember when we were all sitting at a table on the roof of the hotel at Kweilin? The three of you, I, Mr Vinald, the Knightons and Miss Bell. Knighton saw something that astonished him, he looked as if he had had a tremendous, though not unpleasant, shock. I want to know what it was he saw.'

Dr Baumann laughed at that and shook his head from side to side several times as if at some amusing idiosyncracy. The idiosyncracy, though, he seemed to make clear, was Wexford's and not Knighton's. What a question to ask! What kind of answer could he expect?

'I can't say I noticed that,' said Mrs Baumann complacently.

Her daughter looked at Wexford. 'It was that very good-looking girl of course, the one that got so friendly with Gordon Vinald on our way home. Pandora Something. A girl from New Zealand. She walked out on to the roof and all the men were looking at her.' Her voice when she mentioned Vinald had an edge of awkwardness but not perhaps pain. 'I did happen to notice the expression on Mr Knighton's face. He was just startled at suddenly seeing such a very striking—well, beautiful girl.'

'I didn't even see her,' said Dr Baumann in a triumphant way.

'Well, maybe not, Dad, you wouldn't. But I should think every other man on that roof did. I know exactly what Mr Wexford means, I saw it just as he did. I expect Mr Knighton is very sensitive to beauty and there hadn't been much in that line, had there? What struck me about those tour parties was that we were all as old as the hills.'

'Margery!' said her mother. 'A young woman like you! I'm sure I didn't see much to write home about in that Miss Pandora Whatever-it-was.'

'Mrs Vinald now,' said Wexford.

Mrs Baumann looked cross, her daughter wryly amused. 'I'm sure he's welcome,' said Mrs Baumann. 'I never liked the man, he wasn't a nice man at all. And I'm sure he wasn't honest, I don't believe antique dealers ever are quite honest.'

'Oh, Mother! He was very kind to us. You know how

pleased you are with that little vase and you never would have bought it if Gordon hadn't said it was worth far more than the man was asking. And it was too. My father had it valued, Mr Wexford, and the valuer put it at three hundred pounds. Not bad when Mother gave twenty for it.'

She picked up from a coffee table a small blue and white jar and handed it to Wexford. It was inconceivable to him that anyone would give three hundred pounds for such a thing, a whitish mottled thick piece of pottery with a blue bird and some squiggles on it. On its base was a small red seal.

'You can't take anything out of China that's more than a hundred and twenty years old,' Margery said. 'They put the red seal on an antique piece to show you it's within the limit and therefore all right.'

Wexford handed it back. 'Do you happen to know what it was Mr Vinald and Mr Purbank quarrelled about so that they didn't speak to each other after the train left Irkutsk?'

Now it was Margery's turn to laugh. 'I know they didn't but I haven't the faintest idea why. Gordon just said he was a "nasty piece of work" and left it at that.'

He went home to another good, almost elderly, marriage—his own. Dora was watching an old British film on television, *The Snow Moth* with Trevor Howard and Milborough Lang.

'I wonder if people will see old films of Sheila's in thirty years time.'

'Considering she's never made any,' said Wexford, 'they don't stand much chance. You don't want her going off to Hollywood, do you?'

'I'd like her to make just one or two really good films as well as acting on the stage. There's that old TV series of hers, of course, I don't count that. I'd like to think of her—well, her beauty recorded for posterity. In a lovely setting, in a sensitive film like this one. After all, what do you suppose Milborough Lang looks like now? She must be fifty-five.'

Wexford always did his best to jolly his wife out of these alas-for-my-lost-looks moods of hers. To him, of course, she looked much the same as she had done when he first married her. As the credit titles came up he switched off the set.

'I wish to God you'd been with me in Kweilin. You'd have observed people. You'd have talked to people, you always do, you'd have got to know them. You wouldn't have been distracted like I was by—hallucinations.'

She looked a little worried. 'Reg, I wish we knew what those hallucinations of yours actually were.'

'Lack of sleep; Maotai.'

'Oh, come on. I doubt if you had more than a couple of sips of the stuff.'

Wexford shrugged. 'You might have been able to tell me why a man who sees a pretty girl walk across a roof looks more like he's seen the Virgin Mary.'

The phone rang. It was Burden.

'I'm getting more help than I expected from that chap Brownrigg who's the Clerk to Chambers where Knighton used to be. He's a meticulous old boy and he's got records of all the cases they've handled back for twenty years. But what I'm phoning for is because a fellow by the name of Vinald's been on the blower for you three times since midday. I'll give you his number.'

Wexford dialled it. Vinald himself answered. 'Oh, Chief Inspector, how super of you to phone. I've been trying to get in touch ever since my wife said you'd been here.' The voice was hearty, ingratiating. It was also very nervous. 'I really did want to know precisely what you wanted of me.'

'Any little bits of help you or your wife could give me on the background of Mr and the late Mrs Knighton, Mr Vinald, that's all.'

There was a short silence. Vinald cleared his throat. 'There's more to it than that, though, isn't there? I don't think it can be just that, eh?'

125

Wexford thought quickly. He would play along, though in the dark. 'I expect,' he said, 'you remember that last evening in Kweilin as well as I do.'

'Oh, certainly. And I realize a fuller explanation is actually called for here. I suppose I should begin at the point we all met up in that roof bar place . . .'

'Mr Vinald,' said Wexford heavily, 'I don't want to hear this on the phone. I'll come along and see you tomorrow. I'll see you in your shop at noon sharp.'

'Well, of course. I'll make a point of being there. I can assure you there's a perfectly simple and reasonable explanation for the whole thing . . .'

'Good night, Mr Vinald,' Wexford said firmly. Far better to confront the man in the morning and hear it face to face. He rather enjoyed the feeling of suspense, of revelation deferred. Tomorrow, perhaps, indeed probably, Vinald was going to tell him what had so affected Knighton on the roof.

But that, though not in detail, Wexford thought he already knew. Knighton had seen Pandora Vinald. Of course it wasn't the sight of a pretty girl which had brought that look to his face. The people who had suggested that to him simply hadn't thought what they were saying. It was *this particular pretty girl,* and Knighton hadn't looked like that because he was seeing her for the first time but because he was seeing her again, perhaps after the passage of years.

A girl who had once meant a great deal to him—whom he had loved?—had walked out on to that roof and by the merest chance he had been there, had looked up and with joy and wonder and fear had seen her.

PART THREE

12

Inspector Burden was a conventional conservative man who believed passionately in law and order. The slightest offence against those principles irked him and he loathed crime. That curious understanding of the criminal mind and its workings which some policemen have to such a degree that there is not much to choose between them and their morality and the criminals and theirs, was foreign to Burden, was distasteful to him. That perhaps was why he was a less successful policeman than he might have been. For between them and him a great gulf was fixed which grew wider and deeper as he grew older.

He was insensitive and he lacked sympathy. Supporting a cliché he didn't know to be one, he would often say he reserved his compassion for the mugger's victim, the beleaguered householder or even the Inland Revenue. He was a believer in retribution and was one of that majority of policemen—to which Wexford did not belong—who favoured the reintroduction of capital punishment. And this not solely for the taking of the lives of policemen. That the French, who had been sensible enough to keep the guillotine for so long, were now proposing to get rid of it was beyond his comprehension.

More even than young rioters and muggers he disliked recidivists. This was a word his wife had taught him, he had always called them old lags himself, but it came to the same thing. It was just his luck, as he remarked to

Jenny on leaving the house, that he should have to spend the day, maybe the next few days, hunting them out. And that without even the satisfaction of the housewife hunting cockroaches, in that there was nothing he could do to them when he found them.

He had taken an unprofessional dislike to Adam Knighton but he had to see him first. Renie Thompson opened the front door to him. She showed him into the living room where to his mild surprise he saw his chief already there, seated opposite Knighton and in the throes of an enquiry into the topic that was at present obsessing him. Knighton had grown gaunt in the past few days, his feet were in carpet slippers and a grey heavy knit cardigan was wrapped round his shoulders. He had become an old man, all that style and presence gone.

Wexford gave Burden a nod but the other man made a gesture of rising from his chair.

'Don't get up, Mr Knighton,' Wexford said. 'I'd like you to give a little more thought to what I've been asking, if you please.'

Knighton moved his shoulders. He was frowning. 'I told you, I remember very little about it. My memory has been affected by all this,' he said bitterly, as one recalling a tranquil time that can never return. 'It was all very beautiful, wasn't it? The most beautiful view I think I've ever seen. If I looked astonished up on that roof I suppose it was at the beauty of the sight.' A ghastly smile widened across his face and turned it into a death's head.

With a shrug Wexford turned to Burden. He had tried his best. The man was lying, of course, or at least that last sentence of his was highly ambiguous. Burden suggested the possibility that the murder had been committed by someone out to 'get his own back' on the former prosecuting counsel. The smile shrivelled on Knighton's face, he looked almost faint. He took from Burden the lists Brownrigg had compiled.

It took him a few moments to collect himself. But he made the effort. He spoke in an almost normal conversational tone.

'I see Hayward's name is here. Gilbert or "Gib" Hayward. He threatened me, actually threatened me in court. The jury had returned a verdict of guilty and he was awaiting sentence. When the judge asked him if he had anything to say he began shouting threats at me. It was really rather alarming, though of course there was nothing he could actually do.

'I've had anonymous letters too but they won't be much use to you, will they, since they were anonymous?' Knighton was burbling on in this half-crazed way, Burden thought, for the sake of saying something, anything, rather than reveal his true feelings, his deep fears. 'Oh, and there was this other chap here, one Peter Kevin Smith. I was *defending* him. For some reason he thought I hadn't done a good enough job. He went to prison for five years and the next day his mother came in to see me, made her way into chambers, if you please, burst in threatening he'd shoot me when he came out.'

'When you look at these names, sir, does any one or more of them give you a feeling that, yes, here's someone who might have done more than threaten?'

Knighton gave the lists back as if he didn't like holding them, as if he didn't care for the feel of them on his hands. 'None of them ever did. I can't imagine anyone carrying out such a threat against my—my wife. And do men have such long memories?'

'Some do,' Wexford said rather enigmatically, and he added, 'It depends on how much they want to remember.'

Now how to act on the information in the lists?

Those people whom Knighton had successfully defended and those whom he had unsuccessfully prosecuted could be ignored. But this still left so many that Burden realized he was going to have to be ruthless, categorize them according to the circumstances of the case, perhaps decide to disregard all petty crime and go only for killers and perpetrators of manslaughter, robbery with violence and grievous bodily harm. Could he dare assume it wasn't a woman? For a start he thought he could. He just couldn't see a woman not personally antagonistic to Adela Knighton getting her out of bed and forcing her downstairs and shooting her in cold blood. A girlfriend of Knighton's who had had reason to hate or resent Adela, that would be a different thing. But Knighton had no girlfriend.

The murderer wasn't going to be in his dotage either. Knighton's own age was just about the oldest at which Burden could imagine anyone climbing up and squeezing through that window, and Knighton was a well-preserved thin sixty-three. The murderer was going to have to be thin, no more than middle-aged. He had started making his list and on it, prominently, were 'Gib' Hayward and Peter Kevin Smith, the former now fifty-two years old, the latter forty-six. They might be fat, though, they might even be dead.

Hayward had killed a man in a fight outside a West London pub and Peter Kevin Smith had hit an old woman in the stomach, rupturing her spleen, prior to breaking into the till in her tobacconist's shop. Narrowing down, rejecting women, people over sixty-five, forgers, con men, straight burglars, bank robbers—though he didn't know if he could afford to do this—he had ended up with a total of sixteen men. In fact there had been more clients in Brownrigg's records with reason to be grateful to Knighton than inimical towards him. Certainly he had been the kind of counsel newspapers and hardened villains adore, spectacular, unscrupulous, witty, savage and subtle.

He went up to London with Wexford where their ways diverged. Though he had set Martin on to 'Gib' Hayward in Brighton, he intended to see Peter Kevin Smith personally.

'He's still living with that loyal and supportive mother of his,' Burden said as they parted. Wexford kept the car and Burden got into the train for Mile End.

The Pensive Selima was sitting in the shop window this time. Not on the lofty vase's side but on the edge of the blue plush drapery that covered its plinth. She sat cosily folded up into roughly the shape of a fat tawny brown armchair. The woman in the big glasses wasn't there. If he hadn't been seeing him at the appointed time and in his natural habitat, Wexford might not have recognized Vinald. In China he had always worn jeans. He looked quite different in a suit of dark grey fine tweed, pure white shirt and grey tie with a silver zig-zag down it. He looked older, cleverer and much more suave.

'Chief Inspector, do sit down. It's good of you to come.'

Wexford thought this remark strange since it must have been obvious to meaner intelligences that he had come out of duty rather than altruism. He chose a chair which, because he had once apprehended a man who had stolen half a dozen like it, he suspected of being by Hepplewhite. Vinald sat down opposite him on the yellow satin cushion of a love seat. He leant forward in an intimate fashion and, low-voiced, plunged into a—what? The answer to an unasked question? A lecture on iconoclasm? Or just a defence?

'Chief Inspector, China is an extremely long way away and pretty alien to us anyway, I'm sure you'll agree. And who knows how long the present regime will last? What's thirty years? Nothing in historical terms. The next lot to get into power would only do so by bloody revolution. And what's going to happen during any new insurrection? Much the same as happened during the Cultural Revolution. Anarchy. Armies of sixteen-year-old boys told by the highest authority to destroy anything old they could lay their hands on. Did you know that every village in China had its own temple, Taoist, Buddhist or Confucian, and many of them had all three? Where are they now? We know the answer to that. Destroyed. Razed to the ground and the very sites ploughed over as with ancient Carthage. When I hear sentimentalists groaning over our so-called thefts from China in, say, the Boxer Rebellion, I thank God for those—appropriations. Thank God we do have the Dowager Empress's throne in the British Museum. What do you suppose the Red Guards would have done with that?'

Wexford was not at all sure what Vinald was driving at but the man was evidently very very guilty over something. 'What indeed?' he said equably.

'Again only a romantic idealist would insist that the means are never justified by the end. The end here is to save priceless art treasures for the world. And these are not China's but indisputably the property of *all mankind*. They are our heritage, for in art all men are brothers. So therefore I maintain we should get our hands on what we can of it by fair means or foul—not that my means were foul, not at all.' Wexford's mystification, though veiled by experience, was now reaching him. 'And my scale is small enough,' he said more confidently. 'I would hardly have thought it worth anyone's while . . .'

'If we in the force decided that what you call things on a small scale weren't worth our while, Mr Vinald, I think we might very soon have anarchy in our own country.' He would get to the bottom of what Vinald was on about but not now. 'Since you're being so frank with me I'm sure you won't mind answering a couple of questions.' Vinald was looking very nervous indeed now. 'Like where you were on the night of October the first, for a start.'

It surprised him that Vinald didn't have to pause to think. Still, there were people with very good memories, people who in a flash could tell you exactly what they had been doing on any evening in the past fortnight. Wexford himself was one of them.

'I was at home with my wife. You know where I live, just round the corner in the Villas. My wife's mother brought a friend of hers round to meet us after dinner, a film cameraman or some such thing. They stayed till nearly midnight and after that my wife and I went to bed.'

Wexford asked him for his mother-in-law's address and was told she had a flat in Cadogan Avenue.

'I can't tell you where the guy she brought with her lives. His name's Phaidon, Denis Phaidon with a ph.'

As if to leave, Wexford got up and said with deceptive indifference. 'By the by, what *did* you and Mr Purbank quarrel about in the train on the way to Irkutsk?'

'*What?*'

Patiently Wexford repeated his question.

'What can this possibly have to do with it?'

'To do with what, Mr Vinald?'

'My buying antiques,' Vinald muttered, 'or the fact that this Mrs Knighton was murdered.'

'It's just one of those small things we think it worth our while to bother about,' said Wexford.

Vinald shrugged. 'I don't remember anyway. It was a long time ago and no doubt I did my best to forget it and forgotten it I have. The man was simply a very nasty piece of work.'

Cats never make a sound when they move. Wexford was aware that the Pensive Selima had left the window only when he felt the faintest susuration against his trouser leg. She stalked slowly into the back regions as if she owned the place and no one else was present.

The old woman herself came to the door, eyeing Burden with such contemptuous hatred that he knew it would be useless to place credence on any alibi she might produce for her son.

But as it had happened no alibi of hers was needed. For one thing, Peter Kevin Smith had grown far too fat in the ten years since he had come out of prison to have got through that window. For another, his right hand was in plaster and he was a right-handed man. He had broken it falling in the street—drunk, Burden supposed—and to prove the break had occurred before 1 October, exhibited an appointments card from an orthopaedic hospital with appointments listed back to 18 September.

Next on the list was Sidney Maurice Wills of Southwark. He was more interesting than Smith, being thin and wiry and in fit condition. Also he was still in his early thirties, having been out of prison not more than a year. Knighton had been prosecuting counsel in a curious case in which Wills had been found guilty of being an accessory to murder and of concealing a body. He had undertaken to dispose of the corpse of a woman stabbed to death by an acquaintance of his and had subsequently buried it among roadworks.

'What you want to do instead of wasting your time on me is find out who that bastard Knighton paid to do it for him.'

'Oh, he paid someone?'

'Only, natural, isn't it? He wouldn't do it himself, no more than he'd fix up his electric wiring or service his own Rolls-Royce motor car himself. He'd call in a professional. Like Chipstead, for instance. Used to be with Lee's mob, could be dead for all I know, I never mix with them sort of people these days, but he's just an example. Christ, do I have to teach you your job?'

Wills had an alibi nearly as good as Smith's, or would have once it was verified. He had been on a week's holiday in Minehead with a girl he called his fiancée, returning to London on 3 October.

There were eight more Londoners to see. The other men on the list lived in the north of England and would be seen by their local police. Of the London eight, George Lake had been celebrating his Silver Wedding at a restaurant in his home suburb of Wandsworth until 1 a.m.; Mojinder Singh, a Sikh from Southall, had been at home with his huge family of wife, parents-in-law, two brothers and six children; Norman Trimley and Brian Gage were far too fat; Henry Rossi was seventy-two and growing feeble; George Catchpole had been working a night shift; and Walter 'Silver' Perry . . .

'Silver do harm to Mr Knighton?' Mrs Perry screamed at him in the council flat on the top of the Bethnal Green tower. 'Silver worships the ground Mr Knighton treads on. Didn't he save his life?'

Burden nearly groaned aloud. He realized he had muddled the lists. That was what came of doing a task as distasteful to him as this was. Silver Perry had coshed and killed a night watchman and had done so some years before the abolition of capital punishment. Or it was generally believed by every newspaper reader in the country that this was what he had done, yet the skill of Adam Knighton had acquitted him. Burden vaguely remembered the man's story sold to the *News of the World* and, as he was recalling it, a scrapbook was thrust into his hands by Mrs Perry. There was the half page of cutting, the first instalment, yellowed by time. 'I firmly believe I owe Mr Knighton my sanity and indeed my very life . . .' These ghost writers! He was handing the scrapbook back when Perry himself walked in.

He was a tall man, getting on for sixty, with hair like that of an elderly woman who has just had a rinse, styling and 'set'. Silver's hair, however, was naturally metallic-looking and naturally wavy and had looked just the same, according to the *News of the World* photograph, when he was thirty-three. He gave Burden a parsonical look and said gravely, 'I would lay down my life for Mr Knighton.'

'Really? I don't know what use that would be to him.'

Silver went on as if Burden hadn't spoken. 'I was grieved to hear of his great loss, and him such a devoted husband by all accounts . . .'

Burden hadn't heard of Knighton as a devoted husband by any accounts. He left and when the lift didn't come walked down by the stairs, all the hundred and fifty feet.

There was one more man to see. Coney Newton, who also lived in the East End, had raped a girl and afterwards stabbed her, though not fatally. Nearly a year later, when the girl was at last recovered, Knighton had held her up to ridicule in the witness box, but the jury would have none of it and Newton had gone to prison for eight years. No one could say, except perhaps the paranoid Newton, that Knighton hadn't done his best for him.

'I don't bear a grudge, mind. I said to Silver, I don't bear a grudge and I don't hold you to blame . . .'

'Silver?' said Burden.

'Silver Perry. He's a mate of mine. It was on account of him, what he'd said in the papers like, that I was set on getting that Knighton to defend me. I said to them, I want a fella called Knighton and then I'll be OK. I don't bear a grudge, mind, but I might have saved me breath. All that carry-on, that telling the jury the girl was asking for it, that wasn't to help me, that was just for show. Using a lot of long words and making her colour up and getting a laugh, that was for show. What he should have done, what I told him again and again, was just stick to it I wasn't *there*. That was the truth, I wasn't there. All I wanted was him to tell the true fact which was, I wasn't *there*.'

'I suppose that's what you'll say when I ask you where you were on the night of Tuesday, October the first?'

Coney Newton looked narrowly at Burden. He was a thin, gaunt, grey-headed man of perhaps fifty, with a rampart of prominent grey teeth. In every sense an ugly customer. 'I wasn't anywhere I shouldn't have been and that's for sure,' he said, and he went into an elaborate explanation of how on that evening he had been in a pub with someone called Rocky whose surname he didn't know, then at his sister's, then in a club round the back of Leicester Square with 'old Silver'.

'You were in a club with Silver Perry?'

'That's what I said.'

'Till when?'

'Maybe two,' said Newton and he gave Burden another narrow look.

It would have to be checked along with the alibis of Lake, Singh and Catchpole. The club, which Newton said was called the El Video, would very likely be closed at this hour, but Burden had time to kill before meeting Wexford. He got on a bus and went on to the upper deck, always his favourite way of jaunting around London.

Really he should have gone to see Newton first, then he could have checked that alibi with Perry. The last thing Perry would do, surely, was support the false story of someone intending harm to his hero. Still, the El Video first.

It was, as he had expected, closed. With the tightening up of the pornography law, the photographs in the narrow glass case beside the door had been softened to mere languishing close-ups of breast and buttock, succulent mouth and swelling flank. The door itself had a cardboard notice on it which said the club was strictly private and for members only and underneath that a poster advertising a rock concert. There were three bells and Burden rang the middle one.

After a while the door was opened by a young black woman in velvet knee breeches and a red tee shirt. She looked at Burden, said there was nothing doing till six and then it was only by appointment, but then seemed to understand he meant the club. She giggled and said Moggy would be opening up at eight. Burden walked off up the Charing Cross Road, wondering how Wexford was getting on.

Purbank wouldn't tell him what the quarrel was about. He also said he had forgotten the reason for it, though being more restrained than Vinald, he didn't add that the other man was a nasty piece of work.

His flat, on the fringe of Epping Forest, was in an apartment block with huge picture windows which pictured panoramas of tree tops. Purbank turned out to be an accountant who operated from home, in a big room drably furnished in 'safe' shades of porridge, cardboard and mud. Like Vinald he was made highly nervous by Wexford's visit and, when asked if he had been in touch with any other members of the train party since their return, particularly if he had received photographs from any of them, he cried, 'No, no, no!' with the vehemence of someone pleading not to be assaulted.

But of the Knightons he seemed genuinely to know nothing. In the train it was the single people who had congregated, the married couples keeping a little apart, though the Knightons had always made a three with Irene Bell. On the hotel roof in Kweilin he disclaimed having noticed anything out of the way except what he called the 'silly' music and, remembering it, he gave a nervous bellowing laugh.

Wexford thought the chances of his having shot Adela Knighton were about as remote as they could be. But he was rather taken aback when Purbank was unable to account for his movements on the night of 1 October. He could only say that he had been at home alone, or so he supposed, he couldn't really recall, but he thought he had been at home alone and could recall no visitors or phone calls. He seemed a friendless man, not so much a recluse as one whose manner, both boring and blundering, had driven possible friends away.

His head full of China, remembering China and wondering where Adela Knighton's photographs of China had got to, Wexford walked across the lobby of the flats and came face to face with a Chinese man. In other circumstances, even in Kingsmarkham where there was at least a Chinese restaurant, he would scarcely have given him a second glance. But here, in spite of himself, he stared just as those Chinese in Chang-sha had stared at him.

The man spoke pleasantly in an English that was a little high-pitched. 'Good afternoon. Were you looking for someone?'

Wexford collected himself. 'No,' he said, 'thanks all the same.'

He was tall for a Chinese, about forty, professional-looking, in a dark suit and plum silk tie and carrying a dark red leather briefcase. His English was accented but absolutely fluent and idiomatic. 'Nasty day,' he said. 'It's getting very chilly out,' and with a smile walked away to the lift.

Wexford had a look at the names above the doorbells outside. Number 7: Y.S. and M. Hsia. That would be it. And Purbank lived at number 8. Of course there was no reason why Purbank shouldn't have a Chinese next-door neighbour. There must be many thousands of immigrants from Hong Kong, Taiwan and Singapore in this country. They mostly lived in cities and city suburbs, just as well in a flat in Buckhurst Hill as elsewhere. And yet it *was* odd. It made him look on Purbank, whom he had almost dismissed as of nugatory interest, with new eyes.

He picked up Burden at the appointed place by London Bridge. By now it was raining hard and the inspector was standing under his umbrella.

'We'll have a look at Knighton's bank account,' said Wexford. 'See if any large sums have gone out since he got back from China.'

Burden said rather gloomily, 'Can you see that guy hiring an assassin?'

'The wine he drinks is made of grapes. Other men in his station and class of life have done murder. Whatever he may have said on the subject to his wife and children, murder is by no means confined to the working class. And, you know, Mike, it ill becomes him to have said so, it was a fault of character in him that he could say that and it makes me feel his guilt more likely. I don't agree with you, I feel it's more likely he'd have hired someone than done it with his own hand.'

'Well,' said Burden with unexpected shrewdness, 'that might account for why he's so ashamed, why he seems to *hate himself so much*.'

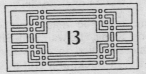

13

IF HE WAS MORE INTERESTED IN THE VINALD FAMILY THAN IN other members of the train party this was because he was coming to believe that it was the sight of Pandora Vinald, then unmarried, which had occasioned that look of ecstatic shock on Knighton's face. Somewhere, somehow, Knighton had seen her before, and if that look was anything to go by, had done more than see her. The next step would be to call on Jennifer Norris in her 'old' house in Springhill Lane.

Today she looked more like her mother than ever. Her hair had received a recent perm and her face was as shiny as a new coin. He had expected to be admitted by a cleaner or the present-day equivalent of a maid and into opulent luxury. It was rather a surprise to find her alone and the room into which she took him sparsely furnished. She didn't ask him to sit down.

'Where did my parents go on previous holidays? Do you mean since Daddy retired?'

'Go back five years, would you, Mrs Norris?' How old was Pandora? Younger than Jennifer certainly. Perhaps no more than twenty-four.

She didn't immediately answer him. It was impossible for her to miss an opportunity of dilating on her family's prosperity and social advantages. 'Mummy had what she called her holiday fund, you know. It was her way of getting the best out of her own money. She wanted real travel, you see, not just the usual winter sports in

January and some Mediterranean beach in the summer everyone has.' This last sentence nearly took Wexford's breath away. He said nothing. 'So Angus invested this fund for her and she drew on it whenever they wanted to go anywhere—well, really super, you know. Like China. Mummy adored travel.'

Wexford nodded. 'Where did they go the first time after this—er, fund was started?'

'Egypt, I think, or it might have been Thailand and Java. I think they went to Mexico some time but I can't be absolutely sure. And once they just went to Jugoslavia and Corfu.' The Balkans were dismissed and put on a level with Bognor Regis. 'But that was at least six years ago.'

Keeping his patience, Wexford asked if they had ever been to New Zealand.

'People don't go to New Zealand for holidays, do they?' She was a girl of limited horizons. 'We have some sort of remote cousin in Sydney or it may be Melbourne, some place down there, and they did go to him for a while, maybe a month.'

'They spent a month in Australia? When was that?'

'Oh, years and years ago, six or seven years.'

It was stretching things a bit. Wexford found it hard to imagine the fifty-six-year-old Knighton popping across from Sydney to Auckland and there falling in love with a girl of seventeen. And what was being suggested, after all? That the girl had still loved him after seven years, had been reunited with him in China and then shot the rival wife?

'Mummy wanted to go to India and Nepal next,' said Jennifer Norris. 'She wanted to go in February, poor Mummy.' For the first time he saw signs of real emotion in her face.

He noticed something on the walls of a kind of study as they passed back through the hall to the front door which set him inquiring of Sergeant Johnson of the uniformed branch as soon as he was back in the station. But Johnson knew all about it.

143

'He's got a gun licence all right, sir, had one for years. Had one long before he was married when he was living in a flat in the High Street here. We do inspect, check he keeps the lethal stuff under lock and key. What you saw on his wall is mostly old fowling pieces, flintlock stuff and so on. He does have modern weaponry. I've a list of what he's got kept up to date.'

'But no Walther PPK?'

Johnson shook his head. 'He was the first one I checked on when your directive went round at the start of the case.'

Of course.

Wexford walked into his office and found two parcels awaiting him with the rest of the post. One had come by post, the other, in a large brown envelope and unsealed, by hand. He looked into that one first. The envelope contained a secondhand copy of the collected short stories of that Victorian writer of the macabre, Sheridan Le Fanu, and a bit of paper torn from a prescription pad with *Len* scrawled across it. Wexford wondered what Dr Crocker could be up to but he had never read any Le Fanu and thought this would do very well for relaxation during the Saturday afternoon and Sunday which he intended to take off.

In the other package, the one that had come by post, there was no clue to the identity of its sender. Wexford removed from their brown paper wrapping eight cardboard folders, the kind that film processors use. The name 'Knighton' was written across the top of each of them. Undoubtedly, these were the snapshots the Knightons had taken during their holiday, sent to him from an unknown source. His name on the wrapping and the address of Kingsmarkham Police Station had been printed. The postmark was a London one, Chingford, E.4.

Carefully, he went through the photographs. But it didn't take much perspicacity to tell that some, three or four, were missing. The appropriate negatives had also gone, the strip of celluloid cut through. It wasn't then just a failure to 'come out' that accounted for their disappearance. But which ones weren't there?

The first six envelopes were all of Eastern Europe and Russia, including one of a Russian railway station which the authorities would certainly have pounced on had they known of its existence. It was from the photographs in the other two folders, the Chinese ones, that the shots were missing. He recognized Chang-sha, the Marquise of Tai's tomb at Mawangdui, the Mao birthplace at Shao-shan. There were several shots of loop-shaped mountains in Kweilin, all apparently taken from the hotel roof. Then nothing till the Five Goats statue in Canton. What had become of the Li River excursion then, the most spectacular trip to be taken between Peking and Hong Kong? Had the Knightons left their camera behind? Wexford knew they hadn't. He could remember Adela Knighton taking shots on deck—of the cormorant fishers, the villages, the boats with their square orange sails. Someone, the sender of this parcel, had for a reason as yet unfathomable to Wexford, abstracted those pictures and doubtless destroyed them along with their negatives.

Knighton put up no opposition to the suggestion that his financial circumstances be examined. Without expression he handed Wexford his latest bank statements, of which he received one every month. When Wexford asked why he had statements so often he explained that this was because, a year ago, owing to a standard order for a direct debit he had forgotten about, he had been briefly overdrawn. Since then his bank had kept him up to date with frequent statements. Prior to his retirement he had had a private account but since then he and his wife had used only their joint account. It was for this account that the statements had been issued. Knighton telephoned his bank and asked the manager to tell Wexford the facts about the private account, that it had been closed for three years.

There was nothing in the statements for the past year

to indicate that any large sum which couldn't be accounted for had been withdrawn. A substantial monthly sum was paid which Wexford took to be from some pension or annuity of Knighton's, and there were injections of larger sums, presumably from interest on Knighton's or his wife's investments. Four thousand pounds had been paid into the account in April, very obviously from Mrs Knighton's holiday fund, and a similar amount withdrawn two weeks later to pay in advance for the train tour. It was evident that Knighton had parted with nothing in fee to an assassin.

Of course there was no way of knowing whether this particular account was the only one he had. But in his previous exploration of the house and its desk and drawers, Wexford had found no cheque book or paying-in book for any account apart from this one and the closed private account of which Knighton had kept his final cheque book.

'Mr Knighton, I'd like you to come down to the police station with me so that we can have a talk. I think it would be profitable for you to have a talk with me and my colleague, Inspector Burden.'

'I see no reason why you can't talk to me here.'

'Perhaps not but I do. It will be more straightforward for all of us at the police station.'

'You mean more intimidating for me? I am quite sufficiently intimidated, I assure you.' Knighton made a weary movement of his head. 'I don't know if it's fear or shock or what it is, but I seem to be suffering from some kind of amnesia, what a mad doctor would call a fugue.' Knighton used the quaint and old-fashioned expression for an alienist without awkwardness. 'I seem to live in a stupefied daze,' he said.

Wexford noted he hadn't included grief among the emotions which distressed him.

'If I am going to be interrogated, I think I should have legal advice.' It seemed a strange thing for such as he had been to say. 'My legal adviser should be present,' he said.

'That's entirely your privilege, sir,' said Wexford more blandly than he felt.

It was a curious interview. And this was because of Knighton's frankness in certain areas and obtuse caginess in others. However, no legal adviser was present. Perhaps he thought that with a lifetime of experience behind him he could advise himself.

They used one of the less cell-like interview rooms. It had a rug on the floor. The chairs had straight backs but padded seats. Knighton sat on one side of the table and Wexford and Burden faced him. He looked ill, his eyes were fast becoming dark holes in his face, some sort of remorse was piling years on him as cancer does. He looked as if he had reached the end of his tether or some eleventh hour. Yet he could make a pedantic lawyer's joke.

It was chilly in the room. The central heating was not due to be started until 1 November. Wexford had a small electric heater brought in and apologized to Knighton for the cold and general mild discomfort.

'*De minimis non curat lex,*' said Knighton with his death's head grin.

The law may take no account of trifles but lawyers do. In accordance with Wexford's expressed wish, Knighton went into long detailed theories of how a potential killer might have known he was to be away on the night of 1 October. Once again he named the people to whom he had spoken of his projected trip to London: his wife; his daughter Jennifer; his son-in-law; village cronies; and his son Roderick. His host naturally had known of it and Dobson-Flint. Whom those people had told he couldn't begin to guess. Suddenly he said, 'You've asked my children and Miss Bell and Adrian Dobson-Flint and a good many others too, I suspect, if my marriage was a happy one. You haven't asked me.'

'In the circumstances,' said Burden, 'we took it for granted you'd say it had been.'

'In a murder inquiry, Inspector, you shouldn't take anything for granted. It was not a happy marriage. It never was. For years it was common knowledge I didn't get on with my wife. My wife felt towards me as many women feel towards their husbands. I was her possession and her protector and she had a right to my continued presence in her life. I don't suppose she ever thought whether she cared for me or not. I disliked her. As the years went by I disliked her more and more.'

Temporarily this silenced Burden. It took more than that to nonplus Wexford.

'Perhaps you feel like making a new statement, Mr Knighton?'

'I'm not going to confess to anything if that's what you mean. I disliked my wife but I bitterly regret her death. I would give everything I have—' he hesitated and Wexford thought he was going to say 'to bring her back' but he ended '—to turn time back to before the first of October.'

Wexford said, 'You were an unwilling husband. Were you a faithful one?'

'For twenty-five years I was. Before that—there was someone I wished to marry but it was impossible and we parted. I had my children to think of.'

'And your career, I daresay,' said Wexford.

Knighton winced. He made a vague gesture in front of his face. 'And my career, yes. I was thinking of a judgeship. As it happened, it never came. Let me say that I knew it wouldn't come if I deserted my wife and children for a young actress.'

They talked to him for a further hour. Gates came in with coffee and a plate of ham and cheese sandwiches. Knighton took the coffee but refused to eat anything. Wexford asked him about his knowledge of guns. Knighton said he knew nothing about the Walther PPK beyond that in fiction it was the gun used in the later James Bond books and that in fact it was used by the Stockholm police force. As the afternoon wore on to five o'clock they let him go home.

Two things of significance happened on Monday morning. One was the collapse of Gordon Vinald's alibi. Mrs

Ingram and Denis Phaidon had been sounded out and both agreed that they had been to visit the Vinalds for coffee and drinks but it had been on Wednesday, 2 October, not Tuesday, 1 October. And Phaidon, in all innocence, made matters rather worse for Vinald by saying that they had originally intended to go there on the Tuesday but had been put off until the next night because, according to Pandora, her husband had been called away on business to Birmingham.

Wexford was reading the report on this and thinking about it, when Detective Constable Archbold who, with Bennett and Loring, was still pursuing a house-to-house enquiry in Sewingbury, came in to tell him it seemed they had at last found a witness. Thomas Bingley, an old man, retired, a one-time agricultural labourer. He had been in the wood through which the footpath from Sewingbury to Thatto Vale ran . . .

'An old man?' Wexford interrupted. 'In a wood at half-past two in the morning? What the hell for?'

'Well, sir, for poaching. Pheasants, it would seem. That's why it's taken us so long to find him, he's been lying low. It was his niece put us on to him, thought we ought to know uncle was often out on that path at night at this time of year. Apparently he sets running snares and goes to fetch his booty in the small hours.'

'And he was there on October the first, was he? I call that adding insult to injury, poaching a man's birds on the very first day shooting officially begins.'

'Cheeky,' Archbold agreed. 'The point is, sir, he says he saw a man on that path. It was a clear night and the moon was shining and he says he saw a tall thin man with grey or white hair walking rapidly along the path towards Sewingbury.'

'With a smoking automatic in his hand, I daresay,' said Wexford.

By chance, thanks to the anonymous parcel, Wexford had photographs of several possible suspects in his possession. In the single living room of Bingley's unsavoury cottage down by Sewingbury Mill he showed the old man a picture of Knighton. Bingley looked at it and scratched his head and said that could have been the man he saw, though he thought he wasn't so tall. Purbank, pictured on the Kweilin hotel parapet in conversation with Irene Bell, he looked at and seemed to consider as a possibility. Then he hesitated and pointed with his little finger, a dirty finger with a broken nail, at someone in the background of the photograph, a man whose hair was covered by a straw sun hat. It was Vinald.

'This feller I saw looked a lot like him.'

'You can't put any credence on anything a bloke like that says,' said Burden when they were outside by the river bank.

'It's a muddled effort to please us in case we do him for poaching. He's one of those who thinks we won't love him if he says he doesn't know.' Wexford surveyed the recently completed concrete embankments, already known locally as 'the weir', through which the Kingsbrook had now been made to pass. There had been considerable controversy over whether it should be done at all. The river which, three weeks before, had flowed between reedy (and often litter-strewn) banks, was trammelled into a symmetrical gorge with a paved sitting area, holes in the paving for trees and a new brickwork arch to the bridge that carried Springhill Lane.

'It doesn't look all that bad now it's finished,' Wexford said. There came into his mind a vision of the Li River and its landscape of looped mountains, the porcelain blue sky, the rippling water—and Wong drowned. 'Purbank has grey hair,' he said.

'Oh, come *on*. Any port in a storm, that is.'

'Not a bit of it. Purbank has no alibi for that night. And he may have a motive.' They strolled over to the car that was waiting for them at the point where the footpath to Thatto Vale joined the road. 'Three or four photographs and their negatives are missing from this set of Knighton's. Suppose it was to Purbank that Adela Knighton sent her pictures? The postmark on the package returned to me was Chingford, and Chingford, according to my map of Greater London, is pretty well next door to Buckhurst Hill where Purbank lives. Suppose one or more of those snaps showed Purbank in a compromising situation, a situation which he would do a great deal to avoid having made public.'

'Like what?'

'That I don't know. I haven't seen them. But Purbank might conceivably have thought Adela Knighton sent them to him, not out of kindness or interest, but to inform him what she knew. *And perhaps she did.*'

'So what do we do about that?'

'Nothing, at the moment. First we're going to find out why Vinald lied and said he was at home having cosy little drinks parties when in fact he was in Birmingham. Or Herstmonceux or Mevagissey. There's no knowing with a liar of his calibre. The really interesting thing about that alibi of his, though, was that it alibi'd Pandora as well. And now it doesn't, nothing and no one does.'

In Birmingham, it appeared, Vinald had done no more than meet the agent of a South American collector of porcelain. He had taken with him certain of the pieces he had brought out of China and two vases more recently acquired. In saying that this had taken place on the evening of 2 October instead of the true date, 1 October, he had made a simple mistake.

Vinald brought all this out very glibly but he couldn't conceal a terrible underlying nervousness. He was afraid of something and his fear was mounting. Wexford and Burden saw him at home, not in the shop, and Pandora came into the room while they were talking. Was it for her that he was afraid?

She was in a dress of white knitted wool today, bronze belt and shoes, her black glossy hair in the current fashion of smooth top and the sides a Renaissance frizz. She looked calm, not at all nervous. Wexford was suddenly sure he had been quite wrong in connecting her with Knighton. It was most probable they had never even spoken to each other.

'So you and your wife were alone here on the Tuesday night?'

They both said yes to that rather quickly and in unison. Their haste made them break off and smile awkwardly at each other. Pandora shrugged, opening her eyes wide.

'I'm going to have to insist on your telling me the cause of your quarrel with Mr Purbank.'

Vinald waited a moment. He smiled stoically, making the best of things.

'If you must know, he persistently made remarks insinuating I was turning the trip into what he called a buying spree.'

'And if you were, how did that affect him?'

'He suggested that every time we went sight-seeing and had a choice of what to visit I opted for the places where there would be artefacts for sale rather than for museums or panoramic views or whatever.'

'That may have been irritating to you but it was hardly offensive, was it?'

'It was the way he said it. It was more in the implication than what was actually said.'

'Mr Purbank says he has forgotten the cause of your quarrel.'

There was no mistaking the satisfaction this afforded Vinald. He smiled gaily. He put his arm through his wife's. 'He's a very nasty piece of work. Frankly, when he said he'd tell our guide it was my object to turn other people's holidays into a commercial venture to feather my own nest, I'd had enough. I slapped him down and we—exchanged no further words.'

Wexford knew he was lying, or rather that he was telling a heavily diluted version of whatever the truth was. As they left, going down the steps, Wexford paused to stroke the head of the Pensive Selima who was sitting among some dead lobelias in an urn. She suffered his attentions, shook herself distastefully, jumped out of the urn and skittered down into the area.

'Not all that tempts your wandering eyes,' said Wexford, 'and heedless hearts is lawful prize . . .'

'What's that?'

'The poem the cat gets her name from. Come on, we're going to the V and A.'

Once Burden wouldn't have been quite sure. His wife had altered all that. 'The Victoria and Albert Museum,' he said to that London expert, Donaldson, and to Wexford, 'What are we going there for?'

'China's gayest art,' said Wexford.

That night, tired but not particularly late home, he finished Le Fanu's novella of vampires, 'Carmilla', and went on to the next story in the collection, 'Green Tea'.

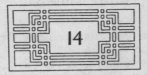

14

HE DIDN'T TELL BURDEN. HE DIDN'T TELL ANYONE BUT HIS WIFE.
Sitting up in bed reading Le Fanu beside Dora reading
Charlotte Brontë, he came wonderingly to the end of the
story and started to laugh.

'You mean,' said Dora as he explained, 'that this man
was writing a book and he got overtired and he kept
himself going by drinking green tea? Tremendous quanti-
ties of it as a sort of stimulant?'

'You might say he chain-drank cups of green tea. And
he was very much frightened by a monkey-like creature
he began seeing in the corner of his room. Then he saw
it in the street and it got on an omnibus with him. Well, I
saw an old woman with bound feet.'

'I suppose it was Len Crocker sent you the book.'

'Of course it was. He realized I'd made myself halluci-
nate in the same way as the Reverend Mr Jennings did
in Le Fanu's story. I chain-drank green tea too, you
know. I must have been drinking a couple of gallons a
day.'

He laughed, remembering. But thinking about it before he fell asleep, he wasn't entirely satisfied with the
explanation. He was relieved, it took a niggling little
load off his mind, it was obvious it had been the green
tea that produced the visions—but was that really all
there had been to it? Surely there had to be more,
though he might never find out what.

*   *   *

154

It made him feel a little strange about drinking his breakfast cup of tea, though this was Twining's Assam and in no way green. After breakfast he looked among his books, found *Masterpieces of the Supernatural,* and saw as he suspected that the last story in the collection was 'Green Tea'. If only he had read on to the end he would have known the answer when his anxiety was at its height.

Now what to do about what the poacher saw? About Purbank and the photographs? Burden was busy with reports from Middlesbrough, Manchester and Newcastle, all of them clearing the remaining men whom Knighton had prosecuted, respectively, on charges of murder, arson and grievous bodily harm. Back in the cottage down by Sewingbury weir, Wexford struggled to get something more satisfactory out of Bingley. But the old man again picked Vinald out from the photograph, qualifying his selection by saying the man he had seen looked more like Vinald than anyone else there. All he was positive about was that he had seen a man walking along the footpath at three in the morning or thereabouts and that man had been walking *back* from Thatto Vale.

Wexford and Burden had lunch together in the Many-Splendoured Dragon. Spring rolls, beef and onions, beansprouts, water chestnuts, Chinese mushrooms. Burden had a pot of jasmine tea but with a restrained shudder Wexford stuck to Perrier. He had been back in his office five minutes when the switchboard told him there was a girl downstairs wanting to see him. A Miss Elf.

'A Miss what?'

'Elf, Mr Wexford. Like, you know, gnomes and fairies.'

He nearly said, 'Is she pale green?' but green for the moment was a dirty word with him. 'Get someone to bring her up.'

Loring brought her in and left at a nod from Wexford. She was a small fair girl, perhaps five feet tall, and she looked very young. Fourteen or fifteen was his first impression. Her face was babyish, innocent, with large soft blue eyes. She wore jeans, a red sweat shirt and a

red and white track suit top, blue and white canvas and
rubber running shoes and, carrying no handbag, came in
with her hands in her pockets.

'Miss Elf?' Wexford said.

'That's right.' Her voice didn't quite match the
appearance.

'What can I do for you?'

'It's more what I can do for you. OK if I sit down?
I've got some info for you. A friend of mine—well, more
a client—he said the police here were looking for this
old guy hanging about H.P.G. in the night time on October the first. So I never let on to my client but I reckoned I'd better present myself to you seeing as I did.
Did see him, I mean.'

It was all very unclear. Miss Elf had aged in his
estimation about two years but he was still mystified.
'You live in Hyde Park Gardens or Stanhope Place?
Your parents live there?'

She broke into laughter. 'No, no. I'd better begin at
the beginning, hadn't I? Tell you who I am and what I
am and what I was doing there at that hour, right?'

'What are you?' Wexford said slowly.

'I'm a whore,' said Miss Elf.

Wexford had begun to guess it. He disliked people trying
to shock him, he wondered when they would ever learn
he couldn't be shocked and hadn't been shockable these
thirty years.

'I suppose you mean you're a prostitute, a call girl?'

'Right.'

'You look very young for that.'

'Well, that's the point, isn't it? I mean, me looking
young. That's what you might say got me into it, me
looking so young always. I'd got a rare commodity to
sell and it was a sellers' market. I'm twenty-four actually.
But wanting to screw twelve-year-olds didn't go out
with the Victorians, you know, and I looked twelve
when I started. I'd pass for fifteen now, wouldn't you
say?'

Wexford nodded. He couldn't resist asking, 'Is your name really Elf?'

Her laughter was loud and harsh, with a coarse note. 'Really and truly. I was born Elf, the only daughter of Mr and Mrs Elf. Piece of luck, wasn't it? But I don't insist on it, you can call me Sharon.'

Of this offer he resolved not to avail himself. He was thinking that most of her clients were probably men of his age and he knew enough of prostitutes to be aware that she would look on him with the same eyes as she looked on them, believe him subject to the same desires and the same perverse needs that made them want little girls. He felt a bit angry and a bit sick over it all and then he told himself that at any rate what went on now was ten thousand times better than in the days when it was really little girls they had.

'So to the night of October the first,' he said coldly.

Sharon Elf fixed her large blue eyes on him. 'This client of mine in Stanhope Place, he's one of my regulars, reminds me a bit of you actually.' She didn't see Wexford wince, or if she did, didn't care. 'He gave me a buzz around eight that night and said would I come and see him at midnight. Half twelve would be better if I could make it on account of he'd got people for dinner and by twelve thirty they were sure all to have gone.'

'Where exactly does this client of yours live?'

'One of those houses facing the back of H.P.G.'

'Hyde Park Gardens, yes, I see.'

'As it happened, I could make it very well. I'd got another client at eleven, that was up in St John's Wood, so I left there around twelve twenty, twelve twenty-five and I got a cab and it got me round to Stanhope Place just before twenty to one. I know you're going to ask me how I can be so sure of the time. The fact was I didn't want to embarrass my client—you know, if his guests hadn't gone on the dot like he said. So I kept looking at my watch and it was just before twenty to one we got there.

'I took a look at my client's house and I saw the light

on in the hall and the bedroom but not the lounge, so I knew that was OK. Anyway, I was paying off the driver when this old fella came out of the back of H.P.G., one of the lower ground floor flats—well, basements really. He came across the road and took my taxi.'

'Did you hear where he asked the driver to go to?'

'Sorry. There I can't help you. I wasn't interested, you see, didn't know any reason why I should be. Not then.'

'How exactly do you know now?' Wexford asked.

She said simply, 'My client in Stanhope Place gave me a buzz last night and I went round around ten. He told me the fuzz had been asking questions. It was the first time I'd seen him for three weeks, you see, or I reckon he'd have told me before.'

Wexford could almost have blessed Purbank or whoever it was had sent him those photographs. They were coming in very handy. There was one of the whole train party together on the Kweilin hotel roof. Only Adela Knighton, who had taken the shot, was missing. Unhesitatingly Sharon Elf picked out Knighton.

'That's him.'

'You're quite sure that's the man you saw in Stanhope Place at twenty minutes to one on the night of October the first?'

'Positive,' she said cheerfully. 'I had a good look. You see, I rather fancied him.'

Wexford's brain reeled. Did it work both ways then? If tired old men were looking for girls too young to criticize or have standards, were the girls looking for surrogate grandfathers? He was glad, though, to see the back of Miss Elf and, feeling a fool, asking himself who was he to sit in judgement, nevertheless opened his window for a little while after she had gone. Perhaps it was only to blow away the smell of rubber soles and Palmolive soap.

He turned his thoughts to what she had told him. There was Bingley's evidence and now this. He pressed his buzzer and said, if Inspector Burden was about, would they ask him to come up? Burden came in carrying a report on the last man on his list, a certain Dudley Preston whom Knighton had defended on charges of manslaughter and drunk driving but had failed to save from three years in prison.

'Do you know your window's wide open? It's like an icebox in here.'

'You can shut it if you like.' Wexford told him about Sharon Elf and what she had seen.

Burden's mouth went down at the corners. But that, Wexford thought, was more on account of Miss Elf's profession than the destruction of Knighton's alibi.

'You believe her? A woman like that?'

'Sometimes you talk like a mid-Victorian beadle. I don't see why a call girl shouldn't be as truthful as anyone else. Look at it how you will, it's an honest trade, it parts with what it's paid for. Enough of this rubbish anyway. She picked him out from a group photograph, so of course I have to believe her.'

Burden shrugged. 'If it's true, and I suppose it is, things look bad for Knighton. The presumption would be that immediately he and Dobson-Flint had retired to their rooms, he prepared to go out again. No doubt he hung about while Dobson-Flint used the bathroom, then he slipped out, taking with him one of the bunches of keys from the hall table. It was too late for a train, so he must have had the taxi take him to wherever he had a rented car waiting. Who knows? He might have rented a car somewhere near Victoria Station and left it parked and waiting for him. He'd have hired that when he got to London and put enough in the meter to last him till six fifteen. With meter charges stopping at six thirty he wouldn't have had to worry. I suppose that means checking on the car hire places round Victoria now.

'If he took the taxi at twenty to one he would have been in Victoria by ten to. I may be ignorant of London but even I know there wouldn't be much traffic at that time of night. By one at the latest he would have been in that car and starting his drive. It wouldn't take him more than an hour so we'll say he got there at two.'

'A quarter of an hour to cut out the pane of glass, maybe a few minutes to steel himself—yes, it just about works out.'

'He didn't have to get through the window, he had a key.'

'He still had to cut out the glass.'

'Of course he did,' said Burden. 'I'm a fool. Of course he did. And he wouldn't have done it *after* he'd killed her. There's one thing, though—can you imagine him hoicking her out of bed and bringing her downstairs and shooting her through the back of the head?'

'There are a lot of things I can't imagine human beings doing but still they do them, Mike.'

'Well, I can't swallow it. Not a woman you'd been married to for over forty years. Not your own *wife*. And Knighton's not one of these yobs I've been hob-nobbing with, is he? Wouldn't we, I mean wouldn't anyone, call him a *civilized* sort of man?'

'Look, there are a lot of things I don't like too. I don't like any of it much but this is evidence we've got, Mike. Sharon Elf saw him at twelve forty slipping out of Dobson-Flint's flat. Bingley saw a man walking back to Sewingbury around three and it wasn't Vinald he saw. Adela Knighton died between two fifteen and three forty-five. The timing works out very neatly. What was he doing, taking a taxi at twenty to one in the morning when his friend thought him in bed asleep, if he wasn't going clandestinely back to Sussex? We have to see him, we have to get him down here again. We have to know where that gun is now.'

'I don't see any motive.'

'Motive sometimes has a way of showing itself rather late in the day. Anyway, someone said that every married man has a motive for murder.'

But as Wexford reached for the phone, it rang. The switchboard again, announcing a second visitor.

'There's a Mr Shah here, sir, asking to see you.' The voice went lower. 'A Chinese.'

'He doesn't sound Chinese.'

Sha? *Shah*? Did they mean Indian or maybe Tibetan? For a moment Wexford was mystified. Then a little tug of excitement caught at his throat. The name might be pronounced more or less Shah but in fact it was Hsia.

His visitor was Purbank's next-door neighbour in Fairmead Farm Court, Buckhurst Hill.

'I'd like you to stay,' he said to Burden.

The tall man in the dark suit that Wexford had encountered in the lobby of the flats came into the office. He was wearing a dark suit of a slightly different shade today and he still carried his briefcase. His black hair was so smooth and sleek it seemed to have been painted on his scalp. His eyes were mild, intelligent, his expression one of gentle impassivity. He held out to Wexford a narrow pale brown hand on which he wore a signet ring in obsidian and gold.

'My colleague, Inspector Burden,' said Wexford. 'Mr Hsia.'

Hsia sketched a slight bow. 'It's Chief Inspector Wexford, I believe? I hope I haven't come at an inconvenient time?'

'Not at all. Won't you sit down? I think we might all have some tea, don't you?' Wexford put his finger on the buzzer.

Sitting down, Hsia kept his arms tensely along the arms of the chair, then, as if by some oriental relaxation technique, lifted them and laid his hands calmly in his lap.

'Chief Inspector, I have come here to tell you something my friend and neighbour Mr Purbank cannot bring himself to tell you. It may seem I am betraying a trust, you see, but while this secrecy goes on I fear very much he will become ill. He is very much frightened, you see, so for his relief I must speak the whole truth to you.' Hsia's face relaxed and he gave a sort of rueful chuckle. 'You may feel, you see, that I am the one who should need to keep the secret, for I am the criminal. May I begin now?'

Wexford nodded. The tea came in. It rather surprised Wexford to see Hsia take milk and two lumps of sugar.

'My name is Hsia Yu-seng,' he began. 'You know where it is I live. I work for the Kowloon and Fuchow Bank in London Wall.' He paused and Wexford thought that 'work for' was probably a modest understatement. 'Most people,' Hsia went on, 'suppose that I am originally from Hong Kong or Taiwan, you see, but this isn't so. I was born in Shao-shan in the People's Republic—in fact, you know, in the very birthplace of the late Chairman, Mao Tse Tung. I was born in that place ten years before what they call liberation.'

'How did you come to leave China?' Wexford asked.

Hsia raised his teacup to his lips and drank a little. 'May I?' he said, reaching the ringed hand out for a Garibaldi biscuit. 'I committed a crime,' he said. 'I was twenty-one. If I had been caught—and I should have been caught, there is no hiding such things in China, you see—I would have been executed.'

Wexford moistened his lips. Inescapably, he associated capital punishment with murder. 'What crime?'

'I raped someone,' said mild sleek Mr Hsia, and he turned up the corners of his mouth in an apologetic smile.

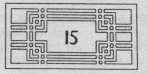

15

Burden made a choking sound over his tea. He wiped his mouth with a crisp white initialled handkerchief. 'Excuse me.'

'*You raped someone?*' Wexford asked.

'I and three others. You don't know how it was, the life there, the deprivation, the oppression, the *re*pression. This girl, she asked us, you see, she teased us, it was an invitation with the eyes, the walk. And then, when it is happening first with my friend, then with me, she is frightened and later she tells her father who is Party cadre.' With the stress of telling, Hsia's English worsened, approaching pidgin. He recovered himself and loosened his clenched hands. 'For this in China there is execution. There was then and there is now. My uncle, my mother's brother, he was a truck driver, driving every week to Canton. He took me in the truck, hid me, and from Canton I got into the New Territories. I am cutting a long story short, you see, but that was how it was. I walked to the border, crossed into the New Territories and came to Hong Kong. English I could speak a little, I had studied it at the University of Chang-sha, so after a while I came to England with my wife that I had married in Hong Kong, you see, and whose father is director of the Kowloon and Fuchow Bank. And from then on all goes very well for me.' He smiled again and this time slightly inclined his head.

Wexford looked at him, the bland parchment-coloured

163

face, the still features that have led to 'inscrutable' being the adjective invariably associated with the Chinese. Undreamt-of adventures, terrors, privations, struggles, lay hidden between the lines of that long story cut short. A less likely rapist than Hsia Yu-seng, Wexford had never seen.

'This is all very interesting,' he said, 'but what has it to do with Mr Purbank?'

'I am coming to it,' Hsia said, nodding. 'I have said all goes well for me and this is true, you see, except in one respect. That is my mother. My father died, you see, in the fighting of 1949 and my mother is widow, living with my brother and his family. But I was her favourite and always I have been very sad that I cannot get news to her. Always I have been afraid for her sake, you see, to send a letter and it is out of question for me ever to set foot in People's Republic. Often I have been thinking of ways to get news but find nothing better than what my father-in-law already has done—send her message only that I am alive. Then one day my neighbour Mr Purbank says to my wife that he is going in a train to China.'

'I begin to see,' said Wexford. 'Mr Purbank's itinerary would take him to Shao-shan and you asked him to deliver a message to your mother.'

'I asked him if he would take a *letter* to my mother. I had heard through my father-in-law that my brother's wife is cook in Wu Jiang Hotel, you see, so I thought to myself, there can be no trouble for Mr Purbank, who will surely eat there when he visits Mao's birthplace, to ask for the cook in order to praise his meal. He was to ask her name and if she answers, 'Mrs Hsia,' to slip her my letter.

'But all this goes wrong, you see, for Mr Purbank lost my letter when some things were stolen from his bags in Russia. And this made him very nervous and anxious to do the right thing, but he didn't know how to do it, you see. So he asked the interpreter to say to the cook, 'Your brother's friend is here,' which he does and my sister-in-law, very excited, you see, sends home for my mother who is an old woman now, more than seventy years old.'

With bound feet, Wexford thought. And when he had seen her that first time, then, when he had seen her as he was lunching in the Wu Jiang Hotel, it was no green tea hallucination. It had been a real woman that time that he had seen standing by the screen and waiting for news of her son. 'Go on,' he said.

'Well, then it was that Mr Purbank became really frightened, for whatever he said he must say through this interpreter, this official guide and interpreter from Lu Xing She. He knew I had been criminal, you see, and feared that if this was known he and the party might be expelled from China, so to my mother and sister-in-law, through the interpreter, he says that he has made a mistake, there has been a misunderstanding.

'But with this my mother was not content. She guessed, I think, that Mr Purbank has much to say but was frightened to say it, so next day when my cousin, the son of my uncle who saved my life, when he drives to Chang-sha she goes with him to look for Mr Purbank . . .'

The second sighting, Wexford thought, on Orange Island.

'. . . and there she finds him but they cannot communicate, you see, except by signs and by then both are afraid, Mr Purbank and my poor mother. Then, as luck would have it, while Mr Purbank is walking in the street in Chang-sha a student called Wong comes to him and asks to practise his English.' Hsia had gone entirely into the present tense now and Wexford remembered reading somewhere that Mandarin has no tenses. 'Perhaps this happens often in present-day China?' Hsia asked.

'Yes, it does.'

'So Mr Purbank has bright idea, you see, of asking this Wong to be interpreter for him. My mother still sits, waiting, in lobby of Wu Jiang Hotel. Mr Purbank tells Wong all about me, how I live in England, work in Kowloon and Fuchow Bank, have wife, have two boys at boarding school, everything about me, and Wong tells my mother who is made very happy and goes off full of happiness when my cousin calls back for her. But this is not, you see, the end of the story for Mr Purbank.

'This Wong is himself perhaps a criminal element or perhaps it's true he wants only to escape from People's Republic. Again to cut the story short, he follows Mr Purbank on the train to Kweilin, pleading with him to get him out of China. Also, Mr Purbank says, he asks always for money, you see, as if to threaten Mr Purbank that he has done a wrong thing that will get him in trouble unless he gives money.'

'You mean this Wong was blackmailing Mr Purbank? Unless Mr Purbank agreed to help get him out of China and gave him money, he would make the whole story of your contact with your mother known?'

'Something of that kind, yes. Mr Purbank was very frightened by now, always to be followed everywhere by this Wong, and although it was dreadful thing to happen he wasn't so very distressed when there was accident on the Li River boat and Wong was drowned.' The still features widened into a reflective smile. 'Mr Purbank then thought his troubles at an end till when he got home, a good while after, this Mrs Knighton, whom someone has shot, sends him photographs of the Li River trip. In them he is talking with Wong, and Mr Purbank is very afraid once more . . .'

'Did you see these photographs, Mr Hsia?'

'No, I didn't but I was told of them. Mrs Knighton's husband, you see, is in some way connected with the law and Mr Purbank thinks, suppose this whole story comes out and causes international incident, you see. So he burns the pictures and the negatives and sends the rest back to you and then he becomes nervous again in case you think he shot this Mrs Knighton . . .'

Wexford very nearly laughed. There was something he knew and Hsia very evidently didn't which stopped him laughing.

'It was wise of you to come to me,' he said.

'I thought it best. And now I shall tell you where Mr

Purbank was on the night of October first till after midnight—with me and my wife in our flat.' Getting up to leave, extending his hand, Hsia added, 'I fear he thinks it safer to be suspected of Mrs Knighton's murder than have it known he associates with such politically dangerous people as ourselves.'

From the window Wexford watched him cross the police station forecourt and get into this year's registration dark blue BMW. Strange to reflect that this sleek capitalist was the son of that old woman with the hoof-like mincing feet, that forerunner and instigator of hallucinations.

'Can you believe that?' Burden said. 'Can you believe Purbank was actually afraid of high-level repercussions because photographs existed of himself in conversation with a dissident Chinese?'

'Hsia believes it.'

'Sure he does. He grew to manhood in a country with perhaps the most repressive political system on earth.'

'I'll tell you what I think for what it's worth,' said Wexford. 'I'll never be able to prove it, I've nothing to go on but my own feelings, but it's my belief Purbank pushed Wong overboard. He was harassed by Wong's persecution and when they were on the boat and he came up behind Wong squatting down in the bows, he gave him a shove and pushed him overboard. Not intending to kill, I daresay, intending to frighten, to show Wong in his muddled way that he wasn't going to be used and battered on in the way Wong hoped.

'Back home I expect he soon forgot about it. We all know the old postulation: if by raising your hand you could acquire a million pounds and kill a Chinaman, would you do it? It's generally believed that few would hesitate long. Maybe it semed a little like that to Purbank. After Wong was drowned I asked Adela Knighton what had happened and she said indifferently that someone had been drowned—"Not one of us," she said. "A Chinese". Purbank had raised his hand and acquired peace if not money and it was all twelve thousand miles off and there are a lot of Chinese anyway . . . until the picture came with his hand reaching towards Wong's back.'

Burden nodded. It was likely enough. Suspects were being cleared, others implicated. Rape had reminded him of Coney Newton and what he had to tell Wexford of the El Video Club. Loring had been there the night before, making inquiries.

'It's managed by a man called Jimmy Moglander—"Moggy" to his associates. Newton was in there all right. He and three or four other men he was with were there until they closed on the Wednesday morning. The lives these villains lead! Moglander and the barman both remember Newton being there. So that seems to clear each and every old lag that might have had a grudge against Knighton.'

'So how about Knighton?'

'He'll keep till the morning, I should think.'

'You're right.' Wexford thrust back his chair and got up. 'I'm going home, Mike. If I hang about here someone'll be bound to drop in and tell me how he saw an old woman with bound feet climbing in through Knighton's loo window. We'll leave Knighton till tomorrow.'

But for Adam Knighton tomorrow never came. It was like *déjà vu*, Wexford thought in the morning, or the rerun of a tape. It was like going to see a film and sitting through the whole programme to see the beginning again. Only you usually did that because you liked the film. He hadn't liked this one the first time round, and as for the second . . .

The same credit titles, the same opening. It started with Renie Thompson phoning the police station at nine, with Burden and the fingerprint man and the scene-of-crimes man and Dr Crocker all going up to Thatto Hall Farm. The sun was shining and there was dew on the grass, and if the Michaelmas daisies were a little more mature and frost had shrivelled the leaves of the dahlias, if the sun was a little higher because the clocks had gone back an hour, only a purist would have noticed. All things up until this point seemed the same. They found a divergence only when they were inside the house, for this time it was Knighton who lay dead and by his own hand.

'Two times in a month,' said Mrs Thompson. 'It makes you think twice about going into a person's house. I thought he must be having a lay-in but the bedroom door wasn't shut, it was like on the jar, so I just gave a tap and put my head round . . .'

Since Wexford's last visit, Knighton had moved back into the room he had shared with his wife and there, on the evening before, he had undressed, put on blue cotton pyjamas and a brown wool dressing gown, lain on his bed and surrendered himself to death. On the bedside table beside him was an almost empty brandy bottle, an empty wine, not brandy, glass, and a cylindrical plastic container that had once held fifty capsules of tuinal.

'His doctor prescribed that for insomnia, presumably.'

'Not me, thank God,' said Crocker. 'I'd have given him mogadon. The only way you can kill yourself with mogadon is stuff down so many you choke to death.'

He closed Knighton's pale blue staring eyes. On the dressing table were two sealed envelopes, both addressed in Knighton's bold and beautiful hand. One of them was to the coroner.

'Who's Mrs M. Ingram?' asked Crocker.

'God knows.' Wexford read the address, Thain Court, Cadogan Avenue, London, SW1, and then he knew. 'It would seem she's the mother-in-law of an antique dealer I happen to know. I see he's provided a stamp but I think I'll deliver this by hand.' Outside, below the window, the gravel crunched. Wexford looked out. 'Angus and Jennifer,' he said and he stuffed the letters into his pocket.

Knighton's yellowish-white waxen face looked as long dead as the Marquise of Tai's. It looked as if it were made of porcelain but a porcelain they had forgotten to colour before the glaze went on.

'Poor devil,' Wexford said. 'There was no loophole left for him.'

'He did kill her then?'

'I didn't mean that. I've a feeling his predicament was a moral one, that it was his conscience he couldn't escape.' They left the room and closed the door. 'I never thanked you for the book.'

'I'm not sure if it would really happen.'

'Well, yes and no,' said Wexford cryptically.

Jennifer and her husband were in the hall. Her expression was as surly as ever. As he came down the stairs Wexford heard the tail end of what she was saying to Mrs Thompson, something about having no help in the house and a shock like this being enough to send her into premature labour. But Angus Norris looked as shocked and distressed as if Knighton had been his own father.

'This is a bad business, Mr Norris,' Wexford said. It was a phrase he used when he found himself in these or similar circumstances. Non-committal, it nevertheless expressed everything needful.

Norris took it *au pied de la lettre*. He spoke with a kind of tragic enthusiasm. 'A dreadful business, dreadful.' His face was rather pale and lined in a way some adolescents' faces are, though this ages them not at all. He looked round for his wife, to comfort her perhaps or be comforted, but Jennifer had gone into the living room and was lying in a chair with her feet up.

He said carefully, in a more controlled tone, 'Was there—a suicide note or anything of that sort?'

'Something of that sort,' said Wexford and he followed the doctor out through the front door.

Roderick Knighton's yellow TR7 had just joined the Norrises' worn-out Citroën on the gravel drive. The barrister got out of it and rushed into the house, closing the front door behind him with almost a slam.

The letters burned Wexford's pocket. He would have been justified in opening the envelope addressed to Mrs

Ingram and reading the contents. A suicide has forfeited his right to privacy and this suicide was also a prime suspect in a murder case. Who *was* Mrs Ingram, apart from being Pandora Vinald's mother? What had she been to Adam Knighton that he had written her a letter from his deathbed?

He wouldn't open it without phoning her first. He picked up the phone to ask the switchboard to find her number for him, then put it down again. On the hotel roof in Kweilin there had been another woman with Pandora, a much older woman, white-haired. In all the thought he had given to the events of that evening at the rooftop bar, in all his recollections of the people involved, that woman had never figured. The beauty of Pandora had eclipsed her.

For him perhaps, for almost everyone who saw them together, but not for Knighton. Knighton, sitting at that table with his wife, had seen her as Dante saw Beatrice and in a moment his life and his hopes had been transformed. But unlike Dante he wasn't seeing her for the first time. Wexford was sure of that. There was a romantic side to his nature that had a weakness for the phenomena of passion, yet he couldn't admit of the possibility of a man of Knighton's age falling in love at first sight with a woman of Mrs Ingram's.

He must have known her before, perhaps years ago. When they had interrogated him he had said that his career would have been damaged if he had 'deserted my wife and children for a young actress'. Mrs Ingram would have been young then, when the Knightons lived in Hampstead during the week and Sussex at the weekends, when Jennifer and Colum were babies, when Knighton by his eloquence was saving at least one murderer from execution.

The interesting thing was that the first time he saw her in London Pandora had reminded him of some famous beauty of thirty years back. He had thought of Hedy Lamarr or Lupe Velez. Thou art thy mother's glass and she in thee calls back the lovely April of her prime . . .

171

Mrs Ingram had friends in the film world. She had brought a film cameraman to meet her daughter and son-in-law.

'What do you suppose Milborough Lang looks like now?' Dora had said, watching *The Snow Moth*. 'She must be fifty-five.'

The letter to the coroner, Dr Neville Parkinson, Wexford delivered in person. Then he went off to meet Burden for lunch at the Many-Splendoured Dragon.

'It's unlike you not to be hungry,' said Burden.

Wexford was picking rather listlessly at his food. 'It's Setzuan here too,' he said. 'Nicer than the Hunan we mostly got served with.'

Burden looked impressed. 'Have you ever heard of a play called *The Good Woman of Setzuan* by a chap called Brecht? The drama society here is doing it at the end of the month. You ought to go.'

'I suppose your wife's playing the lead?' Wexford could tell from Burden's sheepish look that he had guessed right. He dipped in his chopsticks to catch a curl of okra while Burden, resigned to a spoon, watched him warily. Wexford dismissed the versatile Jenny Burden with a wry smile. 'Fishing for trouts in a peculiar river,' he said. 'Knighton was too old for that kind of thing. He was too old to have a mistress and too old to murder his wife.'

'What did Parkinson's letter say?'

'It was very short. I can probably quote it from memory. "This is to inform you that on the morning of 2 October I killed my wife, Adela Knighton, by shooting her with a Walther PPK automatic pistol. As a consequence of that act I shall, by the time you read this, have taken my own life." And he signed it. That was all.'

Burden poured himself a glass of mineral water. 'I wonder where he got the gun and, come to that, what he did with it afterwards.'

'I wonder about a lot of things. Frankly, Mike, I think it's all these doubts I have that are making me—well, I won't say upset. Uneasy.'

'You don't mean you think it's a false confession?'

Wexford didn't answer him directly. 'He was devoured by guilt, wasn't he? You could tell that.' He pushed away his plate. For a moment he hesitated, then he asked the waiter to bring a pot of green tea. 'And certainly he wanted her dead. He left Dobson-Flint's and came back here that night. He must have killed her. Why say so if he hadn't? It's not your run-of-the-mill false confession. The man killed himself. The whole point of a false confession is to attract attention and the kind of hysteric who does that doesn't defeat his own object by committing suicide immediately afterwards.'

'Certainly not,' said Burden firmly.

'Let's go. I have to phone Mrs Ingram and then I have to see her.'

16

FASHION HAD COME FULL CIRCLE AND THE CLOTHES SHE WORE were not unlike those she had been dressed in for her films, a little grey flannel suit with a straight skirt, a pearl-coloured silk blouse with a high pleated neckline, stockings with seams, high-heeled shoes. Her figure seemed unchanged. But that kind of black silk hair is perhaps of all shades the most vulnerable to time. It was whiter than her skin now and that skin itself webbed with lines.

She hadn't sounded surprised by his phone call. Why should she have been? For weeks now she must have been waiting for the police to come to her. *Why* he had come, that was something else again. She greeted him with a gentle, ever so slightly ironical, friendliness.

They went into a living room. The flat was in a small block of apartments for rent on short leases, smart, even luxurious, in one of the most highly desirable residential areas on earth. It lacked any particle of character. It was a suite of motel rooms, biscuit-coloured Wilton on the floors, chocolate-coloured linen at the windows and upholstering the furniture, here and there murals that were blends of Samuel Palmer and Rowland Hilder or montages of beaten tin cans and bits of bamboo. She had added pieces of her own, a pair of water colours, a red, blue and gold ikon, a vase or two that very likely came from Vinald, and flowers in abundance. She had filled vases and bowls with what October afforded in the way of dahlias and chrysanthemums and what October couldn't afford but she evidently could, roses and gladioli and carnations.

She sat down on the sofa, her knees together, her body held a little to one side, her head up, a very Milborough Lang attitude. Suddenly Wexford's heart felt heavy. He was desperately sorry for her.

'I believe you knew Adam Knighton well?' he began.

She was immediately apprehensive. ' "Knew"?' she said. 'What does "knew" mean? I know him, yes.'

This was how the man felt who drew Priam's curtain in the dead of night. And like Priam, she had begun to guess. 'Mrs Ingram, I used the word advisedly. I have bad news for you. I think it will be bad news.' She was very still, her eyes on him. 'You must prepare yourself for a shock. Mr Knighton is dead.'

Her lips parted. She brought her hands together.

'He was found dead this morning,' Wexford said.

'Do you mean—he killed himself?'

'I am afraid so.'

'How?' she asked softly.

'Brandy and an overdose of sleeping pills. He left a note for the coroner and a note for you. I have brought yours with me.'

On the third finger of the thin veined hand she put out to him was a diamond cluster as big as a grape. She wore a diamond watch and diamond earrings. From the neck up she had grown some ten years older since he had told her of Knighton's death.

'It was kind of you to come personally to tell me.' She started to get up. She was politely dismissing him.

'I'm sure you would like to read your letter in private,' he said, 'but after that I'm afraid I shall have to see it.'

She held it against her breast, her hands crossed over it in the traditional gesture of a girl keeping a love letter from father or husband. She was still an actress.

'I shall have to see it, Mrs Ingram. It may be of great relevance to Mrs Knighton's murder. I must see the letter and then you and I must have a talk.'

'If I don't show it to you, could you get an order or a warrant or something like that to force me to?'

He nodded. 'Something like that. But I'm sure you'll let me see it without that, won't you?'

'Yes.' She pushed her thumbnail under the flap of the envelope and began to open it. 'Excuse me if I go away to read it.'

He was taking a small risk but he hadn't the heart to refuse her. While she was absent, the door between the communicating rooms left ajar as if she guessed what he slightly feared, he thought of what Irene Bell had told him about Knighton's attitude towards his family in the past. 'For five years after Colum was born Adela had a husband insofar as there was a man sleeping in the other bed in her room.' Colum Knighton would be about thirty. It fitted. 'And then suddenly Adam came back. He lived at home, he had his meals there, he started taking Adela out—the lot.' What else had she said? 'It was as if he'd had a shock and come to his senses.' What in fact had happened was that after a five-year-long love affair Milborough Lang had left him and married someone else.

She came back and gave him the letter in a quick, almost disdainful gesture. A lamp was on but he took it to the window and read it by the dying daylight.

My darling, I shall be dead when you come to read this. I had dreamed of our being so happy together, I had longed for it and it really did seem within our grasp for a little while. I believed I could live with anything so long as you and I had each other at last, but I was wrong. The love I have for you is the strongest emotion I have ever felt for anyone, stronger than my feeling for my children. I have loved you for thirty years and kept the image of you always in my mind.

But remorse is stronger than love. When I killed Adela I did not know myself. Though I had spent a lifetime in association with evil, I did not know how insidious evil is, how it destroys the joy of everything, even the joy of love. I had never considered that this act which was designed to bring me happiness would instead show me a hell of shame and self-hatred, a hell that is with me night and day, every moment of every day.

That is not something I can live with or expect you to share with me. Therefore I have resolved to put an end to it. Twenty-five years ago my children and my responsibilities and my own fear held me back. This time I think I shall have the courage. Not so much courage, perhaps, as the lack of it, lack of fortitude for a continuance of the life I am living now.

Do you remember how we read the Chinese poems together? Here are two lines from Chang Chi.

So I now return your shining pearls with a tear on each. Regretting that we did not meet while I was still unwed. Good night, my darling, and God bless you, Adam.

She hadn't cried when she read the letter but the sight of him reading it brought the tears. They fell silently, she hardly seemed aware of them.

'Please sit down, Mrs Ingram. Do you feel able to talk about this or would you rather wait a while?'

'It may as well be now.' She spoke the ungracious words graciously. She sat down. 'I should like my letter back, please.'

'Later. You shall have it before I go. Now I should like you to tell me the whole story.'

She made a movement of recoil, she shook her head. 'He didn't kill her, whatever he says. He *couldn't* have killed her.'

'I'm afraid you're going to have to accept that he could and did. Now you're going to tell me about yourself and him. It will be good for you as well as for me. Have you anyone else you can tell it to? Anyone at all who will care enough to listen?'

'No,' she whispered.

He had been thirty-two, she twenty-five. They had met at a dinner party given by that very Henry Lacey who had entertained Knighton on the eve of his wife's death. Adela had been there too. The young Milborough Lang had become famous overnight when her first film was shown, a curious and almost mystical story of a deaf girl called *The Snow Moth*, and she had followed this with a stage success as Petra in Ibsen's *An Enemy of the People*. Wexford remembered seeing *The Snow Moth* when it first came out. As was probably true of Garbo, it was the star's beauty and grace of movement and look of other-worldliness which had brought her fame rather than her acting ability. Milborough Lang had been wonderfully beautiful.

'We were a handsome couple,' she said, seeming to read his thoughts. 'Isak Dinesen says that life is but a process for turning frisky young puppies into mangy old dogs. Only we never were a couple really. Adam had Adela and he had four children. Colum had been born just three months before we met. He told me Adela had had his two younger children to ensure he stayed with her, and it worked, it did ensure that.

'We saw as much of each other as we could. Technically, he still lived with Adela, he slept under her roof. It was very cruel, it was a hateful way to behave to her, I know that. I think I felt more guilty than he did.' She paused and put her fingers to her cheeks to wipe away the drying tears. 'We paid for it, of course. We were punished. The times we had together were always a rush, always a race against the clock. He had to get back to work, to court, to Adela, and I had my career too. I got this Hollywood offer and I went to Hollywood and made that terrible *Mind Over Matter*, but I couldn't stay there without Adam.

'I was the one who made the break. We couldn't have gone on like that. It had been five years but Colum was still only five, and it would have meant another fifteen years maybe of rush and subterfuge and passion and mad muddle. Besides, it had never had the chance to become a real workaday relationship, it was a romance.

'I met Ryan Ingram. He wanted to marry me and take

me away to New Zealand. I think he saw himself, poor dear Ryan, as a sort of new world Prince Rainier, transporting his beloved from the rat race of the screen into a life of wealth and peace. I seem to be predisposed to these romantic men, don't I? Anyway, I did marry him and I did go away with him and Adam and I didn't write to each other or see each other for twenty-five years—until I walked out on to the roof in that place in China.'

Ryan Ingram had died of a coronary three years before. Their daughter Pandora had made a mistaken marriage when nineteen. It was partly to distract her mind from this and from the subsequent divorce that she and her mother had come on the trip that had been intended to take them round the world but had ended, in each case because of a love affair, in London.

'Adam recognized me at once. It must be true that love is blind because I think I've altered more than most people do in twenty-five years. I recognized him, of course. It was an extraordinary sensation, seeing him sitting there, still with Adela.'

She got up and drew the curtains on the dark late afternoon. When the lamp beneath it went on, the rich colours of the ikon, the gold in its border and the Virgin's crown, glowed in the light. Wexford suddenly recalled reading an illustrated article in a Sunday supplement about ikons that looked like that and which came from the neighbourhood of Lake Baikal. . . Milborough Ingram smiled, a little sadly, a little ruefully, and went on, 'Adela went to bed. He came over to our table and said—to be prudent, you know. Oh, that eternal prudence! —"Miss Lang, we met years ago at Henry Lacey's house in London. I don't suppose you remember." "I remember," I said. Pandora was talking to some Australians, I don't think she noticed Adam. The young don't notice, they aren't interested in us. Why should they be? He said—his voice was shaking—"May I buy you a drink?" I excused myself to the others and we went inside the hotel. I never had that drink—I think I'd like one now, though. Will you?'

Wexford nodded. She fetched ice and poured whisky on to it in big glasses.

'We found a sort of banqueting room, a great empty gloomy place, and we went in there and talked. You were in that hotel too, Adam said. Isn't that strange? I wonder where you were then.'

'Being shown his porcelain collection by your son-in-law.'

The delicate dark eyebrows went up. 'He's scared stiff of you because he thinks you're after him for selling something or other to an American. Are you?'

Wexford smiled. 'I think the Chinese would be after him if they knew. China's a long way away.'

'Yes.' Her voice grew grave again. 'China's a long way away. Adam once told me about the Chinese mandarin, how most people wouldn't think twice about killing a Chinese mandarin if they could get a million pounds by doing so. China is so far away, so remote, even today. If one just had to make a sign, he said . . .' She sat down again, looking at him. 'In China, that night, everything seemed simple. Adam could leave Adela. Time had sorted things out for us and we could be together.'

'You still wanted to? After a quarter of a century? After your marriage?'

She delayed answering, drank some of her drink. 'I will be honest,' she said at last. 'I didn't feel the same as I had. How could any ordinary realistic person feel the same? Adam wasn't an ordinary realistic person. I'm not flattering myself when I say he felt just the same, perhaps even more so.

'I wanted to make him happy. I would have liked to remarry and to be married to him. Oh, yes, I would have liked it.'

'So he went home and you and your daughter went to England all on the same plane. Did you speak to Adela Knighton?'

'No. She had seen me once, thirty years ago at a dinner party and naturally she had forgotten me. Adam and I didn't speak to each other again until we saw each other in London. Pandora and Gordon were instantly attracted to each other. That was why it was easy to get straight to London, Pandora wanted it, she would have gone without me if I'd objected. In London I took a lease of this flat and Adam came to see me here. He and Adela used to have days out in London, they'd come up together on the train and he'd go and look up various old cronies while she went shopping and called on some friend of hers in Primrose Hill. I replaced the old cronies.

'It was very much like it had been twenty-five years ago. Patterns repeat themselves, don't they? There was I with my flat and there was Adam living with his wife. We were ruled by the clock as we had been. Almost from the first I knew he wasn't going to leave Adela. I tackled him about it and he—he wept, he actually cried, poor Adam, it was dreadful. He couldn't leave her, he said, not after forty years. He couldn't face her and his children with a thing like that. That quarter of a century might never have been. I'd married and had a child and lived on the other side of the world and he'd become a QC and retired and was a grandfather—but everything was just the same, it was uncanny. And yet he did love me, he loved me more than I loved him, poor Adam.

'And then I tried to break it off just as I had before. I said it was hopeless going on in this way, simply history repeating itself. I said I was too old for that kind of thing and when the lease of this place was up I'd go home to my house in Auckland.'

'You mean you held that over him as a threat?'

She lifted her shoulders and there came to her lips the ghost of a Milborough Lang smile. 'He knew I'd go unless things could be made more permanent, yes.'

The smile angered him. 'You might say then, Mrs Ingram, that you share some of the responsibility for Adela Knighton's murder and hence for Adam Knighton's own death.'

She jumped up, her serenity gone, and cried out to him, 'That's not true! Adam didn't kill her. Haven't I told you he couldn't have killed her?'

'He's admitted it. Before his confession we were pretty certain—all the evidence, circumstantial and otherwise, pointed to his having killed her. He had motive and opportunity and he was there.'

'He was not there,' she said more calmly. 'He was here with me.'

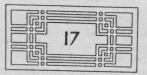

17

'IT SOUNDS RIDICULOUS,' SHE SAID, 'A MAN OF OVER SIXTY SNEAK-ing out of his friend's house and dashing across London in a taxi to be with the woman he loves—a woman of fifty-five. To spend the night with her and go back at dawn. A superannuated Romeo and Juliet. It really does happen, it did happen.'

He believed her. It was so evidently true. 'What time did he come?'

She replied at once. Had it been the only whole night they had spent together? 'A few minutes after one.'

Knighton wasn't the first man to confess to a murder he hadn't committed, Wexford thought. And yet . . .

'No doubt you saw him several times after that?'

'We talked a lot on the phone. I saw him—oh, three times? Four?'

'He never said anything to you to suggest he had killed his wife?'

'How could he have when I knew he was here with me at the time? I could tell he was unhappy, he seemed tormented. But his wife had been murdered and however he felt about her and me, she *was* his wife.' Milborough Ingram put her hand to her forehead and leaned her face forward on it. Her voice had taken on a faltering note. 'He never said any more about our marrying, about our being together. He was different, changed. I thought he was ill. I said he ought to have a holiday and I'd go with him. He just stared at me, he held my hand and stared at me.' She reached for her whisky. 'Oh, God, I mustn't have any more to drink. I'll get drunk and that won't help. Ever since I was eighteen I've had it dinned into me I mustn't drink because it'd spoil my figure and my face, and it dies hard, all that. What does it matter now?'

He got up to go. She was composing herself but hysteria trembled beneath the surface of her composure.

'Would you like me to get your daughter to come to you?'

'I'm better alone. Really.'

He turned his eyes away from that ravaged, once-beautiful face. They lighted on the ikon. He remembered where he had seen it before—in Vinald's bedroom in the Kweilin Hotel.

'I gave my son-in-law two hundred pounds for that.' Wexford heard a rasp in her voice. 'I'm sure it's worth it,' he said politely.

'Oh, no doubt. Only Pandora told me afterwards he gave two pairs of jeans for it and one of those wasn't even his own.'

She had spoken in the bitterness of her heart. It was an anger with the injustice of the world she was venting on Gordon Vinald. Already she looked ashamed of her indiscretion.

'What does it matter now?' she said again.

Wexford made no reply. He said goodbye to her and went down to where Donaldson and the car waited.

Tabard Road, Kingsmarkham, the bungalow that was almost as familiar to Wexford as his own home over the other side of the town. Dora Wexford had dealt with the problem of being a policeman's wife by acceptance, by patience, but Jenny Burden solved it more positively, filling her evenings with learning—and teaching—at classes, with drama groups and string trios. She was out this evening, at a rehearsal, Burden said. He fetched two cans of beer from the fridge.

'Knighton wasn't mad,' Wexford said. 'It wasn't a

matter of having some sort of delusion he'd done it. He knew he hadn't held the gun and squeezed the trigger and shot her. He meant he was morally responsible, he instructed someone else to do it.'

'Not someone he paid. We know he parted with no large sums.'

Wexford said thoughtfully, 'I don't think it was anything as direct as that. I think it was more a matter of nodding, of raising one's hand and killing the mandarin.'

'I don't follow you.' Burden had put on his obtuse look, the one he wore less and less since his second marriage. Once it had inspired Wexford to say he was reminded of Goering who said that whenever he heard the word culture he reached for his gun. Sometimes it came back to make the Inspector's normally intuitive face mulish. 'I haven't a clue what all that means,' he said.

'I can't enlighten you. I'm not being purposely obscure, I don't know any more yet. Let me tell you about Vinald and Purbank instead. I can tell you what they quarrelled about. Vinald pinched a pair of Purbank's jeans to pay for an ikon.'

'He did *what*?'

'I imagine he discovered this ikon in the possession of some peasant in the far east of Russia. Russians are crazy to get their hands on denim jeans, or so I've heard. Probably Vinald hadn't got very long there, wherever it was, or the ikon vendor wouldn't hang about, so Vinald went back to the train and fetched a pair of his own jeans. Because he hadn't any more of his own clean or didn't want to part with them or something he took Purbank's. No doubt he explained to Purbank afterwards and maybe offered to pay for them but Purbank was outraged and refused to have any more to do with him.'

Burden laughed. 'But why not tell us?'

'Vinald wouldn't because it makes him look such a crook. Purbank wouldn't because it makes him look a fool. What could be more undignified than someone nicking a pair of your trousers? It's a kind of vicarious debagging.'

'I suppose it is,' Burden said. 'Put that cat down if you don't want it.'

Jenny's Abyssinian, as lithe and sinuous as the Pensive Selima was stout, had sprung up delicately on to Wexford's lap. He drew his hand down the smooth slippery back.

'Is Vinald a crook, d'you think?'

'D'you remember when we went to the V and A I paid particular attention to the Sung ware? Celadon, they call it. White or pale grey or pale green, an attempt to imitate jade, around a thousand years old. While we were in Kweilin Vinald showed me the Celadon ware he'd bought, trusting, and rightly, to my ignorance. He said it was a hundred years old, Ching stuff, and of course I believed him. He had a whitish bowl, a dull plain thing, and I remember thinking to myself that Dora wouldn't have given it house room. You wouldn't reckon on anyone paying ten thousand pounds for a thing like that, would you?'

'Ten grand? For a white pot a hundred years old?'

'Well, not a hundred years old, Mike. That's rather the point. Say eight hundred? I saw the stick of red sealing wax in Vinald's hotel room and it meant nothing to me. I didn't know then that any antique you bring out of China has to have the government's red seal on it. Vinald was getting hold of priceless pieces from people who didn't know any better, paying virtually nothing for them, and then putting the red seal on himself. Especially that bowl—which he took up to Birmingham on October the first and sold to the agent of a South American purchaser for ten thousand pounds.'

'Can we do anything to him?'

'Like what? Extradite him to China? Do you know what he'd answer if we said to him what I've just said to you? That he gave a fair price for the bowl, believing it to be Ching. Of course it had the seal on it. What can we mean? It was only when he got it home and examined it carefully that he discovered he'd paid five quid for a piece of Sung.'

As Wexford stroked it the cat began emitting a harsh rumbling purr. Still shaking his head over man's chicanery, Burden fetched more beer. Wexford changed the subject. 'When you went hunting up those old lags—what you might call recidivisiting—you had two lists, didn't you? The men Knighton had helped send down and those that had got off or got off lightly because of his defence?'

'That's right.'

'What was the point of the alternative list?'

'You mean the ones he got off?'

'I mean, what was the point of listing people who have had no motive for revenge on him?'

'There wasn't a point really. Brownrigg and I simply made a note of every case Knighton had been involved in that we thought important enough. I put those friendly to Knighton in the right-hand column and those—well, possibly revengeful on the left. I got them muddled too, I . . .'

But Wexford didn't want to hear about that. 'You've still got the lists?'

'Of course I have.'

In the morning Wexford looked at them.

'This Coney Newton seems to be on both lists. What did he get sent down for?'

'Rape and attempted murder,' said Burden. 'He's on both lists because—well, I thought he might have reason to be grateful to Knighton for getting him off with only seven years or vindictive towards Knighton for not getting him off altogether. And funnily enough, he didn't seem vindictive, he just seemed to think Knighton hadn't made a very efficient job of his defence. Anyway, he's got a good alibi for that night and he alibis Silver Perry.'

'That's fine for him then, isn't it, having his word backed up by a really exemplary citizen like that?'

'They were in a club together,' Burden said, slightly offendedly. 'I went to the club. There's no question . . .'

'All right. Who's Henry Thomas Chipstead?'

'Once upon a time he was an East End of London gangster. Around twenty years ago he was up on a charge of grievous bodily harm and Knighton got him off. Wills—' Burden indicated with his finger the name in the left-hand column. 'Wills suggested to me that Knighton might have called in "a professional like Chipstead". Those were his words, not mine. He said Chipstead had been with Lee's mob, might be dead now for all he knew. He's not dead, though, he's alive and living in Leytonstone. But he's over seventy now and in any case we know Knighton didn't pay anyone.'

'And what was this Wills's contribution to the disintegration of society?'

Burden grinned wryly. 'Aiding and abetting. He didn't actually kill this woman but he was an accessory. He concealed the body by night in roadworks on a motorway, only one of the workmen discovered it before they laid the road surface . . . What's the matter?'

'I know where he put that gun,' Wexford said slowly.

'Where who put it?'

'Ah, that's something else. I mean I know where whoever our perpetrator is put the weapon. You just told me. What you said about this Wills and roadworks told me.'

'It did?'

'The weir, Mike, the weir at Sewingbury Mill.'

It was a long shot. Burden's opinion was that 'they' would never be got to demolish all that concrete and brickwork, embankment and paving, for the sake of finding a gun, it wasn't as if it was a body. And the chances, he said pessimistically, were that the gun wasn't there anyway.

'Once I've got a warrant,' said Wexford, 'they'd get on with the demolition if it was a pin they were looking for and Sewingbury Agricultural College they were demolishing.'

Colonel Charles Griswold, the Chief Constable of Mid-Sussex, was as uneasy about it as Burden. And perhaps

Wexford would never have been allowed to swear out that warrant but for the clerk of works who had supervised the construction of the 'weir' for the county authority telling the chief constable that, when the workmen knocked off for the day at five on 1 October, only the paved area remained to be completed. At that time, on that afternoon, he said, the areas waiting to be paved had lain open and uncovered except for a foundation of 'hard core' spread on the soil.

'Suppose we say he left his car in the market square in Sewingbury,' Wexford said. 'He made his way by the footpath to Thatto Vale and got to Thatto Hall Farm at about two. There he either entered by the washroom window or let himself in with a key, having made it appear as if he entered by the window. He woke Mrs Knighton, brought her downstairs at gun-point, shot her, feebly faked a burglary and returned by the path where he was seen by Bingley at around three. At the Sewingbury end of the footpath he spotted the nearly completed paving work on the weir and it would have been the work of only a few moments to bury the gun in the soil under the hard core.'

It was a cold day with a bitter wind blowing. The Kingsbrook, swollen by recent rains, rushed and tumbled under the Springhill bridge and through the new channel constructed for it. The same contractors that had built the 'weir' came to knock part of it down again. As soon as they had the paving stones up, Sergeant Martin and Archbold were to go along and grub about under the hard core for the gun. Wexford looked in for a few moments at the inquest on Adam Knighton. Angus Norris was there but otherwise the family was not represented.

Wexford knew there could be no possible outcome but that the inquest be adjourned. Dr Parkinson was reading aloud Knighton's confession and now and then quoting Wexford's own words that Knighton could not himself have been physically responsible for his wife's death. Wexford crept out of the court. At the far side of the quadrangle that divided the courts from the police station Donaldson was awaiting him at the wheel of his car, Burden already seated in the back. The wind struck him with a sharp gust and blew out his scarf like a flag.

'The river bank is no place to be this morning,' said Burden, rubbing his hands.

'You sound like Mole.'

'Who?'

'It doesn't matter. We're going up to the Smoke anyway. Or near enough. The Haze, we should maybe call it. Is Leytonstone the sort of place we can get lunch in, Donaldson?'

But the London expert, to his own evident chagrin, didn't know, he had never been there.

'Chipstead, I suppose,' Burden said.

'Henry Thomas Chipstead, fifty-two Dogshall Road, Leytonstone. He's seventy-three and doesn't seem to have been up to anything in the hit man line since Knighton got him off the hook when he was fifty. But he'll do for a start.'

'I wish you'd explain to me what you meant about that killing the mandarin.'

They were on the motorway now, heading for London. The wind was so strong that gusts of it shifted and swayed the heavy car. Occasionally spatters of rain in large drops dashed against the windscreen.

'I think that years and years ago,' Wexford said, 'Knighton had reason to be in contact with some villain who was a professional assassin or hit man. Defended him, presumably. After the case he went to Knighton and said to him something on the lines of, if there's ever anything I can do for you, Mr Knighton sir, you've only to say the word, you know what I mean, nudge, nudge, anything you want done on the quiet, and Knighton, no doubt, got all upstage with moral indignation, but later on he got to thinking about it. Much later on and when it would really have suited him to have someone put out of the way.

'No money would have to pass, you see. That would

be the beauty of it. He wasn't going to have to be specific with this old lag, wasn't going to have to give him three or four grand in used oncers or anything like that. Beforehand he might even be able to think he wasn't really the instigator. Suppose it was no more than a matter of making a phone call and saying something like, My wife's going to be alone on the night of October the first? Suppose it was even more subtle and slight than that?

'But afterwards the remorse and the guilt, to a man like Knighton, would be as great as if he had paid an assassin or pulled the trigger himself.'

'Well, he'd be just as guilty,' said Burden.

'Of course he would, but a good many men wouldn't *feel* just as guilty. That's the analogy with the mandarin. One of China's teeming thousand millions is just as much a human life as one's wife or child, but it doesn't feel like that because it's so remote, so far out of sight. And if one only has to raise one's hand . . . I think maybe Knighton only had to raise his hand, or do something as slight as that, to rid himself of his wife and have Milborough Ingram.'

They came into London through the Blackwall Tunnel. From its northern end it wasn't far to Leytonstone. Dead leaves from the fringe ends of Epping Forest whirled in the wind. Dogshall Road was a long straight street that passed with a hump over one suburban railway line and in a dip under another. The gutters were choked with leaves, the trees in the pavement, three times as tall as the little squat terraces of houses, were shedding leaves into the wind. There was a red brick church and a pre-fab church hall with an asbestos roof but nothing else to relieve the long monotony of Victorian terraces, the long double row of parked cars. Donaldson pulled into a gap a little way down from number seventeen.

'Moralizing would be out of place,' said Wexford, 'but this is a fine illustration of how crime *doesn't* pay, don't you think? Chipstead made his living for years, for most of his life, out of violent crime. I'm not saying it was in vain, it wasn't, it caused a lot of suffering, it damaged society, provoked fear, made work for the police, cost the taxpayer money. But it didn't profit Chipstead himself much, did it?'

The three men looked at what Chipstead had got out of it, a hundred-year-old brown brick box with six feet of concrete, on which stood a dustbin and a dead geranium in a tub, separating it from the street. There were only three windows at the front of the house and at all of them the curtains were drawn. Wexford got out of the car and Burden followed him.

The house had a dead empty look as if its occupants had closed it up and gone away, and Wexford, banging hard on the knocker, for there was no bell, had very little hope of an answer. But after a moment or two a woman's voice was heard saying something and then footsteps sounded on the stairs.

The door was opened to them by Renie Thompson.

18

'HENRY WAS MY BROTHER,' SHE SAID.

They stood in the hall. There was a light on upstairs and women whispering.

'Was?' said Wexford.

'He's dead, isn't he? You mean you didn't know? Today's the funeral. To tell you the truth, when you knocked I thought it was the undertakers come.' She wore a grey coat and a black felt hat. She looked at them truculently, at their dubious suspicious faces. 'You'd like to make something out of it, wouldn't you? I know. There's nothing to make.'

'Give us the raw materials, Mrs Thompson, and we'll decide that.'

A woman had begun coming down the stairs, evidently a sister. She stood there, staring, listening, holding the banister.

'I'd worked for Mrs Knighton since nineteen sixty. Him and her, they was the best employers you'd find anywhere. Henry had to come up in court for something he never done and I said, you want Mr Knighton to speak up for you and he got Mr Knighton, Mr Knighton was on his side on account of knowing *me,* and he got Henry off, of course he did, considering Henry never done it.'

The woman on the stairs clicked her tongue.

'Henry thought the world of Mr Knighton.'

'So did you too, Renie,' said the woman on the stairs.

'You a Sewingbury family, are you?' Burden asked. They both nodded, eyeing him warily. 'Had your brother been ill prior to his death?'

The third sister now came down, buttoning herself into a black astrakhan coat.

'In the hospital six months,' said Renie Thompson. 'He had it in his chest, you see, the lung, and then it went to his spine.'

The door knocker rattled. The woman in astrakhan went to the door and the wind blew a dead leaf in to cling to her coat. Two men in black stood outside, their hats in their hands.

'All right,' said Wexford, 'we won't trouble you any more at the moment.'

Among the other parked cars two black Daimlers now waited, one empty, one bearing the body of the former gangster in a coffin laden with flowers. Wexford and Burden went back to their car. Donaldson said a message had come through on the radio that the gun had been found under the paving stones at the 'weir'.

Wexford nodded. He was watching Chipstead's house. Until now it hadn't occurred to him that there had been others inside as well as the three sisters. These people, no doubt, had been sitting in silence behind the bay window with the drawn curtains, waiting to follow Chipstead's body to the grave or the fire. They came trooping down the path, an elderly man and woman arm-in-arm, a boy of eighteen in a borrowed black jacket and tie, a little man with red hair, a fat man with practically no hair, a tall man with silver hair.

'Silver Perry,' Burden said.

'Were they old pals or something?'

'Evidently. It wouldn't surprise me.'

The Daimler took the sisters and the old couple. The rest of the mourners got into an old dark blue Ford Popular.

'Where do you suppose they're going, Donaldson?' asked Wexford.

'City of London Crematorium, Manor Park, sir,' Donaldson said promptly. 'Twenty minutes there, twenty minutes for a hymn and our-dear-brother-to-the-fire, twenty minutes back.'

'We may as well go and have lunch then.'

The wind had dropped and it became very dark, dark enough to have the light on in the front room at 52 Dogshall Road. The light shimmered through unlined green curtains. The boy was the first to leave, dressed in leathers now and carrying a crash helmet. He got on the Yamaha parked next to the Ford Popular and roared off in the direction of the bridge. A little while later the front door opened again and Silver Perry came out. Conventionally dressed in a dark suit and dark waisted overcoat, he had something of a look in the fading light of Adam Knighton, but of Knighton debased, vulgarized, roughened. He was a little less tall and lacked the presence of the man for whom he had said he would do anything, would lay down his life.

'He used those words?' Wexford asked.

'Well, in a newspaper,' said Burden. 'I was going to tell you, I nearly did tell you only you interrupted me with your idea about the gun, they remember Coney Newton being in the El Video till three or whatever and Newton says he was there with Perry but no one in the club said a word to me about seeing Perry.'

On the doorstep Perry kissed Renie Thompson and then walked quickly away. Wexford thought he would get into the Ford but evidently it wasn't his, he had come on foot. And on foot he was departing through the thin grey drizzle that had now begun to fall steadily. The street lights had come on, lozenges of fruit drop orange among the stripped branches of the trees. Perry turned up the collar of his coat and trudged along, hands in pockets. He was heading, probably, for the tube station, a quarter of a mile up the hill past the hump in the road.

The car crawled after him, Donaldson driving very slowly. A van behind started hooting but Donaldson took no notice.

'He thinks he's going to cross here,' said Wexford. 'Pull round the corner.'

Donaldson turned sharply to the left just as Perry approached the edge of the pavement to cross the street. The side of the car presented itself in front of him like a wall. Silver Perry took a step back as the car door was thrown open and Wexford got out.

'Care for a lift, Silver?'

Wexford had his warrant card out but he need not have troubled. Perry belonged in that category of men who could pick out a policeman on a nude beach or at a fancy dress ball. It was child's play to him to detect three of them in a London suburb, in a car, in the rain. For all that, he looked for a split second as if he might try making a run for it. In that second his face showed the spark of hope, the flare of panic, the commonsense realization that quenched them. He shrugged and got into the car. Rain was running off the glossy white cap of hair.

'D'you know where Cyril Street, Bethnal Green is, Donaldson?' asked Burden.

'I can find it, sir.'

'Off Globe Road,' said Perry.

'Or do we take him straight back with us? Your gun's been found, Perry. Shooters usually do turn up in the long run.'

'Shooter? What shooter?' asked Perry.

'Cyril Street first, I think,' Wexford said, 'and then maybe we can think again. Enjoy yourself at the funeral, did you, Silver? By God, but you niff of Cyprus sherry.'

'I suppose you think you're funny. I didn't go to enjoy myself. Henry Chipstead was a lifelong friend.'

'And we all know how good you are to your friends. Laying down your life and so forth. Or laying down other people's lives.' Wexford looked into the man's pale blue eyes, watery eyes, narrower and shiftier than Knighton's. 'You've no alibi for the night of October the first. And you were seen near Thatto Hall Farm. You were seen walking along the footpath to Sewingbury from Thatto Vale at three in the morning.'

Silver Perry said nothing. The car wound its way along a one-way street system, through back doubles, from the eastern suburbs into the East End of London. It was raining hard now and the wipers were on at high speed.

'You left your car in the market square at Sewingbury,' said Burden. 'You must know the area well.'

Perry admitted nothing. In a low voice he said, 'Renie and me—like a hundred years ago I used to know Renie pretty well.'

'When you came back you saw the building works and you buried the gun, knowing it would be concreted in next day.'

Perry tapped Donaldson's back. 'Second one on the left now, son.'

'I reckon Knighton must have given you something for your trouble,' said Burden. 'Reimbursed you for the shooter at any rate.'

Perry sighed. 'The wife's out, round at her sister's. I wouldn't want her brought in on this.'

The tall stalk of a tower, punctured all over now with squares of light, and its fellow stalks, vertical dormitories. There were several hundred cars now on the shiny black wet tarmac that was clean of shed leaves since there were no trees here to shed them. Wexford sent Donaldson off for a cup of tea in a Globe Road café. The lift took them up what felt like ten miles to Perry's eyrie and the kind of view that would once have made men gasp but now is commonplace to air travellers and frequenters of revolving restaurants.

No one was at home. The place was dark. Perry put on a light or two and took them into the room that had nothing in common with the accepted notion of a penthouse except altitude. He said, 'I'll tell you about it. It's too late to worry about Mr Knighton now. There's nothing can harm him where he's gone.'

The cheap sentimentality of these people! Wexford thought. It was typical. Perry had once shot a man in cold blood, had since then done appalling violence, to say nothing of accepting Knighton's commission to kill his wife, yet he talked like some guiltless and gullible old woman.

'You, however,' said Wexford, 'aren't yet in that happy hereafter and there's plenty of harm can come to you.'

'You mean you're going to caution me?'

Wexford shook his head. 'Not yet. Tell us about when you first knew Mr Knighton.'

'It's twenty-five years. More. But for him they'd have hung me.' Silver looked at Burden. 'You know how it was. I wrote my story for the paper and I cut the piece out and sent it to Mr Knighton. He never answered, naturally he didn't, a man in his position. I waited for him in Lincoln's Inn one evening and we got talking.'

'Just like that?' Wexford tried to imagine it, this shifty tyke and Knighton meeting, getting 'talking'. Knighton would surely have frozen him with a stare and, if he persisted, threatened him with the police.

'Not "just like that",' Silver said. 'I never pestered him, I never annoyed him. I just said I wanted to thank him properly, I said it quiet like. I told him there was nothing in the world I wouldn't do for him.'

And then Wexford did see. Knighton's integrity was already shaky, he was already becoming corrupted. For five years he had been Milborough Lang's lover but by then he knew they couldn't continue on that impermanent, uneasy basis. She would go and he would be left with Adela. Unless . . .

'By all this "anything in the world" claptrap you meant you'd get rid of his wife for him, didn't you?'

Silver winced at the plain speaking. 'He knew what I meant. I knew and he knew, there wasn't no need to put it into words. Help him get what he wanted, that's what I meant and he knew what I meant.'

'How did you know what he wanted?' asked Burden.

'I said I waited for him. It was a few times I did that and I followed him before I got him alone and we got talking. A couple of times I saw him meet this girl. Actress, she was, world-famous.'

'Still, Knighton didn't take you up on your generous offer?'

'He had a lot of scruples, had Mr Knighton,' said Silver with a kind of sage reverence. 'Well, you have to in his position. I said to him I'd never forget what he'd done for me and any time he wanted you know what, any time, he'd only to let me know. I wouldn't bother him, I said. I knew a man in his position don't want to be seen with the likes of me, I understood that. I was living in rooms in Cambridge Heath then. When the council put us in here I dropped him a line with my address and my phone. He never answered, naturally he didn't.' Silver looked up, straight into Wexford's eyes. 'It used to bother me, I used to think about it a lot, the fact that I'd never done a thing to repay him, I had it on my conscience.'

'Your *what*?'

'I know the meaning of gratitude, the same as other folks.'

'No, not the same as other folks, Silver,' said Wexford. 'The way you know it is pathological.' He shook his head reflectively. 'What was he supposed to do, give you a ring and say he'd changed his mind?'

'I told you we never put it into words. It was subtle like, we understood each other. He had to give me a ring, yes. I arranged it, I knew he wouldn't want to ask me outright.' Silver shifted in his seat. He had kept his black overcoat on but now he pulled himself out of it and threw the coat across the arm of a chair. Behind him the glittering view twinkled like a million fallen stars. 'I said to him, if ever you want you-know-what, you give me a tinkle. He never said a word. I looked him in the eye. You don't even have to say it, I said. You dial my number, I said, and when I answer you say one word. Any word you like, I said, so long as I know it.' There were beads of sweat on Silver's forehead now, up near the wig-like white hairline. 'He never answered me direct. He just looked at me and started telling some story about a Chinese mandarin, I don't recall the ins and outs of it now. That's it, I said, mandarin. You give me a call and when I answer you say ''Mandarin'' and I'll know. That was all of twenty-five years ago, nearer twenty-six. ''Mandarin'', I said, ''any time, you say that one word and I'll know—and I'll do it''.'

What had passed through Knighton's mind at the time? Had he conceived it as possible even in those days? Or had he merely been humouring Silver Perry, jollying him along, preparatory to getting rid of him for good? Wexford supposed they had been in a pub or even on a park bench somewhere. Just the one meeting, he was sure of that. Perry eager, grateful, gratified that this august man would condescend to converse with him, Knighton inexpressibly shocked, horrified, yet tempted. Raise the hand, say the word, do nothing more and she will die and you may have your heart's desire. What evil wicked nonsense! Better take one's own life in one's misery than countenance this, than even stay here listening to this. But 'Mandarin', one word. . .

'But one day, not long ago, he did ring you and he did say the word,' said Burden.

'Early in September it was. I picked up the phone and no one spoke for a bit, though you could hear breathing, and I was just thinking this was some joker when this voice says it. Stuttered a bit and spoke very low. The funny thing was, I'd *forgotten*. I mean I'd never seen Mr Knighton all that time, I'd never heard his voice. I'd had a bit of news via Renie over the years, but not for a long time, I never even knew he was retired, I never knew they lived in Sussex permanent like.

'The voice said this word. I could hear it started "man" and I thought what it said was "managing", but the receiver was put back before I could say anything. But I must have like recognized it in my subconscious or whatever on account of it kept haunting me all day. And suddenly it came to me. After all those years I could repay Mr Knighton at last, I could fulfil my promise.'

Wexford got up and turned his back. 'You make me sick.' He stood at the window, looking down on lurex-embroidered London, up at a homing aircraft laden with lights, breathing steadily to command his anger. 'Get on with it,' he said, 'and we can dispense with the noble sentiments.'

'You went ahead on that single word, a word you didn't even hear properly?' Burden put in.

'I *knew*,' said Silver. 'I hung about his chambers but he never come out and then I saw his name gone from the list at the door. I went up to Hampstead but I only had to take one look to see the place was full of bleeding Arabs. A couple of times I rung Thatto Hall Farm and he answered the first time and she answered the second but that didn't help me any.'

'Help you?'

'I had to know her movements, didn't I? I had to get her alone. Then one day I saw him. Coming out of Victoria Station it was, round about four in the afternoon, Wednesday, October the first. He was carrying this over-night bag, I knew he'd gone away for the night.'

'What were you doing at Victoria?'

'I have to work, don't I? I've got my living to earn. I was driving the mini-cab, I'd just dropped a fare. He was looking for a taxi, Mr Knighton was, and I thought to myself, why don't I offer him a lift to wherever he's going? But I knew I was the last person he'd want to be seen with. Besides, I'd had a better idea. Seeing that overnight bag gave it to me. He'd come up to town for the night and she'd be alone. I reckoned on her being alone. I'd been to see poor old Henry in the hospital, you see, a couple of weeks before, and Renie was there and she said the daughter was married and expecting a kid and all. So I reckoned on the old woman being alone. I reckoned if I was going to do it I'd better get on with it, I'd better get it over with that night.'

Wexford thought he heard the front door click. There were sounds of movement in the hall and the woman who had screamed at Burden came in. Like her husband, she knew policemen by instinct and she gave Wexford a look others reserve for a thief or a vagrant. Wexford and Burden went out into the hall.

'Do we take him back with us and charge him?'

Wexford shrugged. 'Nothing to charge him with. I doubt if we could even make conspiracy stick.'

When they went back into the room the woman had disappeared and Silver Perry was drinking something that looked like whisky. It appeared to have been rationed out to him, as if for medicinal purposes.

'I was working till midnight. I got on to a pal of mine, never mind who, it don't matter now, I got on to him to say I'd been with him at the El Video if there was questions asked. Anyway, my last fare kept me a good half-hour over the odds and it was gone two, more like two fifteen, two twenty, before I got to Sewingbury. I left my vehicle in the market square and I walked. I came back by the footpath but I went by the road, not being too sure of my bearings if the moon was to go in.

'It was well after three when I got to Thatto Hall Farm. I got out my glass cutter and cut out that pane in the toilet window. Must have taken me ten minutes, maybe fifteen. The house wasn't that dark inside because of the moon shining in. I took my shoes off and went upstairs.

'All the bedroom doors was open and I went in the big front one, thinking to find her there. There was twin beds and one of them had the bedclothes turned back. I went back there later and took her jewel box and chucked some of her bits and pieces away to make it look like an outside job. He was an amateur, you see, he didn't know what's what. But first I looked in the other rooms and when I couldn't find her I went downstairs again. I was beginning to wonder what was up, I can tell you.'

Silver drank his drink and put the glass down heavily.

'I found her on the floor. She was dead, she'd been shot dead. I knew what it was right away, Mr Knighton had got there before me and done it himself.'

19

WEXFORD HELD THE GUN IN HIS HANDS. EVERYTHING THAT COULD be deduced from an examination of it was in the report on the desk in front of him. It was a Walther PPK 9 mm automatic and approximately halfway along the barrel, on the underside, was a minute wart-like fault in the metal which would mark each bullet that passed through it with a fine hairline scratch. Burden, looking over his shoulder, said, 'What was Perry going to use? His bare hands?'

'I daresay. They're weapons you don't have to dispose of. A strange business, wasn't it? Perry was sure Knighton had killed her, not knowing she didn't die till some eleven hours after Knighton's departure for London. He thought Knighton had got tired of waiting for him to keep his promise and had killed her himself.' Wexford put the gun down on the desk. 'I've no time for a villain like that, Mike, but I believe him when he says he was ashamed of himself for having failed Knighton. Because he had shilly-shallied since the beginning of September, Knighton had been driven to do it himself. And because he thought Knighton hadn't done a sufficient job of faking a break-in and burglary, hadn't done any sort of job of that at all, he himself took the jewel box out of the house and having no great opinion of our acumen, scattered its contents about the front garden.'

According to Perry, in spite of his ploy with Mrs Knighton's pieces of jewellery, in spite of the evidence of break-in, he had expected Knighton to be arrested and charged with his wife's murder almost at once. He had cursed himself for the delay which he saw as having led Knighton to commit the crime. When nothing had happened to Knighton he had simply put this down to police ineptitude. If he had ever doubted Knighton's guilt, that doubt had been dispelled by his suicide.

'And certainly Knighton believed Perry had killed her,' Wexford went on. 'From the moment he came home on October the second and I told him his wife had been shot he believed Perry had done it and done it on his instructions. That accounts for the feeling we always had of his being surprised yet not surprised, guilty yet innocent. That day he phoned Perry at the beginning of September—I wonder what impelled him to do that, what particular thing happened? We shall never know now. Had Adela found out about Milborough Ingram and threatened or ridiculed? Had Mrs Ingram begun to talk of going home? Or had Adela begun talking of another long holiday—we know she wanted to go to India and Nepal in February—which would take him away from Milborough again? Whatever it was, a temptation that was a quarter of a century old came back and this time he succumbed. But I can't think he really believed in it, Mike. It must have seemed like fantasy. With anyone but Silver Perry, who isn't, I think, quite sane, it would have been fantasy.

'You can imagine him leaving Milborough Ingram's flat late one afternoon, going off to meet Adela and travel home with her. Maybe it was on a street corner or in a station that he saw the empty call box and remembered the past, remembered "Mandarin".

'Of course it was all nonsense, it could never happen now. "Mandarin" was all he had to say and the murder would be done and his happiness secured. In fantasy, in dreams, not really. But he went into the phone box and he dialled and he said it. At any rate he said something like it and then he went off and met Adela and no doubt told himself what a fool he was.'

Burden came round the desk and sat down. He was frowning.

'He must have wondered if anything would happen.'

'Perhaps. Nothing did, though, did it? Three or four weeks went by and nothing had happened. He must have thought Silver Perry had forgotten ''Mandarin'' or got old or reformed or had never really meant it in the first place. But as soon as Adela was killed he knew. But happiness wasn't secured. There was no freedom, no future, no joyful looking-forward. Not happiness, but remorse. For he believed Perry had done it on *his* word, though that word was a muttered whisper given after a gap of twenty-five years.'

'He killed himself in vain,' said Burden. 'He killed himself for an illusion. He might have been happy, he might have re-married. He'd done nothing and Perry had done nothing.'

'The intention was there, Mike,' Wexford said thoughtfully. 'And it was more than just a wish for his wife to die, wasn't it? However slight, it was an express instruction and he had delivered it to a dirty little crook and murderer he shouldn't have lowered himself to speak to. Even if we'd found someone for this job while he was alive he'd still have had that on his mind, wouldn't he? On his conscience, disgusting him with himself and, I suspect, pretty well poisoning the feelings he had for the great love of his life. Men like Knighton had better not commit crimes even vicariously, they had better not be involved in crimes they *imagine* they have committed vicariously.'

Burden looked at his watch. 'He should be in by now. It's just gone ten.' When Wexford didn't respond he said more sharply, 'The one that really committed it, I mean. You said you didn't want him fetched from home.'

'Not in the circumstances, no.' Wexford sighed. 'Not that it's going to make much difference, maybe a couple of hours. I'm not planning on talking to him much, we don't need a confession. It's all as clear as glass. I should have seen it from the start, only China intruded, China and what went on there confused me. Not that China didn't have a good deal to do with his motive, it did.'

'He bought the gun,' said Burden, 'quite openly from a very respectable gunsmith's, Warrington Weapons & London Wall. It was easy. And it makes our task easier.'

'The books he was keeping, or not keeping, are going to be pretty damning evidence too. We'll be spending the rest of the day looking into his financial juggling, Mike. Come on, then, let's go and take him.'

They had finished. There was nothing more to do until the special court in the morning. It had been dark for hours, the damp foggy dark of November. Wexford picked up his coat and slung it over him. 'I feel like a drink.'

'Come back to my place,' Burden said.

Wexford felt deeply tired, as tired as he had been after those white nights in China. His head floated, it seemed full of a crowding of figures and prevarications and lies. Yet there was nothing to think of or talk about except what they had done that day and he went on talking about it.

'But surely it was Perry that Bingley saw in the wood?' Burden had asked.

'How can it have been? Confused as Bingley was, he was sure the man he saw was walking back from Thatto Vale, not going towards it. Besides that, Perry went by the road and only came back by the footpath. Now if Perry didn't get to Thatto Hall Farm till three, took ten to fifteen minutes cutting out that glass and another ten going over the house and finding the body, it would have been more like ten to four before he passed the spot where Bingley was. Or had been, for by that time Bingley had certainly gone off home.'

They got into Wexford's car. Jenny had taken Burden's. Wexford drove slowly because he was tired.

'It was a grey-haired man he saw,' Burden insisted.

'But was it? He came to see us in the first place because his niece told him he ought to. He had seen a man walking that footpath back to Sewingbury at three in the morning of October the second. But he was nervous about coming to us because he'd been poaching. So to please us he makes his story as near to what he thinks we want as he can. Knighton is tall and has grey or silver hair. He either knows Knighton by sight or has seen his picture in the paper. Therefore he describes the man he saw as tall and with grey hair. But when I show him photographs that's a different matter. He is reminded then of what the man in the wood *really* looked like. Of the figures in the pictures he's shown he doesn't pick out Knighton, who resembles Silver Perry more than any of them. He picks out Gordon Vinald who doesn't resemble him at all but is youngish, dark, rather short and slightly built.'

Burden's porch light was on. The bungalow itself was in darkness. Wexford got out of the car and walked up the path towards the light and something soft and slinky came out of the shadows and rubbed itself against his trouser leg. He jumped because he was weary and it had been a long day. Burden unlocked the front door and Wexford followed him into the house, holding the cat in his arms.

'Bingley couldn't pick out the man who killed Adela Knighton from the photographs because he wasn't in them. So he picked out the man most nearly like him. He chose the only man in the group who was also young, dark, short and slight.'

The centre light in the living room came on but the bulb in the table lamp flashed, fizzled and went dark. The bright glare from the middle of the ceiling made Wexford wince and blink. Burden switched it off.

'I'll get another bulb. I'll just have to think where it is Jenny keeps them. And then what? Scotch?'

'I shouldn't,' said Wexford in much the same way

Milborough Ingram had, though he was thinking more of his health than his face and figure. 'But I will.'

He sat in the dark, a little light coming in from the hall. The back door slammed as Burden went out to the garage. The cat began doing that uncanny thing cats do, staring at nothing, following nothing round the room with its eyes. It slid off Wexford's lap and sat with its tail faintly moving, gazing towards the doorway and the light.

An old Chinese woman with bound feet, in dark trousers and a quilted jacket, walking with small mincing steps, came out of the light—out of nowhere, it seemed—and stood on the threshold. His heart simply stopped. It felt as if it had stopped and the restarting, the thuds of its beat, were almost painful.

'Why are you sitting in the dark?' Jenny Burden asked. 'Where's Mike?'

He managed to speak in his normal voice. 'Gone to find a light bulb.'

She retreated into the kitchen, the high wooden-soled sandals she wore restricting her walk, and came back at once with a bulb. The table lamp came on and showed him Burden's wife, made up to look Chinese but not to look old, a black wig covering her fair hair. The cat rubbed itself against her, winding in and out between her ankles.

'The Good Woman of Setzuan, I presume?'

'It was our dress rehearsal. It was dark so I thought I might as well come home just as I was.' She kissed Burden who came in with their drinks. 'If you'll excuse me, I'll go and take all this lot off.'

'My God,' said Burden. 'I wonder you didn't think you were hallucinating again.'

Wexford said nothing. He took his whisky with a steady hand.

'So it *was* Angus Norris that Bingley saw?' Burden said.

'Of course. Having let himself into Thatto Hall Farm with his wife's key, got his mother-in-law out of bed, brought her downstairs and shot her, he made his way home again along that footpath, thus enabling Bingley to see him at three o'clock.'

'I suppose he told her,' said Burden, 'that his wife had been taken ill or gone into early labour or some such thing and they hadn't been able to get through on the phone. He shot her through the back of the head because, like the gentleman he is, he let a lady procede him into a room. And that wife of his is having a baby any minute . . .'

'I hope it may be a consolation to her,' Wexford said sombrely. 'Mother, father and now this. Norris was shattered by Knighton's suicide. Did you see his face? He hadn't expected that. I daresay he thought he was doing Knighton a favour, killing Adela. Mind you, I don't think he planned it, or not very far in advance. He didn't go up to London and Warrington Weapons and buy the gun with that in mind. He bought the gun because he collects firearms. Then—maybe not till the very day of October the first—his wife told him her father would be going to London for the night.

'Jennifer slept soundly because she was sedated. She would have been unaware of it if he was absent for an hour. I think he was desperate. He had married someone who expected to be kept in the style of her mother, of her older brothers and their wives, but he couldn't make the grade. He had only what he earned as an assistant solicitor with Symonds, O'Brien and Ames. I'm guessing here but I hardly think it can be otherwise, that he bought that house on a mortgage far above what he could afford. The cost of living went on rising and mortgage interest rates edged up too. It's apparent the house isn't even adequately furnished. We've seen enough of his financial affairs today to know that he was substantially in debt. And now there was a baby on the way which probably meant Jennifer would demand some sort of living-in help.

'He was frantic with money worries. He took his gun

and walked to Thatto Hall Farm and killed Jennifer's mother, believing it would be thought she had come down and admitted some stranger who had knocked at the door. Norris, you see, is tarred with the same brush as his wife's family—he thinks he belongs to an élite that is above suspicion of criminality.'

Burden said, 'His firm were Mrs Knighton's solicitors, they drew up her will for her, so he knew what was in it—fifty thousand pounds for his wife.'

'That was a contributory motive only. That was a bonus. His motive was Mrs Knighton's holiday fund.'

'We didn't find a single record of that, not a word referring to it.'

'I daresay Norris felt it was safer that way. I daresay he even had a bold dream that if ever it came to the crunch he could deny that his mother-in-law had entrusted him with a large sum to invest. But to do that would have meant cutting himself and his wife off from her family entirely and certainly losing that future inheritance. Anyway, he didn't have the nerve. He only had nerve enough to kill her.'

'I suppose he had drawn on the fund for his own use and was hoping against hope that by some means or other he could make up the deficit before Adela demanded a really large sum.'

Wexford nodded. 'After all, last April he had had to provide her with four thousand pounds to go to China, a substantial amount for one holiday.'

'But that was more than six months ago. Why kill her now?'

'Because she asked for more. She wanted to go to India and Nepal in February. What would that have cost for the two of them? At least as much as the China trip. Very likely he didn't even have that much remaining in the fund. With Jennifer's inheritance he could pay his debts. He could make good what he had helped himself to out of the fund and present the money intact as soon as Knighton or a brother-in-law started asking questions.'

'Strange, isn't it, that a man would rather do murder

211

and thereby shut himself up for fifteen years, not to mention losing his wife and child—for I'm sure he will—he'd rather do that than stand up and confess to having lost a sum of money?'

Wexford shrugged. 'We're all cowards one way or another.' He looked up and smiled as Jenny came back dressed as herself.

ABOUT THE AUTHOR

Ruth Rendell has received enormous acclaim in the mystery field, winning three Edgar Awards from the Mystery Writers of America, *Current Crime*'s Silver Cup, and the Crime Writers' Association's Golden Dagger award. The *Boston Sunday Globe* calls her "the best mystery writer...in the world today," and the *Los Angeles Times* says she "gets better and better, bolder and bolder" with every book she writes.

Ruth Rendell lives in Polstead, England.